Wartime Brides and Wedding Cakes

ALSO BY AMY MILLER

Heartaches and Christmas Cakes

Amy Miller

Wartime Brides and Wedding Cakes

bookouture

Published by Bookouture in 2018

An imprint of StoryFire Ltd.

Carmelite House
50 Victoria Embankment
London EC4Y 0DZ

www.bookouture.com

ISBN: 978-1-78681-324-4
eBook ISBN: 978-1-78681-323-7

‘What do we live for, if it is not to make life less difficult for each other?’—George Eliot

January 1941

Prologue

Audrey Barton was fast asleep when her husband, Charlie, left. Kitbag slung over his shoulder, he carefully closed the bakery door behind him, quietly slipping from one life into another. The ink-blue sky peppered with stars, Audrey hadn't stirred when he'd dressed, silently, in the darkness, tying the laces of his heavy leather boots with trembling hands. She had slept on under the rose-print eiderdown, as he propped a handwritten note on the dressing table, glancing back at her dark blonde hair fanned on the pillow and breathing in the fragrance of her Pond's face cream, locking his wife's image into his heart.

I can't say goodbye, he had written.

When Audrey had awoken before dawn that freezing cold morning, to join Charlie in the bakehouse as she did every day, she discovered the note. Pulling her nightgown closer to her body, shivering slightly, she bit down hard on her bottom lip, quickly unfolding the paper to read his troubling words.

'Charlie Barton!' she cried, screwing up the note and hurling it across the room. Clenching her jaw and blinking away tears, she quickly processed what he had done. Of course, she knew he was joining up. He'd wanted to join the British Expeditionary Force since Britain declared war against Germany in September 1939, but because he was a baker, his occupation was 'reserved', and so he had food production duties at home. After fifteen grim months of war and in the midst of the Blitz, unimaginable calamity across the country and with millions of people's lives in peril, Charlie had eventually persuaded the authorities to let him enlist, on the proviso that the bakery could continue to run without him. Yes, Audrey knew he was leaving, but he hadn't told her when. She had planned on organising him a farewell meal with his favourite dishes, herring plate pie and marrow surprise, and on packing him up with all the comforts she could think of: knitted socks, gloves, long johns, balaclava helmet and a gingerbread cake for sustenance.

A kiss at the very least.

'How could you?' she muttered, dashing to the window, the gnarled floorboards creaking underfoot. She lifted up the blackout blind and threw open the window, leaning out into the bitingly cold January air, to peer up and down Fisherman's Road, the street in east Bournemouth where they lived. There was nobody in sight. Whereas once the lamplighter would have been putting out the gas lamps, at this hour, to make way for dawn, the blackout meant the only light was provided by a sliver of moon hanging in the sky like a fingernail clipping, shining onto the deserted, snow-covered street.

Audrey spotted a trail of Charlie-sized footprints in the snow, leading away from the bakery, continuing past the butcher's and the post office, their blackout blinds still closed. He had gone. Audrey didn't cry easily, but this morning, she wept.

'Oh Charlie,' she said to nobody, her voice quavering. 'What kind of husband leaves his wife without saying goodbye? Goodbye might be all we have.'

Tears streamed uncontrollably down her cheeks as her thoughts flew to the argument they'd had the previous night. Heavens, she knew not to go to bed on an argument, yet that's exactly what she'd done. It had blown up out of nowhere when Audrey had been getting Mary, the eight-year-old evacuee girl billeted with them, ready for bed.

'Your hair is so soft,' Audrey had said, brushing the little girl's hair while sitting in front of the roaring fire, where a line of woollen stockings and gloves dried in the heat from the crackling flames. 'It feels like rabbit's ears, or butterfly wings, or the softest velvet you can imagine. Mary, I do believe you have the hair of a princess. You're a special girl, do you know that?'

She'd noticed Charlie's face dark as a thundercloud when he'd walked past, heading down to the bakehouse to knock back and prove the dough for the next day's bread, but it wasn't until Mary was tucked up in bed and Audrey was elbow-deep in washing up the crockery that he told her what was on his mind.

'You shouldn't fill the girl's head with such fanciful rot,' he had said, his muscular arms folded across his chest. 'You're setting her up for another fall. She's not a princess but a kiddie with more problems on her shoulders than Winston Churchill. Her brother's dead, her mother topped herself, she's got no home to go to and her father's fighting on the front line, if he's even alive. Mary needs toughening up, not softening up.'

Audrey had stopped pot washing and stared for a moment at the shelves in front of her. The jewel-coloured bottles and jars of rosehip syrup, pickled cucumbers, apple chutney and carrot jam she'd made in the summer months in preparation for winter blurred in front of her eyes. Placing the dishcloth down on the Belfast sink, she had turned to face her husband, hands on her hips.

'That girl has seen enough sadness to last her two lifetimes,' she said coolly. 'I will do everything in my power to raise a smile on her sorry little face and give her a taste of what childhood should be. There can be no denying that the horrors she's seen are unimaginable to us, Charlie.'

'Not for long,' he had challenged, raising his chin. 'I'll be going out to the front line with my eyes wide open. I'm prepared for anything, nothing can shock me.'

Suddenly weary, Audrey shook her head. 'I don't know what's got into you, Charlie Barton,' she said, 'but the man I married was not bloodthirsty, or begging for a fight. You should open your eyes to what's around you. Folk are managing to put a smile on their faces, like a sticking plaster, but families are being pulled apart; husbands, sons and brothers dead before they've even started their lives. Millions of children just like Mary have been evacuated hundreds of miles away from home, not knowing if they'll see their parents again. What the world needs is more simple kindliness and common humanity.'

'You think I don't know that?' he said, incredulous. 'Are you suggesting I don't go and fight for our country?'

Unsure of quite what she was saying, Audrey sighed. She knew, deep down, that Charlie had a heart of gold and had married him because of his dependability, kind nature and strength. She shook her head.

'No, I'm not saying that,' she said, her shoulders sagging. 'Nothing I can say will stop you wanting to fight, even though this bakery and the neighbourhood depends on you for bread in a time when people are having to forgo foods other than what is absolutely necessary. It's like you've been somewhere else since the war started. You might as well have already gone!'

Audrey knew she was treading on thin ice, but she couldn't help herself. The prospect of Charlie leaving the bakery – leaving and potentially never returning – was hanging over them both and tearing her apart. She knew she was being unfair. She knew that Charlie wanted to defend his country against Hitler and the potential threat of invasion, to help put a stop to the horrific pain and suffering that people across the globe had so far endured, but the fear of losing him deeply affected her. Though she would never admit as much, when she met and married him seven years ago, he had, in some ways, rescued her. Their marriage, the bakery and his extended family had plucked her from the lonely road she was travelling, giving her direction and strength. Without him, would she fall apart?

'You don't understand,' said Charlie, but she turned her back on him and plunged her hands back into the soapy water.

No, you don't understand, she thought.

'I should get this done,' she sighed, her cheeks burning. She felt Charlie's eyes boring a hole into her back for a long moment, but she didn't turn to face him, much to her deepest regret.

Now, he was gone. She stared at her wedding band and rotated it slowly around her finger, the gold bright and smooth to touch. Her thoughts went back to their happy wedding day and she glanced at the photograph on the dressing table of the two of them about to cut their wedding cake. She had baked and intricately iced the rich, fruity celebration cake herself, carefully positioning the hand-painted bride and groom wedding cake topper she kept, to this day, wrapped in tissue paper in her jewellery box. Averting her gaze, she tried to work out what to do. Should she follow the footprints in the snow to try to find Charlie? Or should she respect his wishes and not say goodbye?

Realising he had probably left hours earlier and as through the window a flurry of light snow began to fall and cover his footprints, she wiped her eyes and quickly dressed in her bakery overalls, pinning back her hair and fixing the bakery cap on the top of her head. She pushed her feet into her wooden clogs and looked in the mirror at her twenty-seven-year-old self. Slim in build and naturally pretty, Charlie used to say her blue eyes changed shade depending on her mood. This morning they were dark and gloomy as the bottom of the sea. Her beloved Charlie was joining the thousands of other men away from home, who might never return.

I can't say goodbye.

Pushing back her shoulders, standing tall, Audrey took a deep breath and raised her chin. The faint noise of the clattering of loaf tins came from the bakehouse, where she knew Charlie must have arranged for his Uncle John to step in and take over his baking duties. In a time of rationing, when shipping losses meant that food imports had radically fallen, bread was an essential part of everyone's diet and, as the local family bakery, the neighbourhood depended on Barton's bread. She thought of their small but spotless shop downstairs, the shelves waiting to be filled with warm golden loaves and counter goods, to satisfy empty bellies. The locals said the smell of Barton's bread was so good it was impossible to walk past without coming in. Offering everyday comfort and sustenance in an uncertain, tense and dangerous time; she would never, ever, let her customers down.

Giving her reflection a long, hard stare before turning away, she picked up Charlie's screwed-up note and placed it in the dressing table drawer for safekeeping.

The lengthy list of what needed doing that morning pressed on her mind. She would need to open up the shop in a matter of hours and paint on a smile for her customers. There were hotel orders to fulfil and a celebration cake to be baked. Life must go on. Today, she would show fortitude and strength, however heavy her heart.

Chapter One

Summer 1941

Like a nightingale at dusk, the sweet sound of William's harmonica drifted from the open attic window of the bakery, stopping Audrey in her tracks.

'Are my ears playing tricks on me?' she asked Elsie, William's fiancée, as she paused from pushing a sodden apron through the wooden rollers of the mangle to listen, staring up at the window in disbelief. It was the first time in six months since her brother William had returned home from the front line, severely injured, that she'd heard him play, and his mournful notes plucked at her heartstrings. Her cheeks pink with the exertion of scrubbing dirt from the bakery's aprons, caps and overalls, Audrey's eyes misted over. Hearing him play loosened the knots across her shoulders; in truth, she had been worried sick about William for months.

'I've never been more pleased to hear the blues in all my life,' said Elsie, a huge dimpled smile exploding onto her pretty face. 'When he starts playing boogie-woogie, we're going to throw a party.'

Audrey smiled at this remark and watched as Elsie quickly dropped the apron she was wringing soapy water out of, dried her hands on a towel and pulled the red headscarf from her black curls, which fell around her face in soft ringlets. Walking away from the mangle to go inside the bakery and see William, Audrey gently caught hold of Elsie's wrist.

'Wait,' she said, her eyes sparkling as his mournful music continued. 'Let him play a while undisturbed. That harp will be better for him than any dose of medicine.'

Elsie nodded her agreement and the two women shared a glance that conveyed a myriad of emotions. Since William had come home, Audrey knew only too well that life had been difficult for him and Elsie, to say the least. The couple were supposed to have been married the previous year, but William's injuries had kept him away from Bournemouth on the wedding day. Thinking of the tension that day – not knowing whether he was going to turn up or not – made Audrey feel quite sick. When he had finally come home, they'd discovered that his right foot had been amputated and the right side of his face, including his eye, severely burned, so he'd misguidedly thought Elsie would no longer want to be his bride. He couldn't have been more wrong, but expecting the couple to take up where they left off was a mistake. It wasn't just William's body that had been injured. It felt, to Audrey, as if part of his soul was lost in no man's land. Not knowing what he'd seen in battle, or exactly how he'd suffered in France when his truck was hit by a bomb killing all the men travelling with him, meant that she and Elsie tiptoed around his dark moods as if the floor were covered in eggshells.

The knowledge that William was up in his room at the bakery, a mere shadow of his former self, while Elsie struggled to keep their relationship going, pained Audrey immensely. Though he volunteered as one of the neighbourhood's fire-watchers, struggling on his crutches, with binoculars pinned to his eyes, for several hours every night, on the lookout for incendiary bomb fires, he was otherwise sullen and distracted. Her lovingly made hotpots and casseroles seemed not to tempt him, her freshest, warm cakes too indulgent in a time of austerity, and long walks along the coast too physically painful for him. She'd tried discussing the news with him – with Yugoslavia and Greece under his belt, in an operation with the codename 'Barbarossa', Hitler had now invaded the Soviet Union – but William seemed to shrink even further inside himself. He preferred to stay in his room writing letters to soldiers in his regiment, or would sit out in the bakery yard absorbed in simple tasks such as podding broad beans or scraping clean the carrots. The doctor said it was a matter of time – and warned that some men returned from war in body but not in mind. It certainly seemed that William's mind was elsewhere, perhaps Audrey feared, trapped in a memory too horrific to fade, but maybe, just maybe, there was hope.

'When he plays it's almost like before the war, isn't it?' said Elsie. 'When everything was normal and ordinary. Can you remember those days? Feels like a different lifetime.'

Before the war, William had worked alongside Charlie in the bakery as his apprentice. When he wasn't hard at work, he'd perch on a flour sack to drink a cup of tea and play on his mouth harp, earning him admiring comments from their customers and neighbours on Fisherman's Road. He'd fallen for Elsie and everyone was delighted to hear they were to marry. Just the thought of him as the sorry soul he was now, who had opted out of the world and who spent far too much time stewing on his own, made Audrey blanch. Where had her valiant, bold and musical brother, who was desperately in love with Elsie, gone? Well, she'd be damned if she was going to let him disappear forever.

Audrey took a deep breath as she listened to him play, enjoying the fragrance of the red geraniums bursting out of pots in the yard and mingling with the scent of the onions, tomatoes and lettuces growing in soil, disguising the roof of the Anderson shelter. Perhaps his playing was a sign that better times were ahead.

Appreciating the sight of the bright white washing on the clothes line flapping in the warm July breeze against the blue sky, her heart lightened a little. This moment was a welcome relief from the last few months of running the bakery without Charlie – an arduous task. Uncle John had gladly come out of retirement to take over his nephew's baking duties and Barton's had reduced the numbers of delivery orders it took on, but even so, the old man was tired, Audrey knew that. She was tired too, she thought, staring at her fingers that were red raw from all the scaling, moulding, baking, serving, scrubbing and cleaning she did. Not that she was alone in running the bakery. Maggie, the shop girl, was a good egg and Audrey's stepsister, Lily, who'd arrived in a 'fix' last year, now lived at the bakery with her baby, Joy, and helped out whenever she could. So why did Audrey feel as though she'd been through the mangle herself?

'It's the sleepless nights in the shelter and all the worry,' she muttered to herself, running her eyes over an advertisement on a sheet of newspaper on the floor, where earth-covered spuds were piled up, ready for scrubbing and preparing and cooking for tomorrow's dinner. The typeface was bright and bold, its message clear: *Your courage, your cheerfulness, your resolution, will bring us victory.*

Audrey gave a gentle laugh. There was no time for tiredness in wartime, was there? And she had no right to be tired, she told herself. Not when Charlie was away facing goodness knows what, and folk were having to live in shelters because their homes had been bombed out.

She began pegging out more washing. The strange thing was, despite being exhausted, when her head hit the pillow she couldn't sleep. Instead, she lay there awake, worrying. Oh, there was so much to worry about – not least when the next air-raid siren would sound. Since the beginning of the year the siren in Bournemouth had sounded dozens of times. There had been heavy air raids all over Britain – and though Bournemouth hadn't suffered a pounding like London, Coventry or Bristol, the Woolworths building in the Square had recently taken a hit, and swathes of Westbourne, Branksome Park and Moordown had been destroyed by parachute bombs. Churchill had been on the wireless, warning that Hitler may try to invade Britain 'in the near future' too and that civilians should prepare for gas, parachute and glider attacks. It didn't bear thinking about.

'No wonder we're all tired!' Audrey said to herself, shaking her head.

Then there were the wedding cake orders, of course. Audrey often made wedding cakes at short notice, because sweethearts had just days together before the groom had to return to active service, and often didn't know, until the last minute, when those days might be. She never turned down a customer; Charlie always insisted they pull out all the stops for the customers.

Charlie. Of course, what she worried about most was whether Charlie was safe. She missed him dreadfully. Painfully. It was a difficult and complicated thing: love in wartime.

Looking sympathetically at Elsie, who was leaning with her back against the wall, her arms gently folded, listening to William's harp, her eyes closed in relief that he'd started playing again, Audrey was heartened. Elsie would never give up on William, that was clear.

'Go on up,' said Audrey to Elsie. 'You should be together. Of course, you should. It'll do him more good to be with you than anything. I'm sorry to have delayed you.'

Watching Elsie rush inside to see William, hoping he would welcome her with open arms, Audrey's crowded thoughts were interrupted by the arrival of little Mary running into the yard, leaving the wooden gate swinging and creaking on its hinges. Dressed in her blue school frock, one sock up and the other down, her fringe sticking up from running, she pushed aside the sheets hanging on the washing line, gasping for breath.

'What is it, Mary, love?' said Audrey. 'You look like you've run twenty miles.'

Mary was a different girl from the silent creature who had arrived at the bakery a year ago, refusing to speak a word. She'd had so much to cope with for a girl of seven, what with witnessing the death of her little brother, Edward, when a bomb hit their house, and then, poor girl, her mother taking her own life at Christmas. Finding the words to explain that to Mary had been one of the hardest things Audrey had ever had to do. Mary's high-pitched, horrified scream was etched on her memory for the rest of her life. But, despite her losses, away from the smoky chimney pots and the slum district she had previously lived in, the sea air, busy bakery life and simple kindnesses were doing the little girl good. Other women she knew hadn't taken to their evacuees, but Audrey, unable to have a baby of her own, felt vehemently protective of Mary and had grown to love her as if she were her own flesh and blood.

'It's Lily,' Mary said, in tears now. 'She's in trouble! She's lost the baby!'

Lost the baby? Audrey's stomach somersaulted and her jaw dropped.

'What on earth do you mean, "lost the baby"?' said Audrey, the clean washing slipping from her hands to the muddy ground. Mary gripped hold of Audrey's hand and pulled her towards the gate.

'Please,' said Mary, tears spilling. 'Help her!'

And just as suddenly as William's sweet music had started, it stopped.

Chapter Two

Earlier that day Lily had taken Joy out in the pram, to try to soothe her. After months of being banned, sea bathing was now allowed on small areas of the beach where gaps had been made in the barbed-wire sea defences. With holidaymakers discouraged from travelling, to avoid creating traffic and wasting precious petrol, the beaches were bare. The sun warm on her skin, Lily pushed the pram along the promenade, past the signs warning people to 'bathe at your own risk and do not take photographs', hoping the motion would rock Joy to sleep. And, for a precious few moments, where nothing but the gentle lap of waves on the beach was audible, the child was quiet.

'Why don't you have a sleep?' Lily had said, suppressing a yawn and peering into the pram as Joy chewed on a wooden clothes peg. 'You must need a nap, I know I do.'

Though Lily had done everything the maternity nurse had instructed – nursing, bathing and clothing Joy the right way – the baby girl was 'fussy' and didn't feed well. When she did feed, she cried and cried afterwards, her face boiling red and flushed. Her tiny fists would clench and she'd arch her back, drawing her knees up to her tummy as if in pain. She slept for, at the most, three-quarters of an hour at a time, and though everyone's advice was to not be a martyr to Joy, Lily couldn't leave her wailing in her crib because she'd wake up everyone else at the bakery and probably down the whole of Fisherman's Road. Instead, the baby was strapped to her almost continuously.

She couldn't admit it to anyone, since she'd taken the enormous decision to keep the child despite being an unwed, single mother – risking bringing shame and scandal to Audrey's home and business – but having a baby was more exhausting than she could ever have imagined. The starry-eyed feeling she'd experienced on the day Joy was born had well and truly evaporated. Six months on, she longed for someone to take Joy off her hands, for just a few hours. She knew how selfish that sounded, especially when she knew that Audrey was desperate to have her own baby and couldn't. But it was true. How she wished to read a book, write a letter or just be able to think clearly, but Joy had other ideas. As if reading Lily's traitorous thoughts, Joy began to cry and her little fists flew up and down as if fighting off a swarm of bees, sending her wooden peg hurtling to the ground.

'Poor little soul,' Lily said, all out of energy. 'Won't you ever stop crying? Are you so unhappy?'

By the time they had walked for another quarter-hour and reached a shaded and empty spot on the beach, Joy had thankfully cried herself to sleep, and Lily took the opportunity to dip her toes in the sea while Joy slept in her pram. Ignoring the ugly sea defences all around, she stared at her pale feet on the slithery, cold pebbles in the shallows, lifting up the skirt of her cotton dress. She was struck by a memory of Jacques, the young French soldier who had stayed at the bakery for respite last year, and who was now missing, presumed dead. He had been evacuated to Bournemouth from Dunkirk, after waiting in the sea for hours to be rescued by boat, all the while under attack from the Germans. Lily's blood ran cold; she couldn't bear to think that she would never see him again. After leaving the bakery, he had written her an incredible love letter, but she had never had the opportunity to reply or to tell him the truth about her pregnancy. That fleeting moment, that possibility of love, was gone forever. She shook her head in dismay and, glancing back at the still-quiet Joy, lifted her skirt higher and went deeper still into the water.

Shivering now, her thoughts went to Joy's biological father, Henry Bateman. He had been Lily's boss in her previous job, and she had been so foolish to fall for him. Why had she never questioned whether he was engaged before becoming intimate with him? How could she have been so reckless and naive? Lily loved Joy, of course she did, but now that she was trying to be a mother, she could tell she was not a natural.

Privately, she felt envious of other girls her age who had war jobs. There were dozens of Land Girls working on the farms in the area who shared an enviable camaraderie. There was the Women's Royal Naval Service (WRNS), where girls were working as coastal mine-spotters and repairing ships. Elsie was one of twenty-eight female 'conductresses' working on the Bournemouth buses, and the Women's Auxiliary Air Force (WAAF) girls were in the cockpit, flying aircraft on reconnaissance flights. Even the window washer on Fisherman's Road was a girl, who came to work in her overalls, hair in a scarf and a ladder over her shoulder.

Lily sighed. Shouldn't she be playing a vital part in the struggle like them, instead of fading into obscurity? She sometimes felt she'd woken up in someone else's life.

And what of her heart? The one man she'd had genuine feelings for, Jacques, was gone, and Henry Bateman – who she never wanted to see again – had turned out to be a cheat and a liar, and was now married to another woman.

Squinting in the sunlight, she quickly unbuttoned her dress and dropped it on the beach, where Joy was still sleeping. In just her slip, she walked into the sea and dipped her shoulders in and out of the water, gasping at the cold. Glancing once more at the pram, with the gas-mask boxes slung over the handle, she waded even deeper until her whole body was submerged. Holding her breath and dipping her head under the water, she opened her eyes to see her hair streaming through the seawater, like copper-coloured seaweed. Releasing breath from her lungs and watching the bubbles rise to the surface, shot through with shafts of sunlight, she waited until she couldn't stand it for a moment longer, then pushed her face up through the water, gasping in the air. Starting to swim now, she found it so refreshing and soothing, and the water so cold and clear, that her mind emptied of all thoughts. She swam and swam towards the horizon, feeling quite free, not thinking of anyone or anything but the sensation of the cold water against her pale skin.

*

Now, Audrey dashed out into the street to be confronted by a portly elderly gent in ill-fitting battledress and cap, from the Home Guard, an organisation of local volunteers guarding the coastal defences, carrying baby Joy in one arm, and pushing the pram with the other hand. Unclothed besides her pilchers, poor Joy was furiously kicking her little legs and screaming at the top of her lungs. Her darling face was beetroot red, topped with a tuft of copper curls.

'Is this your baby?' he said crossly. 'The poor wee thing was abandoned in her pram on the beach, screaming so loud you could hear her in France!'

Audrey gasped and stretched out her arms to take Joy and opened her mouth to answer the man when Lily came running up behind them, soaking wet, her thin slip clinging to the outline of her body and her undergarments, her copper hair sticking like strands of seaweed to her forehead and neck. In one hand, she carried her shoes and her dress and she leaned over to catch her breath, hands on her knees.

The man, taken aback by Lily's appearance, shielded his eyes with his hand, muttering under his breath and shaking his head. Audrey blushed on his behalf, astonished by Lily's brazenness, instinctively wanting to cover her up and protect her from his judgemental glare. The older generation couldn't help but judge, and didn't she know it. Having Lily, an unwed young mother, in the bakery had caused quite a stir amongst some of the older customers.

'You look half-drowned!' said Audrey, handing Joy to Lily, then throwing a white sheet over her shoulders. 'What's going on?'

'Thank heavens!' Lily cried, shrugging off the sheet, standing straight, taking Joy and kissing her chubby cheeks. 'I thought I'd lost you!'

The man cleared his throat and rocked on the balls of his feet, averting his gaze from Lily's snow-white plumage. Audrey knew he was about to voice his disapproval of Lily and felt impatient with him, wishing he would go away.

'I found this baby on the beach,' he said. 'I was calling out, hollering at the top of my voice, for the baby's mother to come forward, but anyone I spoke to on the beach said they didn't know who she belonged to. There was no identity card near the baby. I was about to take her to the police station and report her as an abandoned child, but this young girl here insisted the baby came from the bakery.'

'I didn't *abandon* her,' said Lily, frowning and holding Joy close to her body. 'I…'

'It wouldn't be the first time a baby has been abandoned,' the man continued. 'Did you hear about the child that was found in the porch of the Coolmain Nursing Home on Porchester Road? The poor little mite was left with his soother and his milk. I heard that the mother who left the baby was a young girl…'

'Never mind what you've heard,' interrupted Audrey. 'Better to keep a still tongue in a wise head these days. This was obviously a misunderstanding, isn't that right, Lily?'

Lily nodded, but her eyes had misted over and her bottom lip was trembling. Wet through, she looked a sorry state. Audrey whispered to Mary to run into the bakery and bag up a few leftover rock cakes for the man. When she returned moments later, she handed them over.

'Please, take these for your trouble,' Audrey said. 'I'll look after it from here. I'm sure you have more important things to attend to. I've heard about the weapons training the Home Guard has been undertaking lately, and we have a great deal to thank you for.'

The man's chest puffed out. The compliment and the smell of the sugary rock cakes had cast a spell on him. All of a sudden he regained his composure and relaxed. Audrey allowed herself a small, internal smile. She was happy enough to give this man his due – the Home Guard had suffered a lot of taunts, dubbed the 'Broomstick Army' as there were not enough weapons for all the volunteers and men were literally training with broomsticks in place of weapons, but there was no doubt that they were a solid part of the coastal defence and would help delay – heaven forbid – an enemy invasion.

'Yes, well, of course I do, but…' he began, his eyes resting on the cucumbers growing in a small greenhouse in the bakery courtyard. 'They're four shillings and sixpence a pop now, you know, cucumbers. The price of food has rocketed, don't you think, ma'am?'

Audrey quickly plucked one from the plant and gave it to him. She resisted the mischievous temptation to tell him that perhaps he could use the cucumber instead of a broomstick in weapons training.

'I see you have hens,' he said. 'Are they good layers? Eggs are such a luxury these days, aren't they, what with rationing and all?'

'The hens have been on strike this week, I'm afraid, but thank you again,' said Audrey, gently taking hold of his arm and steering him out of the bakery gate and closing it behind him, widening her eyes in mock disbelief.

'Right then,' she said, facing Lily, who, shame-faced, was shivering in the early evening air. 'Let's get dinner on before I look at tomorrow's orders. You look like you need a hot meal. Why don't you get dry and then help me?'

Silently cursing Lily for being so daft, Audrey got to work in the kitchen, the warm cosy space where she spent much of her time when she wasn't in the shop or the bakehouse. With a view of the Overcliff and sea through the window, it was the room where she experimented with new ration-friendly recipes, cooked up meals to feed her family and friends – and where she liked to sit, on a rare break, for a cup of rationed tea or to write to Charlie.

'What was Lily thinking?' she said to herself, shaking her head as she imagined Joy alone on the beach. Lily was such an unpredictable young woman. She liked to take risks, was impulsive and if she hadn't got herself in a fix by getting pregnant with an unavailable man, Audrey had no doubt she'd be one of those girls to have a thrilling war job. She wasn't the domestic type, and though Audrey would never say it out loud, Lily was not particularly maternal. But as things were, she must concentrate on being a good mother to Joy. With no father on the scene, it wouldn't be an easy journey, there was no doubt about it.

'She's going to need your help, not your judgement,' Audrey muttered to herself, as she soaked a large slice of stale bread in milk, then mixed together the precious minced meat cuts, onion, grated potato and oatmeal, before mashing in the softened bread, for the meat roll. Once it was cooking – the tantalising smell of meat making Audrey wish the meat ration was bigger than the meagre 1s 2d it had been since January – she made a hot drink. From the hooks nailed in a row above the sink, she selected the teacup she always gave to Lily; decorated with blood-red flowers and trimmed with gold, it seemed to suit her stepsister's air of drama.

'Something smells good,' said Lily, carrying Joy on her hip.

Audrey smiled and pulled out a chair at the kitchen table for Lily, placing down a steaming cup of weak tea in front of her. Mary came into the kitchen too and sat down at the table, quickly becoming engrossed in a jigsaw puzzle on a wooden tray that she'd half done the previous day.

'What happened today, Lily love?' asked Audrey, trying to keep the anxiety and annoyance out of her voice as she fetched down a board and deftly chopped up a cabbage.

'I hadn't intended on leaving her like that,' said Lily slowly, tears welling up in her eyes. 'She had been screaming so hard and then suddenly she fell to sleep and I just wanted a few minutes… a few minutes to do something else. I went for a swim, but once I was in the sea, I couldn't stop swimming. I almost reached the pier.'

'The pier!' said Audrey, her eyes wide. The pier was a good distance away and had last year been partially blown up by the Royal Engineers to prevent enemy landings, so was dangerous too. 'For goodness' sake, Lily, what was going through your head?'

'I don't know,' said Lily. 'I was thinking about Jacques and Henry and the war and whether I could volunteer to help, and about the future—' But before she could continue, there was a loud thud and shouting from upstairs, the banging of a slammed door, then a clattering of footsteps on the stairs.

Audrey stood immobile, listening, when Elsie flew into the kitchen and grabbed her bag from the kitchen chair. Upstairs, William banged on the ceiling with his crutches. Audrey frowned and shook her head in confusion.

'Goodness, Elsie,' said Audrey, feeling as if her head was spinning. 'What's wrong? I'm making meat roll. I thought you were staying for din—'

'Your pig-headed brother!' Elsie snapped, before storming out. 'That's what's wrong!'

Chapter Three

Elsie's worst fears had come true. After all these months of trying to keep her courtship with William going, despite his black moods, he'd called their engagement off. Grabbing her beaten-up Raleigh bicycle from where it was leaning against the bakery wall, she cycled the short journey home in utter despair. Too shocked to cry, and only thinking of how much she truly loved William since the very first day they met, she couldn't believe it was all over. There were girls she knew who had lost their loved ones in action and, in some dark and twisted way, she envied them the telegrams reporting their deaths. Yes, the man she loved was alive but would now never be hers. She would have to live for the rest of her days with the knowledge that he was living and breathing without her, and that he didn't want her.

Furiously dumping her bike where the front gate used to be, before the neighbourhood's metal was salvaged to put towards building Spitfires, she rushed into the house without saying 'hello' to her mother, kicked off her shoes and dashed upstairs into her bedroom, where she found her eleven-year-old twin sisters, June and Joyce, making a den. The bedsheet was stretched out from the chest of drawers to the bedpost, as a makeshift roof, and the girls had on their gas masks and were imitating the sound of the air-raid siren and bombs going off. When Elsie lifted up the pillowcase that was the entrance to their den and glared at them, they both screamed 'Invasion!' and fell into fits of giggles.

'Oh, quieten down and get out of here, will you?' Elsie snapped, pulling down the roof of their den. 'Go on! Go and help Mother with the potatoes.'

Unused to their older sister's sharp tongue, the girls fell silent, yanked off their gas masks, discarded them in the corner and scurried off downstairs.

Elsie sat heavily on her bed, angrily looking around the bedroom, wanting to punch and kick the walls. She couldn't take it out on the house, though. It had been fixed up and repaired since it was bombed last year, with help from the Assistance Board, but much of their furniture and belongings had been damaged or destroyed or burned in the blaze, and so the house felt as if it were a shadow of their former home, held together by safety pins and string. Leaning her head against the wall, she wrapped her arms around her middle and squeezed her eyes shut, images of William rolling across her eyelids, forcing herself not to scream.

'Elsie,' said her mother's voice from the doorway, 'I heard you rush upstairs. What's upset you? Well, apart from the news that Russia's losing, which is enough to give anyone a migraine.'

Elsie opened her eyes to her mother's face peering into the room, her huge brown eyes watery and eternally kind, with the twins either side of her, also brown-eyed, all of them wearing a worried expression. It took all of her energy, but Elsie made herself smile. Since her dear father Alberto had been taken to a POW camp on the Isle of Man the previous year because he was an Italian national, Elsie had become the family member that everyone depended on. There were things she'd heard about the Isle of Man, from her cousins, that she had never told her mother – the substandard boarding house accommodation behind barbed wire where 'aliens' had to sleep, sometimes two to a bed; the poor-quality food and the lack of communication from the outside world. Though their father was permitted to write letters home twice a week, Elsie wasn't convinced he was receiving *their* replies at all. She protected her mother, Violet, from all of this because she didn't want to make her suffering worse.

'My engagement to William is off,' said Elsie, matter-of-factly. 'I don't want to talk about it or think about him ever again!'

Her mother and sisters gasped, entering the room and sitting on her bed all at once, Violet clutching Elsie's hands. June held out a precious humbug and offered it to her sister. Elsie shook her head and stroked June's hair in thanks. Her throat was thickening with the need to cry and she swallowed hard.

'But why?' said Violet. 'Did he explain why, for goodness' sake?'

Elsie shrugged, gave a quick shake of her head, raised her chin and stared defiantly out of the window. She felt her mother's shock transforming into anger.

'That foolish young man doesn't know what he's doing!' she said. 'How could he break my daughter's heart? I wish Alberto were here to talk some sense into him. Sometimes I wonder if William had all the sense knocked out of him when his truck was hit that day! I was so looking forward to you and him getting married. It's what I want for you, Elsie dear, to have a happy marriage like your father and I. Oh, how I miss my dear Alberto!'

At the mention of Alberto, Elsie watched her mother's eyes mist over.

'My heart will mend,' said Elsie reassuringly, taking a deep breath and trying to be brave. 'I will use the time I have spent with William to work more. We need the money, don't we, what with Papa away? Apparently they're taking girls on as bus drivers now, as well as conductresses, so I will register for the training and become a driver.'

'You don't always have to be brave and take everything on your shoulders,' said Violet gently, tucking Elsie's hair behind her ears. 'Come here, my lovely girl.'

Elsie's body was rigid with determination and she resisted the comfort at first, but as her mother gently pulled her into her bosom and her sisters threw their arms around her waist, her resolve weakened and she couldn't hold in her sadness and crushing disappointment for a moment longer. As she wept in the failing light, she felt she might drown in her own tears if it wasn't for her little family holding her up, keeping her afloat like a lifeboat.

'It's this blasted war,' said Violet softly. 'It's turning all our lives upside down. Hitler has a lot to answer for. How I wish it were all over.'

Chapter Four

'Room service,' said Audrey, knocking three times on William's door, holding a tray containing a steaming bowl of OXO and a doorstop slice of bread and margarine, since he hadn't come down for dinner. She knew she probably shouldn't be indulging him like this, but he was her brother and she had to take care of him. Their estranged mother, Daphne, certainly hadn't stepped up to the job. Though she'd written to tell her about William's return – and the injuries he'd suffered – Audrey hadn't heard a squeak since she had visited before Christmas.

'Yes?' William said. 'Come in.'

Pushing open the door, Audrey tried hard not to let disappointment show on her face when she realised that William was still in his pyjamas, and that he had not even washed or been outside that day at all, since his fire-watching duties the previous night. The skin of the left side of his face, the undamaged side, was almost grey from the lack of sunlight and the light in his blue eyes well and truly extinguished. His hair, normally swept back and held in place with pomade, had flopped down over his forehead and his shoulders were drooping. He looked a sorry state. The air in the bedroom was thick and sour with sleep and, after putting the tray down on the desk, Audrey threw open the window, taking in a gulp of fresh sea air and appreciating the view of the sun setting over the sea, like a giant knob of butter melting into the horizon. Though she'd lived at the bakery for seven years, she knew she could never grow tired of that view and wondered why it seemed to have no effect on William's spirits.

'Dinner for you, Lord William,' she said, trying to be light-hearted. 'Soup and bread. Had to put your actual dinner in the pigs' swill bin! We can't let food go to waste, you know, it's a criminal offence these days. You'll get thrown into jail for not being hungry!'

She had hoped for a small smile at least, but there was something different about William's demeanour. He seemed less defeated than usual, but angrier, as if he was just keeping a lid on a very dark mood. Audrey frowned, wondering what he and Elsie had argued about, hoping it wasn't too serious.

'Don't be like that,' he said, leaving the food where it was, untouched. 'I told you I'm not hungry. I meant what I said.'

Audrey sighed and twisted her wedding ring around her finger, registering that rationing and all the rushing around she did had meant she must have lost weight, since it was very slightly looser than normal. As a small boy, William had been so happy-go-lucky. With his mouth harp stuffed into the pocket of his shorts, even then, he'd play a tune to whoever would listen. Growing up in London, he was the mischievous one, scaling lamp posts or playing Knock Down Ginger and always dodging a hiding because of his handsome looks and winning smile. She longed to see a glimmer of that version of her brother again, but how should she find him?

'You can't go on like this, William,' she blurted out, half angry, half sad. 'I know you're suffering, but Elsie is suffering too… I thought, when you started to play your harp earlier, your spirits might be lifting, but—'

William glared at her with something like resentment, even dislike, in his eyes, and feeling stung, Audrey immediately stopped talking.

'I've called the engagement off,' he said, rearranging some papers on the writing desk. 'It's over between us.'

Audrey's hand flew to her throat as she tried to absorb his words. Her heart broke for Elsie – she had become like a sister. They'd shared so much together in the last year and Elsie was one of the family. William couldn't just cast her aside. Audrey couldn't hide her fury.

'You absolute clot,' she cried. 'Why would you do anything so senseless?'

William was leaning on the back of his desk chair, but he grabbed his crutches and hobbled over to the drawer in the small bedside table by his bed. He yanked it open, making everything on it wobble, and pulled out a letter, from which fell a photograph.

Audrey bent down to pick up the photograph, her heart sinking when she saw the image of Elsie with Jimmy, the pilot officer who had invited her to a Christmas party for evacuees last December. Jimmy had draped his arm over her shoulder, and Elsie was smiling, radiantly. Mary stood between the two of them, holding a Christmas parcel. Audrey knew what William was thinking, but this was just one fleeting moment in time. One moment during months and months of him being away. Her eyes flicked up from the photograph to William, who was staring at her, accusingly.

'Did you know about this?' he said, his voice wavering. 'Did you know they were courting, while I was away?'

Audrey shook her head in despair. 'Elsie hasn't been courting anyone but you,' she said quietly. 'Where did you get this letter?'

'I found it in her things,' he said, not meeting Audrey's eye. 'I saw the photograph and the words "thanks for the memory" on the back, whatever that means! What does that say about her feelings for me? I—'

Audrey held up a hand and interrupted: 'It says nothing about her feelings for you—'

But William spoke over her: 'And I was perfectly right in thinking that I shouldn't have come home,' he said. 'I knew Elsie would want to move on with another man, and now she feels trapped with me covered in ugly scars and hobbling around without my foot! What use am I to her? Perhaps I should write to this Jimmy myself on her behalf? Perhaps then she'll have a chance of happiness and be rid of me once and for all? At any rate, it's clear that it's not me she wants.'

Audrey's eyes darkened. Wanting to grab her brother by the shoulders and give him a good shaking, she felt dismayed. She would not listen to him talk himself into this knotted, muddled-up way of thinking.

'Don't say such daft things!' she cried. 'Elsie loves you. She's been as loyal as any girl could be. She went to a party with this chap out of goodness. Bournemouth was heaving with military personnel looking for a companion last Christmas, most of them away from their homes and families. He met her on the bus route she worked, I believe, and he invited her along to a party for the child evacuees, that's all. It doesn't mean a thing. She took Mary to that party and came home early because Mary sprained her ankle when she was dancing. I remember it was the same night that Lily went into labour. I can't speak for that pilot, but I know Elsie thought nothing more about it. I'm surprised at you, William, jumping to such conclusions about a girl like Elsie.'

'But look at her eyes,' he said, staring down at the photograph, his own eyes firing. 'They're full of life and laughter. When she looks at me now, all I can see is pity. She feels sorry for me, doesn't she? Who wants their sweetheart to pity them? What can I give her?'

'Everything,' Audrey said. 'Love is everything.'

William sat down on the bed and hung his head.

Impatient with his self-pity, Audrey went to leave, but before doing so, turned back to face him. He had laid down on the bed, his head on the pillow, weary with the world.

'On your wedding day last year, when you didn't turn up to the church without even offering an explanation, Elsie's heart was truly broken,' she said steadily. 'She thought perhaps you didn't love her, but she remained loyal to the hope that you would return. Hope was all she had. For the last six months, since you've been home, you've barely shown her any love or affection, despite her visiting you here almost every day after her shifts on the buses. Blaming her and treating her with suspicion says nothing about the way she's behaved, but a great deal about the man you seem to have become. I know what our father would have said to you.'

'What?' said William, his eyes blazing. Audrey had stepped over the line – there was an unwritten code between them never to use their dead father's name in an argument like this, but he had pushed her too far.

'Stop shilly-shallying around,' she said. 'And, for goodness' sake, *act like a man.*'

Leaving the room and closing the door behind her, Audrey stood in the hallway for a moment and held her hand on her heart. It was thudding like a bass drum in her chest.

'You're the only sane person around here,' said Audrey to Uncle John late that evening when he was shifting a twenty-stone bag of flour from one side of the bakehouse to another, as if it was as light as a feather. She raised her eyebrows at John's strength; four decades of bending over a trough, hand-mixing the dough and lifting flour sacks had made the man as strong as the carthorses that ploughed the fields.

'If that's the case, things must be bad,' he laughed, facing her and winking, before he collected up the pale dough that had spilled over the trough, like lava from a volcano, pushing it back in and knocking it to prove up again. In another few hours, he would weigh off the dough, mould it up, and prove it again, ready to bake and fill the shop and neighbourhood with the irresistibly comforting smell of fresh bread. He moved with ease and was such a natural, he could probably bake in his sleep. 'Perfect,' he said, smiling at her, standing with his hands on his waist.

She smiled back, suddenly overwhelmed with gratitude. Uncle John had stepped up when Charlie left, to take on the baking, and he had not let her down. In his white overalls, which he kept spotlessly clean, he had the highest standards. He kept all the utensils clean, diligently whitewashed the walls, always mixed and prepared the dough by hand and on time, and took the baked loaves and rolls out of the oven at the same time every day, like clockwork, ready for delivery and the customers. He took the baking life in his stride – the yeast going bananas in the July heat; a telegram from the Ministry of Food explaining that calcium was to be added to flour to combat the epidemic of rickets the Land Girls were suffering. He even cooked the neighbours' roasts in the bakery oven on a Sunday morning, just as Charlie had done, to help save the neighbourhood's already rationed fuel. Charlie had learned most of all he knew from John and Audrey held him in high regard.

'Thank you from the bottom of my heart for everything you've done for the bakery,' she said. 'Since Charlie left, I don't know what I'd have done without you.'

Feeling a little embarrassed, for she knew John didn't like fuss, she looked down at her fingers, which were stained red from sorting redcurrants, strawberries and gooseberries, ready for jam making and bottling.

John gave a gentle laugh and shook his head to indicate that her thanks were unnecessary. 'There's a lot of tradespeople on the lookout for customers these days,' he said. 'I promised Charlie I wouldn't let the Barton standards drop and I won't. Besides, I'm happy as a pig in mud here. There's nowhere I'd rather be, apart from maybe fishing for roach in the River Stour.' He grinned at her, before continuing: 'I'm too old to join up, but I can do my bit here.'

'You're a trooper, John,' said Audrey. 'Thank you.'

With his index and middle finger, he made the 'V for Victory' sign that Winston Churchill had been photographed making in the paper and now everyone was chalking or painting on walls, or tapping out in Morse code – three dots and a dash.

'The V sign is the symbol... of the unconquerable will... of the occupied territories... and oh, my old brain is goin',' said John, imitating Churchill's voice and repeating part of a speech he'd recently made on the wireless. 'Summat like that anyhow.'

Audrey laughed and John doffed his cap, which fell to the floor. He bent over to pick it up and when he stood back up straight, she noticed his breathing was wheezy. She frowned while he stopped to catch his breath, but then he started coughing. He spluttered and coughed for a good minute, with Audrey patting his back, before he returned to normal, his face bright red and clammy.

'That cough has been getting worse since this time last year,' Audrey said, shaking her head. 'You need to get it seen to. Are you even taking anything for it? I've got some blackberry syrup upstairs.'

'Port wine and brandy is my medicine,' he said, spluttering. 'It's nothin' but a bit of flour in m' throat.'

'That may be, but it needs seeing to,' she said. 'It worries me. Pat told me you're hiding it from me.'

John shook his head, rolling his eyes at the mention of his sister, Charlie's mother, Pat. A tireless volunteer for the WVS, when she wasn't involved in the local 'meat pie scheme', cycling meat pies to the Land Girls working in the surrounding villages and fields, she was running knitting and clothes mending groups, or boiling up a sheep's head to make a stew. She was a remarkable woman, but she did have her finger – and nose – in every pie.

'Trust her to be makin' a meal out of my ailments,' he said. 'There's nothing for you to worry about, love. Speakin' of worrying matters though, how's that brother of yours? I saw him heading out for fire-watching duties not half-hour ago, but he barely grunted at me. I know it ain't easy for him with his injuries, but it looks like he's got the weight of the world bearin' down on his young shoulders.'

Uncle John shook his head and Audrey sighed, folding her arms across her chest. She thought of poor Elsie and the words she'd had with William earlier. She regretted being so short with him, but felt increasingly infuriated by his behaviour.

'He's not well,' she said. 'It's like he's gone into himself. All he can see is darkness. He's gone and broken off his engagement to Elsie too.'

'He never has!' said John. 'Get 'im to come down here tomorrow. The boy can 'elp me.'

'But it's his foot, he's…' Audrey started. 'I don't know if he's able to…'

'He's got two working arms, ain't 'e?' John said. 'He doesn't need two feet to 'elp me out. I've known men more injured than 'im in the Great War get back on their feet without complainin'. In my mind, that boy needs less sympathy and more orders.'

'I'll speak to him,' said Audrey, privately dreading the conversation.

John returned to work, while Audrey lingered. It was these hours, late on, when the rest of the bakery slept but there was still so much to do, that she missed Charlie the most. They'd always done their talking, debating and deciding in the bakehouse while he worked on the bread. He seemed to think more clearly when he was busy working with his hands. She felt the same when she was mixing the ingredients for a cake or the counter goods – the methodical process helped her think straight.

'What else is on your mind, my girl?' said John. 'I can tell there's somethin'.'

Audrey thought about telling him about her fears for Lily and how she was coping with motherhood, but decided against it. Going by his advice for how to deal with William, he wouldn't have a lot of sympathy for Lily.

'I'm all right, John,' she said, forcing a smile. 'I'm still getting no end of orders for wedding cakes from young couples getting wed while their sweethearts are home on leave. How they'll make their marriages work, I don't know; they'll spend more time apart than they will together.'

'Absence makes the 'eart grow fonder,' said John. 'Or so I've 'eard.'

'I'm having to make the dried fruit spread very thinly now,' Audrey mused, thinking of the dwindling supplies in the storeroom. 'Course, I can't ice the celebration cakes anymore since icing is banned and I'm using the plaster of Paris cake covers, but folk still want a delicious cake inside, don't they? I thought we had more raisins and a box of glacé cherries in the storeroom, but I can't see them anywhere. I've lost track of a bag of sugar too, and I'm panicking since every spillage, wastage or lost item has to be recorded and reported to the Ministry. You haven't moved anything in store, have you?'

John shook his head and stopped what he was doing. 'Nobody's pilferin', are they?' he said. 'None of the delivery boys got their 'ands in the stocks?'

She shook her head, confused, trying to imagine anyone at the bakery taking ingredients. Nobody would do that. Perhaps she had misplaced them; her mind was overflowing these days.

'Maybe you put 'em somewhere else,' John said. 'Remember, we got that leaflet about what to do in an invasion a few weeks back? "Hide the sugar" was on that list. Maybe you took heed and hid it! There'll be an explanation. Only someone downright desperate or stupid would steal from the 'and that feeds 'em.'

Chapter Five

Maggie perched on a wooden stool in front of her dressing table, one of the few pieces of furniture that had escaped being chopped up and burned for fuel during the freezing winter months. Taking the turquoise and gold hairbrush and handheld mirror from the silk-lined vanity set her sweetheart, Pilot Officer George Meadows, had gifted her, she brushed through her cloud of strawberry blonde hair one hundred times and applied a bright slash of lipstick to her lips. Sitting on the floor were her two younger sisters, Nancy and Isabel. Nancy was darning the heel of her stockings, while Isabel was cutting the toes off her shoes to make them into sandals.

'When I get married to George,' said Maggie dreamily, 'I'm going to wear my hair like Veronica Lake, to the wedding. You know, her "one-eyed do". Like this.'

Isabel put down her shoe and smiled in admiration at her older sister. 'Oh, you'll look so pretty, Maggie,' she said. 'If only I had half your good looks, maybe I could find a husband and wouldn't be condemned to spend my life working in that rotten laundry.'

Maggie left one side of her shiny hair tumbling over her left eye and pouted her lips, resting her hands on her crossed knees. Though her sisters might be called plain-faced, she knew very well how pretty she was, and wanted to stay lovely for George. But it wasn't just her sparkly eyes and white teeth that had won him over. No, she believed he had fallen in love with her determination not to give in to the misery of wartime. Some women – and her grandmother, Gwendolen, who she lived with was a shining example – wore the grave hardship of wartime on their faces like a slap and had a fit every time there was an air-raid siren. But Maggie made sure to stay fresh-faced and bright whatever she came up against.

Looking more closely at Isabel, she frowned. There was a bruise on her sister's cheek that hadn't been there last time she looked.

'Is that boss of yours giving you a hard time?' said Maggie. 'Where did you get that bruise?'

Isabel's hand shot to her cheek and she blushed, pulling her brown hair over her face and staring down at the shoes she was working on.

'He's got a temper on him all right, but it was my fault for being clumsy,' said Isabel quietly. 'He pushed me because I wasn't working fast enough – jabbed me between my shoulder blades – and I tripped and hit my face on the corner of a shelf, that's all.'

'That's *all*?' said Maggie, pinning back her hair. 'How dare he! If he lays a finger on you again, Isabel, you come and tell me. I'll not have anyone hurt you.'

Maggie and Nancy shared a concerned glance. Whereas Nancy could look after herself, Isabel was vulnerable and always had been. The youngest sister, she'd had her pigtails pulled at school and stones thrown at her by the neighbourhood boys, just for being shy and awkward. In truth, she was a gentle and loving soul, and whenever she was on the sharp end of their grandmother's tongue, Maggie tried to protect her. Maggie knew Isabel hated her job at the laundry, but she also knew the family desperately needed all the girls' wages. Keeping your job – even one with a cruel boss – was paramount.

'And what will you wear for a dress, Maggie?' said Nancy, deliberately changing the subject. 'Your bakery overall? You can borrow my dungarees from my night shifts in the aircraft factory, if you like.'

'A beautiful wedding dress of course, made with the finest silk and handmade lace!' said Maggie, winking at Isabel. 'No, but it will be lovely, if I can get enough coupons to buy some decent fabric, that is. Rationing has made it difficult, but I have my ways...'

Clothes had been rationed on 1 June 1941, as supplies of wool and cotton had fallen, with an announcement on the wireless from the President of the Board of Trade, Oliver Lyttelton. You were allowed sixty-six clothing coupons per year and you could spend them how you wanted, but with a mackintosh taking nine coupons and a woollen dress eleven coupons, women were panicking about their wardrobes. It was a good job, thought Maggie, that she had a plan in place.

'You could make a dress out of parachute silk,' said Isabel, looking relieved that the conversation had moved on from her bruise. 'Some girls are doing that, y'know. Last time a parachute came down in Bournemouth the silk was stripped off it in seconds. I could get you some, probably, though it might be bloodstained.'

Maggie pulled a face. Isabel was talking about enemy pilots crash-landing, but German landmines were also dropped on silk parachutes, so when locals got wind of one landing, they'd be at the site in minutes, just for the fabric, undeterred by danger.

'No, thank you,' she said in disgust. 'No, I'm going to have a gorgeous gown made from the best fabric I can buy. I'll not have gravy browning down my legs either, but real silk stockings, and my shoes will be—' She paused and put her finger to her lips, while dreaming of her shoes.

'Wooden clogs?' giggled Isabel. 'Like you wear to work?'

Maggie stared at her in mock disapproval.

'Has he even asked you to marry him yet?' said Nancy, frowning. 'Does he even exist? You've never brought him home.'

'How can I bring him home?' Maggie said wearily, putting the brush and mirror back into the leather vanity case, closing it and pushing it under her bed, the only place it would be safe from her grandmother's beady eyes.

She looked around the room that she shared with her sisters: the floral wallpaper peeled, and damp crept across the walls like ivy, the creaky beds complained every time anyone climbed onto the thin mattresses, empty candleholders were lined up on the windowsill, waiting to be refreshed. The two-up, two-down cottage that the girls lived in with their grandmother since their parents had passed away was a poor excuse for a home.

Their grandmother, Gwendolen, squandered money on home-made alcoholic concoctions such as dandelion wine, nettle beer or ethyl alcohol mixed with hawthorn berry juice, illegally sold by a shady neighbour, and each day they only just managed to put food on the table. Maggie's job at the bakery helped; Isabel earned a pittance in the laundry and Nancy worked at the aircraft factory. But Maggie was fed up with scraping through. She wanted a better life and believed that George Meadows was the key to that. Since they'd met, she had worked hard to give the impression that she was from a good, well-educated family, who had a nice house in a decent area of Bournemouth. She couldn't tell him the truth – that her grandmother loved the drink and they were completely poverty-stricken.

'He hasn't asked you yet, has he?' said Nancy and quickly held up her hand to catch the powder puff Maggie was hurling at her. 'You're not going to do much damage with that!'

Regaining her composure, Maggie smiled briefly.

'No, he hasn't asked yet,' she replied, 'but I can sense it's only a matter of time. Look, I better get to the bakery. See you tonight, girls. Isabel, if that man touches you again, come and tell me. I'm not afraid to tell him what I think of him. When I'm married, Isabel love, you can go into that laundry and tell him he can stuff his job!'

Isabel beamed at Maggie, and Maggie silently vowed she would improve her sisters' lives, no matter what. She blew them a kiss and headed down the narrow staircase, pausing at the door of the room where their grandmother slept in an ancient rocking chair, her woollen stockings rolled at the ankles, revealing sharp and knobbly, vein-ridden knees. Maggie shivered; sometimes her grandmother resembled a corpse.

'Goodbye, you old bag,' she whispered. 'It won't be long until I say goodbye for good.'

A shadow of guilt passed over her as she left the house and stepped into the street. She thought of the clandestine meetings she'd had with the neighbourhood's women in alleyways to 'trade', some with their loot hidden in prams alongside their babies, but she shrugged off the guilt as quickly as it had arrived. You didn't get anything by waiting, not in wartime. She would pay back everything she'd 'borrowed' one day, but for the time being, she had one goal: George Meadows, her ticket to a better life.

Walking quickly down the street, she took off her cardigan and carried it folded neatly on her arm. It was a hot day – women would be hatless and stocking-less – but not Maggie, whose standards would remain high, no matter what other women did.

Arriving at the bakery at 8 a.m., the front step sparkling clean, the gold 'Bakery' lettering on the window polished, and a row of honey-coloured loaves already on display and the scent of fresh bread in the air, she slowed down when she heard raised voices from inside. It was Audrey and a man having some kind of heated discussion. Maggie frowned. Heart thudding, feeling suddenly paranoid, she gingerly opened the door, releasing the jingly bell, and went inside.

Chapter Six

Lily was upstairs in her bedroom, fastening the safety pin on Joy's nappy – who was blissfully quiet and distracted by Bertie, Lily's budgie, fluttering around the room – when she heard the muffled sound of Audrey's raised voice from the bakery shop below. There was a male voice too, but it was quieter and she couldn't work out to whom it belonged.

'Whoever can that be?' she said, frowning. Audrey was rarely het up and never did she raise her voice to a customer. Indeed, she gave every customer her personal attention, ensuring they were completely satisfied.

For a split second, Lily imagined that the old Home Guard man from the beach had come back with a police officer in tow, to arrest her for being a bad mother and 'abandoning' Joy. A wave of guilt washed over her as she was struck again by her careless behaviour on the beach. Her porcelain white cheeks turned pink at the memory: how could she do such a thing? What if the ARP warden had sounded the gas rattle when she'd been in the sea? Baby Joy would have been left exposed on the beach, with no one to fix on her gas mask – an awful great thing that looked like a diving helmet. The hairs on the back of Lily's neck bristled at the thought.

'I'm so sorry,' she whispered to Joy, who was furiously pedalling her little legs in the air. 'I don't know what I was thinking.'

There was a side to her own character that Lily couldn't quite fathom; the same recklessness that had got her in this situation the previous year with Henry Bateman, who, unbeknownst to Lily, was engaged to be married. Any girl with a sensible head on her shoulders would have refused to become intimate with Henry without the security of a ring on her finger, or at least an assurance that he was single. But seventeen-year-old Lily hadn't been cynical enough to question or doubt him, and besides, she wasn't interested in marriage. As far as she could tell, it meant a life of domesticity and Lily had never wanted that. She had also wanted independence and freedom from her father, Victor's, watchful eye. Well, that particular wish had come true in spades: her father had refused to meet baby Joy and accept Lily's indiscretion, no matter what. Though she had written to him in London several times since the child's birth, he hadn't even replied. Thank goodness for Audrey, who had welcomed her into the bakery family and given her a home.

'Your silly grandfather is an old curmudgeon,' she said to Joy, her playful words belying the sadness she felt. In truth, she missed Victor dreadfully, and despite thinking she would manage motherhood without his support, privately knew that she was struggling. Keeping Joy was her choice, she thought, kissing her baby's soft cheek. When Joy was born, Lily realised she could never have given her up for adoption. She loved her deeply and wanted to protect her and be a good mother and, with Audrey's help, it had seemed altogether possible. The problem was – and Lily wouldn't admit this to anyone – fear that she was a complete and utter disappointment to her own baby gnawed at her confidence. All the crying Joy did, the fitful nights and the refusal to sleep, felt to Lily as if she was saying: '*You're hopeless, you're getting it all wrong, you never wanted me in the first place.*'

Lily's eyes pricked with tears and she sighed, shaking her head. *I'm losing my mind*, she thought.

Lifting Joy and placing her on her hip, where she seemed to fit like a jigsaw piece, Lily opened the bedroom door to listen to the raised voices coming from the shop. Heading down the stairs, she hoped it wasn't another customer with bad news about one of their relations on the front line. Some of the outpourings of grief she'd seen in the shop took her breath away. Audrey, however, seemed to take it all in her stride and have limitless love and compassion for all her customers, neighbours and friends. The shop overflowed with warmth in more ways than one.

'Gracious me,' she said, stopping dead when she reached the bottom step of the stairs and the voices became discernible. The blood drained from her face and her heart thudded in her chest when she recognised the male voice. She could hardly believe her ears. After swearing he never wanted anything more to do with Lily or to see her again and making her promise she would never contact him, it was *Henry Bateman.*

'I want to see her, Mrs Barton,' he was saying, his voice firm. 'I do have a right to see her and you can't stop me from doing so.'

Panicking, Lily squeezed shut her eyes and held Joy closer to her chest. Flickering images, like the end of a film reel at the pictures, flashed across the insides of her eyelids. Henry in the office at the Ministry of Information, holding her around the waist and staring adoringly into her eyes. Henry telling her he was engaged, his expression unreadable. Henry drunk, shouting at her, telling her that her unborn baby was a 'dirty little secret'. Henry's well-spoken wife, Helen, immaculately turned out, looking down her nose at Lily in that way that said: *you will never have what I have.*

Hearing footsteps approaching, she pulled opened the store cupboard door and wedged herself and Joy inside, crouching by the bags and boxes of dried fruits and nuts, cinnamon, spices, sugar, butter, cocoa powder and chocolate. The fragrance was intoxicating. Her heart thumped as the footsteps came nearer and the door was flung open.

'Whatever are you doing in here?' Audrey asked, her expression thunderous, then immediately softening into an amused smile. 'Come out, will you? He's gone, but would you believe he thinks he can just walk in and demand to see you? It beggars belief! I told him he was most unwelcome at this bakery after how he treated you last time he called, but he insists he wants to bury the hatchet and to apologise for his actions. He asked me to give you this.'

Audrey passed Lily a handwritten note. She accepted it and held it in her fingertips as if it might explode.

'He says he's changed,' Audrey said quietly, peering into the store cupboard and frowning. 'I'm all for forgiveness and second chances, but I have to warn you, Lily, some leopards never change their spots.'

*

'What can I get you, Mrs Cook?' Audrey asked, back in the shop, serving customers. 'Your normal order of half a dozen rolls, is it?'

The door was wedged open to let in the breeze, and Mrs Cook flapped a copy of the *Echo* in front of her face. The grim headlines caught Audrey's eye and made her heart sink: *SOUTH COAST IS NAZI TARGET: CHILDREN AMONG THOSE KILLED*. Behind the counter and out of the customers' sight, Audrey sighed and stepped out of her wooden clogs for a moment, cooling her hot feet on the floor tiles.

'Yes, please, Audrey love,' replied Mrs Cook. 'And a dozen egg custards would be nice.'

Audrey, putting the headline out of her mind, let out a laugh. 'You'll be lucky!' she said. 'Now wouldn't that be lovely, egg custards back on the menu? I for one can't wait until this war is over and I can go back to making some of my favourites. No iced buns, no meringues, no egg custards – what's the world coming to, eh?'

'Hitler has a lot to answer for,' said Mrs Cook. 'If he turns up on my doorstep, expecting me to surrender, I'll tell him what for, that's for sure.'

'You say that,' said Flo, another customer in the queue, 'but look at the poor folk in the Channel Islands. Those that didn't evacuate before invasion didn't have a choice! The German army marched in and took their cars, their food and their documents, paraded down the high street, threatened to arrest or shoot anyone who tried to escape to England and that's it! What can you do?'

'This,' Mrs Cook said, lifting up her handbag and swinging it violently through the air.

The women laughed darkly as they contemplated the awful prospect of invasion.

Audrey loved her customers – despite the shocking headlines and the bad news from the eastern battlefront, their humour and resilience never failed to impress her. Listening to their gossip, she continued to serve the fourteen-strong queue and thought about Henry Bateman. Though she was pretending to be calm about it, his arrival at the bakery had shaken her up no end. Last time he'd been near, Charlie had threatened him never to return or else he'd throw him in the bakery oven, but Charlie wasn't there to wave his fist this time, was he? Besides, Henry had insisted he must see Lily to make amends, and what could Audrey do about it?

'Any word from Charlie?' Mrs Cook asked, interrupting Audrey's thoughts. 'I can taste the difference in the bread, you know. It's still good, but there's a lightness to Charlie's bread and the crust is perfect. I miss him.'

Audrey smiled and rested her hands on the counter. She'd heard this numerous times from customers; some disgruntled that their baker had gone to the front line, others full of admiration. Thinking of her husband and suddenly missing him terribly, she twirled her wedding ring around her finger.

'He occasionally writes, but he doesn't tell me an awful lot. He's a man of few words, as you know. In his last letter, he asked me to send him a Dorset apple cake in the next comfort package,' said Audrey, smiling. 'By the sound of it he's missing his home-cooked food. I sent him the cake, of course, wrapped in brown paper and packed in a tin. Heaven knows if it'll reach him.'

'That's his way of saying he's missing *you*, Audrey love,' Mrs Cook said gently. 'My son Richard says that when he's in battle, he thinks about me sitting in the garden, sunning my face and enjoying the chrysanthemums. I wanted to write back and ask him when he thinks I have time to sun my face, what with turning the garden into a vegetable patch and running around after eight grandchildren, shopping, queuing, juggling the rations with an empty larder, and dashing to the air-raid shelter every other night, but if that thought helps him get through, then so be it. And how's that brother of yours?'

Audrey opened her mouth to reply, but at that moment Maggie's sweetheart, Pilot Officer George Meadows, came into the shop, causing a stir in the queue. His hair was cropped close to his head, framing a smooth tanned face and grey eyes that crinkled around the edges when he smiled. He was straight off the silver screen.

'Morning, beautiful,' George greeted Maggie, offering her a paper bag filled with aniseed balls. Sweets hadn't been rationed yet, but there had been rumours that it wasn't long before they – and chocolate – would be.

With her mouth in an 'ooh' shape, and with delicate fingers, Maggie took a sweet and popped it in her mouth.

'Here he is,' she said, beaming, 'my knight in shining armour.'

The ladies in the queue were transfixed.

'He's lost his white 'orse by the look of it,' muttered Flo, rolling her eyes.

'No, he ain't,' said Maggie, dashing out from behind the counter. 'Horse and carriage are waiting outside, aren't they, George?'

George laughed heartily as she draped her arms around his neck and quickly kissed him on the cheek, coquettishly kicking up her right leg behind her. He took off his hat and pretended to faint, which caused a murmur of laughter and tutting in the queue.

'Well I never!' said Elizabeth, another regular customer. 'I only wanted bread, not a night at the pictures.'

Maggie delved in her pocket and held out some smelling salts under George's nose, which he pretended had revived him. The ladies in the shop were enjoying the show, but, aware of Audrey staring at her, Maggie quickly resumed her position behind the counter and got back to serving, while George leaned on the edge of it, chin resting in his hand, admiring the woman he was obviously smitten by.

Maggie leaned over and asked him: 'Now, what can I get you, sir? A rock cake, carrot cake or a jam tart?'

'I can think of many things I'd like to try,' said George flirtatiously.

The queue gasped. Hands were flapped in front of faces and eyes rolled.

'Gracious, it's hot in here!' said Mrs Cook.

'You should make an honest woman out of our Maggie,' called out Flo. 'We could do with something to celebrate, couldn't we, ladies?'

Other customers in the queue murmured their agreement and George raised his eyebrows before taking a bow.

'It just so happens,' he said, 'that I have a certain question to ask a certain girl. I'm to be posted overseas soon. So, Maggie Rose, will you do me the honour of becoming my wife?'

The women gasped as Maggie's hand flew to her chest, where she pointed, as if to say, *Me?*

George nodded, laughing once more.

'Yes!' Maggie squealed. 'Yes, I will!'

Running out from behind the counter again, this time followed by the saucer-shaped eyes of the customers, Maggie jumped up at George and he spun her around. With her head nestled in his neck, both of them fell about laughing, before they stopped spinning and locked lips, causing a spontaneous round of applause from the waiting women.

'Bless us and spare us,' muttered Mrs Cook.

She and Audrey exchanged a good-humoured glance while Maggie jumped up and down on the spot, like an excited child.

Uncle John, who had come into the shop from the bakehouse to see what all the fuss was about, broke out into a hacking cough, quickly disappearing again.

'I expect you two lovebirds will be needing a cake?' Audrey asked, walking out from behind the counter to hug Maggie. She was such a slight thing and so young, but clearly so happy.

'Oh yes, please,' said Maggie, clasping her hands together. 'Three tiers high, iced with pale pink icing, and those beautiful roses you make from royal icing resting on the top, please.'

Audrey laughed, as they both knew iced cakes had been banned, but she wished she could fulfil Maggie's wishes. She'd do anything to protect her joy. In fact, she wished she could bottle it. In wartime, happiness was a precious commodity. One had to snatch it, however fleeting, hold on to it and refuse to let it go.

Chapter Seven

'This will be the last time I do this,' whispered Maggie to herself, at the end of the working day when she crept into the store cupboard, while Audrey was bagging up the 'stales' in the shop to sell off for a penny. Straining to reach the top shelf, her dress brushing against the back of her knees, she knocked her knee against a wooden crate and snagged her stockings.

'Blast,' she said, staring at the run. 'Not another pair ruined!'

Ever since George's proposal that morning, her mood had been sky-high, but now, with a shiny future dangling precariously in front of her like a new penny on a string, it was more important than ever that she didn't trip up. This was her chance to get away from her sour-faced grandmother and live a better life with the man she loved, wasn't it? No more shabby clothes, no more rinsing out her sisters' one pair of stockings every night in cold water so they could wear them again the next day, no more burning the furniture for fuel in winter, or suffering their grandmother wasting the girls' earnings and cursing her luck. She'd have to see to it that her sisters were looked after too, particularly Isabel, who wouldn't cope alone. Hopefully George wouldn't mind if they came to stay, wherever they chose to live. He came from Hampstead in London, so when the war was over, she'd no doubt live with him there, where she imagined them taking dinner at the Savoy, or going to the Lyceum Ballroom in her finest glad rags. Oh, it would be so very exciting!

'I love you, George Meadows,' she sighed.

Carefully, with light, nimble fingers that trembled just a little, she cut a hole in the bottom of a packet of sugar with a sharp knife, and held her empty gas-mask case underneath it, watching the pure white grains silently flow into it. When the bag was half empty and the box almost full, she adjusted its position on the shelf to stem the flow. Heart thumping in her chest, she quickly sealed the case shut: done.

It's not that bad, she reasoned with herself, as she swept up a few spilt grains with her hands.

Spotting a half-empty tub of beautiful red glacé cherries on the shelf above her, she quickly lifted the lid, took one and popped it in her mouth, letting the gorgeous sugary sweetness burst onto her tongue. She closed her eyes and chewed, pushing away the guilt that was pressing against her brow. Besides, as she understood it, whatever stock Audrey reported to the Ministry of Food as sold one monthwas allocated again for the next month, so it wasn't as if the bakery was losing out, was it? What the spivs and drones were doing in London made her activity seem harmless. She'd heard from a friend of a friend in the city that when a high-explosive bomb had hit the Café de Paris ballroom in March, rescuers found that looters had got to the site before them and were pulling jewellery off the revellers' bodies. Now, *that* was wrong. *That* was downright shameful. Borrowing a bit of sugar and some dried fruit to sell or swap for real or 'buckshee' clothing vouchers was all she was doing. The war made you have to do things you wouldn't normally do, didn't it? You had to be crafty. If she waited until peacetime again to get what she wanted, she might be waiting a lifetime. Besides, she'd do pretty much *anything* to keep George Meadows, and was more determined than ever to collect enough coupons to keep up appearances during their courtship and be a proper bride on their wedding day. So far, she'd managed to keep him away from her home and there was no way she could let him meet Gwendolen, her grandmother.

When she'd mentioned George to her, she'd asked: 'What on earth does he see in you?' – no less than Maggie had expected. If there was one person who had taught her you had to look out for yourself in life, it was her grandmother, but she'd done that without even meaning to.

'Maggie?' said Audrey quietly, suddenly standing behind her in the store cupboard, where the door had silently swung open. 'What on earth do you think you're doing?'

'Oh, I…' said Maggie, turning on her heel, stunned, the gas-mask case slipping from her fingers. Hitting the hard, tiled floor, the box flew open and the sugar spilled out. Flushing bright red, her eyes wide with terror and fury at being discovered, Maggie left the mess on the floor and shoved past Audrey. Without collecting her things, she ran through the shop and out into Fisherman's Road, where people were scurrying home past the sandbags heaped along the shopfronts, the windows criss-crossed with bombproof tape. She looked left and right and saw, in the far distance, George Meadows walking towards the bakery. He'd arranged to meet her after work, to take her for a fish and chip supper.

Head down and walking in the opposite direction, she caught sight of her reflection in the butcher's window – make-up running down her cheeks like railway tracks. He couldn't see her like this! But if she wasn't at the bakery when he arrived, Audrey might tell him what had happened, and then what? George was an honest, respectable man. If he got wind of Maggie's lies, the engagement would be off. *Blast*, she thought. *Damn and blast.*

'Maggie!' she heard Audrey call from behind her. Without answering, Maggie changed direction again and made off up the street towards George, hot tears pricking her eyes. Using her thumbs to clean the make-up from under her eyes, she pinched her cheeks for a makeshift blush, whipped off her apron to reveal a pretty frock she'd traded with a neighbour for a few ounces of sugar, and plastered a smile on her face, before running headlong towards the future, into George's outstretched arms.

'Maggie Rose,' he said, holding her tight, 'where is your gas mask and why are you in such a rush?'

*

Audrey stood with her hands on her hips in the bakery doorway, watching the figures of Maggie and George melt into the distance. 'Well, blow me down,' she said, biting her lip and looking up at the postcard-perfect, blue sky. 'I would never have expected that to happen. Not in a million years.'

It was the most beautiful evening, she thought, following a swift's flight over the tops of the houses and watching a group of schoolboys having a raucous piggyback fight in the street, but you couldn't trust the sky. It seemed innocent enough, but as Audrey knew only too well, at any moment a formation of planes could appear on the horizon, as they had done all through the Battle of Britain, carrying and dropping bombs to blow apart people's lives.

Trust, thought Audrey, picturing Maggie's horrified face when she'd been discovered in the store cupboard. She had thought she could trust Maggie – and now look what had happened. She'd caught her red-handed, stealing sugar from right under her nose.

Shaking her head in dismay, Audrey changed the shop sign to CLOSED, feeling upset rather than angry. Hadn't she always treated Maggie well? Hadn't she packed her off home at the end of the week with her wages and a fresh loaf? Didn't she involve her in all the bakery's comings and goings – at knitting parties and clothes mending evenings, or simply for a slice of pie and a cup of hot tea, treating her like one of the family? Hadn't she offered to bake her a wedding cake that very morning?

Wishing that Charlie was there to talk to, she went into the kitchen and put the nettle soup on the range to heat up. While it bubbled in the pot, she looked out of the window into the courtyard garden, where Mary was sucking the sweet nectar from a white nettle flower, while William was on his knees, weeding the small patch of garden they'd turned over to growing vegetables. John, she knew, would be in the Carpenter's Arms, enjoying an ale and discussing military operations, before returning to the bakery later. Audrey wished William would go with him – it would do him good.

Averting her eyes from the stump that used to be William's right foot, she ran her gaze over his wooden crutches, which were leaning against the bakery wall next to the delivery bicycle. At least he was out of his bedroom – that was something to be grateful for. But she hadn't seen hide nor hair of Elsie since the other evening when she'd run out of the bakery after the argument with William. And now Maggie had run off too. Everyone was running away, it seemed. She was going to have to do something about that, wasn't she? It was up to her to keep her ramshackle family together and safe through this war, and she wasn't about to give up. Thinking about all the people she loved, her throat thickened with sudden emotion.

'Gracious me, this won't do at all,' she tutted, cross with herself, stirring the nettle soup, then pulling herself together and throwing open the window to call to William and Mary: 'Soup's ready.'

'What do you think I should do?' she asked John, after dinner, when William had gone to talk to the ARP warden about his fire-watching rota, and Mary was back outside, petting her rabbit. She'd had no intention of talking about Maggie's pilfering to anyone, but found the words rushing from her lips before her brain caught up.

John's mouth was agape, revealing gaps where several of his teeth once were. He wiped his forehead with his handkerchief and leaned his weight on the big wooden table, shaking his head in shock.

'String her up!' he said. 'The little devil! I wouldn't have pegged Maggie as a wrong'un! Now we know why she's always laughin' and smilin'. How dare she? When times are so 'ard too. Folk are eating paraffin cake to get by without luxuries, and she's got her 'ands in the sugar! Well, I never.'

'She's young, John,' said Audrey quietly. 'Barely out of school. Maybe her young man put her up to it? He was in the bakery shop proposing to her this morning. Perhaps it's something to do with that. Maybe she's in trouble and she's not letting on.'

'She'll be in trouble when I get my 'ands on 'er!' he said, widening his eyes. 'If Charlie knew about this, he'd go straight to the police and report her for thievin', I tell you. Have you 'ad words with 'er?'

Audrey shook her head and felt uncharacteristically lost for words.

'If you don't, I will,' he said. 'I can't believe she could be that daft. What's she taken then?'

Audrey explained what she thought Maggie had pinched over recent weeks.

John thudded down on the baking table with his hands, coughing as he did so, until he was almost doubled over. Gripping the table's edge, he held his hanky up to his mouth as he continued to cough, the top of his balding head and his face turning boiling red.

Rushing to the tap, Audrey fetched him a tumbler of water, placing it down in front of him on the table. Resting a hand on his back as he carried on coughing, he seemed unable to catch his breath. Audrey's eyes darted around the bakery, as she tried to work out how to help him.

'John,' she said calmly. 'John, try to take a breath and have a sip of water.'

But John was shaking his head and couldn't stop coughing, the hacking motion making his body convulse, his face turning a horrible shade of dark purple, his eyes watery and bulging. He was holding his hand up to his neck, loosening the collar of his shirt. Was he choking?

'It's all right, John, just try to breathe in through your nose and out through your mouth,' Audrey said, her voice quivering. Though she was trying to remain calm, John was in trouble and she didn't know what to do. Racking her brain, he started to hyperventilate.

'Oh goodness, try to calm down, John,' she said, kneeling down in front of him, her eyes huge and wet.

Catching sight of Mary in the doorway, her rabbit still in her arms, Audrey was just about to ask her to get help when John made a wretched gasping sound and keeled over, falling off the chair and landing with a loud thud on the bakehouse stone floor.

'John!' Audrey shrieked, holding her fingers to his pulse. 'Mary, quick! Run to Old Reg and ask him to telephone for an ambulance. Tell him it's John and it's an emergency.'

With her rabbit tucked under one arm, Mary fled the bakehouse, rushing to find help.

Audrey crouched on the floor, stroking John's forehead, trying her best to make him comfortable but fearing that life was slipping from him in front of her very eyes.

Chapter Eight

'You've hardly eaten a thing,' said George, gesturing to the fish and chips growing cold on the newspaper wrappings on Maggie's lap.

They were sitting on a bench in Bournemouth's Pleasure Gardens eating supper. Guilt was making her behave strangely and she was grateful to the band that was playing in the bandstand, to give them something to focus on. Since the bombs that fell directly on the Square earlier in the year, destroying Woolworths and nearby shops, the centre of Bournemouth had come back to life and was now ablaze with dahlias, geraniums and musical offerings from the Bournemouth Municipal Orchestra. Children holding fishing nets played in the stream with their trousers rolled up, and posters advertised the dances held at the Pavilion. There was something steely about the residents of the town; it would take more than the Luftwaffe to crush their spirit and bring the seaside resort to its knees. Despite the coastal defences, requisitioned hotels, thousands of uniformed men and women stationed there, the bomb damage and lives lost, Bournemouth fought hard to cling to its holiday atmosphere, though Maggie wasn't sharing in it today.

'Lost your appetite?' continued George.

She stared at the fish and chips growing cold. It was true, Maggie had barely touched them and her stomach churned with nerves.

'I don't want to turn to fat,' she said, smiling, and putting her hands around her tiny waist, as she forced herself to swallow down a couple more chips and then offered the remainder of her fish to George.

'No chance of that, Maggie,' he grinned, willingly eating up the fish, making her wonder where he put it all – he was as skinny as a whippet. 'You're a natural beauty.'

Forcing her troubling thoughts of Audrey aside, she told herself to forget what had happened at the bakery and simply focus on George.

'Truth is, I'm excited,' she said unconvincingly, though she was absolutely genuine. 'To be your fiancée. I can't stop thinking about what our wedding will be like. It's going to be the happiest day of my life.'

Their toes were touching and she hoped George wasn't aware of how scuffed and battered her shoes were – she would have to find a new pair somehow. Tucking her feet underneath the bench, and once the fish and chip supper between them was finished, they sidled up close to one another, until the sides of each of their warm bodies were touching. Maggie blushed as she imagined the two of them laying side by side in a bed on their wedding night. As if reading her mind, George confidently draped his arm around her shoulders, flexing his jaw as he smiled with pride. Her head rested against his shoulder and she closed her eyes for a brief moment, wishing she could stay there forever.

'Have you told your family yet?' he asked. 'I was thinking I should do the right thing and meet them to ask permission for your hand. I know it's wartime and everyone's rushing and grabbing girls to marry while they have the chance, but I would like to do things properly. I know my parents would like to meet you, too. They're fine people, with hearts of gold, and I know they will love you. I've written to my mother about you and she says she'd like to write, so she can get to know you. It made me realise there's so much about you I don't know. I don't even know where you live. You always insist I drop you on the corner, or at the bakery…'

His words trailed off and Maggie blushed crimson and looked down at her hands. They'd only been on a handful of dates in the few months they'd known one another – and she had deliberately not talked about her family, other than to say she had sisters. Thinking of her sisters, her thoughts went to Isabel and the bruise on her cheek. The thought of her suffering at the hands of that horrible man at the laundry made Maggie all the more determined not to ruin this opportunity.

'Oh, there's no need for formalities like that,' she said airily, in her mind going through the awful scenario of introducing George to her grandmother, who would probably be drunk, a fag hanging out the corner of her mouth, cursing at the room as if it were filled with enemies, and probably make up some dreadful story about Maggie.

'But there is,' said George kindly. 'I want to do this properly. I've fallen in love with you, Maggie, and I want to know everything about you. Thoughts of you will keep me going when I'm posted away, like my own personal photograph album.'

Maggie sighed to herself. She feared George would run a mile if he knew the truth about where she was from; the hovel she called home did not match the image of her life she had portrayed. Feeling utterly depressed by the prospect and racking her brain for what to do for the best, she was suddenly struck by an idea.

'I'll take you to meet them now, if you like,' she said, to George's astonishment, standing and taking his hand. 'It's a bit of a walk, though.'

Walking hand in hand through the centre of Bournemouth, past military personnel and civilians taking a turn around the Square, and then up towards Wimborne Road, George chatted easily about his family and his brothers, who were all in the services and who were now scattered around the world. Not for the first time, Maggie was touched by how much he cared about them. How he prayed that all of them were safe, for his mother's sake as much as his own.

'She had three boys in their twenties and my younger brother was just eighteen,' he explained. 'She cried and cried when we were called up, but makes up for us not being there by writing every week.

My father said he wouldn't be able to stand the quiet in the house when we left – we were a noisy lot and loved to sing songs around the piano or play cards – but after the Blitz bombing in London, I should think he's grateful for some quiet.'

Maggie could listen to George talk for hours. She loved the sound of his family and longed to be part of it. As was usual when they met, she didn't talk about personal matters, but instead about music and dance halls and their shared dream to see more of the world in peacetime. Before they knew it, they were standing at the entrance of the Wimborne Road Cemetery, near the entrance lodge, where there was a crater from a bombing earlier in the year and a low wall, once the base for decorative iron railings that had since been removed for the war effort.

'That bomb must have shaken the bones of the dead,' said George. 'What are we doing here, Maggie?'

The cemetery was peaceful as they walked in the failing light past the chapel, and towards a corner of the graveyard where plain tombstones stood in irregular rows. Birds or bats swerved and swooped overhead, landing on the outstretched branches of a tree, their little black bodies looking like musical notation.

Maggie stopped and turned to George, who looked at her with a combination of amusement and confusion in his eyes.

'I thought you wanted to meet my family,' she said, pulling him by the hand to an undecorated headstone, under which her parents lay. 'I'm sorry to say that this is them. My parents both died from TB. They went into the sanatorium and never came out. These days, my family is just me and my sisters.'

As she spoke, she felt a distant tremor of sadness shoot up her spine. Suddenly wondering what she was doing there – and hoping this would put an end to George's questions – she let out a small, sweet laugh, held her palms up in the air and shrugged.

'Let's get out of here, shall we?' she said. 'I don't fancy being in here when night falls.'

'So there's nobody else?' he said. 'Apart from your sisters, you're all alone?'

She sucked in her breath, wary of the lie she was about to tell, but before she knew it the words were out of her mouth.

'I suppose the people at the bakery – Audrey, Charlie, John and William – have been more of a family to me than anyone,' she said, not meeting George's gaze. 'I've had more teas in Audrey's kitchen than I can count.'

Her words stuck in her throat as she realised the irony of what she had said about the Barton family, after what she had been doing right under their noses. She blushed and closed her eyes in shame. How foolish she felt.

George, reading her expression as grief for her dead parents, wrapped his arms around her waist and pulled her in for a sweet, soft kiss.

'I'll take care of you, orphan Maggie,' he said. 'You've got me now.'

Chapter Nine

It was late when Audrey and Mary returned from the hospital; clouds had gathered above the setting sun, turning the sky shades of purple and pink normally seen in a flower bed, over a flat, silver sea. Not that Audrey noticed. She was too concerned about poor Uncle John's ill health and how long he'd been hiding his problems from her.

'Hello?' she called, letting herself and Mary into the back door of the bakery, but there was no reply. The entire building was empty and quiet; Lily and Joy had gone to Elsie's house for tea and she didn't know where William had got to.

'Gosh, Mary,' said Audrey, 'there's an awful lot to do in the bakehouse now that John's been taken ill! Let's get a cup of Ovaltine and some toast before your bedtime. Then I shall have to see to the dough. I think John had mixed the ingredients before he was taken ill, bless his heart.'

They'd left John being cared for by a young nurse called Ida, sweet and fresh as summer rain. Audrey had spoken to her and discovered that she had been overseas in France, helping injured soldiers, but had been returned home for some reason she clearly wasn't willing to share. Audrey had thought John would be happy to have a young lady take care of him, but he lay there wearing a furious expression, not meeting Audrey or Ida's eye, through fear, she suspected, of showing how upset and shocked he'd been by his collapse. Some men seemed to think they were invincible, thought Audrey, an image of Charlie popping into her head, making her miss him suddenly and dreadfully, like a punch in the stomach. She hoped to God that Charlie *was* invincible.

'Why have you brought me in here?' John had complained, trying to sit up, but breaking into another hacking cough, until he was breathless. 'There's nothin' wrong with me. I just need a nip of port and brandy and a breath of sea air. That will see me right. What you told me about Maggie threw me, that's all.'

Ida had told Audrey a different story in private. The doctor suspected John was suffering from 'baker's lung' – an occupational hazard all bakers feared but often ignored until it was too late – and he needed rest and recuperation. When Audrey thought back over recent years, she realised he'd been coughing for a long time. Trouble was, John had nobody to take care of him. His wife, Hazel, was dead – they'd had no children – and John point-blank refused to stay with his sister, Pat. 'Much as I love 'er,' he said. 'I'd rather stick a pitchfork through my eye than stay with 'er. It was bad enough when we were nippers.'

Audrey heated some water on the range, feeling exhausted. Her mind was working ten to the dozen, trying to think how she could organise the sleeping arrangements so that John could stay with her, at the bakery. If he was under the same roof as Audrey, she could keep an eye on him at least, and make sure he was really getting the rest and nourishment he needed.

'I don't know what we're going to do without old Uncle John,' she said to Mary, trying to sound cheerful. 'The bread's not going to bake itself.'

Though it was one of those warm summer nights when the air smelled of the flowering geraniums and rosemary bushes growing in pots outside, Audrey shivered. For a moment there today, she'd thought the worst, that John was dying, and it had deeply shaken her. For as long as she'd known Charlie, John had been a part of the bakery furniture, like the worn and weathered trough he used to hand-mix the dough. With his warmth, wit and loyalty, he had become rather like a father to Audrey. Since her own beloved father, Don, was dead having died from tubercular meningitis, and her stepfather, Victor, had rejected her, she had grown close to John and enjoyed spoiling him rotten with a warm, freshly baked scone and a spoonful of home-made blackcurrant jam. Seeing him struggling and vulnerable had made her realise how precarious the survival of the bakery was. Without him working the dough, how would she manage to do everything? The thought was too bewildering to contemplate.

Reading the worry scrawled across Audrey's face, Mary ran to her side and clutched hold of the skirt of her dress. Audrey rested her hand on the little girl's shoulders and smiled down at her, struck by the fear in her dark brown eyes. She was so quick to feel afraid, poor dear.

'Is Uncle John going to die?' said Mary, her little voice high and thin.

Audrey's heart went out to Mary, whose bottom lip was trembling. In all the years of trying and hoping, a child of their own was the one gift that she and Charlie had not been blessed with, and she was privately greatly saddened by the fact she'd never be a mother, but beginning to wonder if it had been somehow mapped out in the stars that she and Mary would find one another instead. She loved the little girl dearly, as much, she imagined, as if she was her own daughter.

'Come and sit here, love,' she said, sitting on a chair at the kitchen table and lifting Mary onto her lap. 'He's just a bit poorly, that's all. He's got a bad cough from all the flour. It gets stuck in his lungs, a bit like how snow sits on branches in the winter.'

'But is he going to die?' said Mary, eyeing Audrey suspiciously.

Audrey smiled kindly; she had always been honest with Mary, even though that had at times been difficult.

'No,' said Audrey. 'He just needs to rest, he's been working too hard. Speaking of which, I need to get the dough proved and knocked back or we won't have any bread tomorrow. Then what would we do? The customers would be up in arms! Can you take yourself up to bed, love? Don't forget to brush your hair.'

Mary lingered in the room and Audrey looked at her questioningly.

'What is it?' she asked. 'Do you want a drink?'

Mary shook her head. She opened her mouth to speak, then closed it again. Though Mary had been speaking again for six months, there was a lot she still couldn't find the words to say.

'I won't be able to sleep,' said Mary. 'I'm frightened.'

Audrey kneeled to Mary's height and held her around her waist. 'When I can't sleep,' she said, 'I think of a mossy pebble in the bottom of a clear stream, rolling along with the water. In my mind, I listen to the gentle trickle of water and to the birds singing in the trees by the stream. Why don't you climb into bed, close your eyes and try thinking about that pebble? I'll wager you'll fall asleep sooner than you know it. I'll be up to check on you shortly and to tuck you in. I must get on with the bread, else people will have nothing on their plates tomorrow. Some folk depend on having bread to eat, see? They might only have bread and perhaps a bit of potato or carrot to go with it. Not much else. We can't let them go hungry, can we?'

Mary nodded in understanding, smiled a tiny smile and disappeared upstairs, light-footed as a fairy, leaving Audrey alone in the kitchen, which had been thrown into gloom. She went through what she needed to do to get the bread out, and felt a creeping sense of unease. Yes, she'd helped Charlie out on countless occasions with the main bread-baking, as well as being responsible for the counter goods and the shop service. Yes, she knew the process like the back of her hand, but getting it right was a physical challenge and a huge responsibility. Not everyone could bake good bread, it was a highly regarded skill.

She yawned and stretched her arms up towards the ceiling, feeling the knots in her back spasm. Catching sight of her reflection in a small mirror, from which hooks held various sets of keys, she channelled all the young women who were rising up and stepping into the jobs of men who had gone off to war, and pushed aside her fears, headed into the bakehouse, rolled up her sleeves, and got to work.

Chapter Ten

Lily waited in the lobby of the Jetty Hotel in the centre of Bournemouth, as Henry had requested in his short note. Holding a wriggling baby Joy in her arms, she sat on a red velvet settee, nervously watching military personnel and well-heeled civilians mill around on apparently important business, their shoes tapping out busy rhythms on the chequered ceramic floor tiles. Playing in the background was a jazz pianist, and the smell of Virginia Leaf tobacco smoke permeated the air.

Thrilled by the bustle of the hotel and the sparkling cut-crystal glass chandeliers suspended from the ceiling, Joy was, for the time being, quiet, if not still. Nervously jigging her leg, Lily craned her neck to see if Henry was in sight, her heart thumping in her chest. She caught a glimpse of the hotel's dining room, where waiters were attending white-clothed tables set with silver cutlery for dinner and ladies sipping Martinis seemed to have bypassed the austerity measures of war. By the look of the food being served – veal cutlets and cheese soufflé – the wealthy were getting their fill of luxuries, regardless of rationing. But there was no point being affronted, thought Lily, catching Joy's dribble in a cotton hanky and stuffing it in the pocket of her dress; money was the main reason she had swallowed her fears and come to the hotel: money and justice.

'I'm pleased to see you came,' said Henry, suddenly appearing by her side, as if in a puff of smoke.

Shooting up from her seat to stand, slightly bouncing a now-grizzling Joy in her arms, Lily found a smile from her reserves and pasted it on her face. Registering Henry's appearance, she was taken aback. Still just as smartly turned out as he was when she first met him in her job at the Ministry of Information, in a dark, well-cut suit, his face now seemed drawn – as if marriage had aged him – the skin under his sunken eyes a bruised colour and his face pale. Henry's eyes, so much darker and more inscrutable than Lily remembered them, brightened when he looked towards Joy, who let out a perfectly timed giggle.

'And this must be…' he began, letting her grab his forefinger with her hand.

Unspoken words hung in the air between them, like dirty washing pegged on a line. *And this must be… our illegitimate baby.* Lily remembered Henry's verbal attack before Joy had been born and that he'd said he wanted nothing more to do with Lily. Clearly something had changed, and if she could use it to her advantage, she would. She nodded and smiled.

'Joy,' she said. 'This is Joy. She was born just before Christmas…'

Lily studied Henry's face, watching for his reaction, but he was impossible to read. Joy started to cry and Henry frowned, his face written over with concern.

'May I hold her?' he said.

Lily, thoroughly confused by Henry's behaviour, thought there was no harm in it. If he liked the child, perhaps he would be willing to financially support her. She carefully handed Joy to Henry and, as if by magic, she immediately stopped crying and giggled.

Henry glanced at Lily and smiled, surprise and delight registering in his eyes. Lily returned the smile, for once feeling validated as a mother and not the usual failure. The thing about babies was, no matter what unhappiness and difficulties were going on, nobody could resist being calm and peaceful and happy in their presence.

Standing there in the lobby, both staring at Joy, Lily was struck by how peculiar it was that the three of them were bound together biologically as a family, yet were not a family in any other sense whatsoever. The people at the bakery were more of a family to Joy, even the customers who loved to make a fuss of her and asked to hold her – despite sharing no genes.

'Shall we go through?' Henry asked, handing Joy back to Lily. 'I thought we could have a drink, though I should imagine Joy will need to go to bed?'

Walking together through to a dimly lit room, just off the side of the main bar, Henry showed Lily to a table.

'She doesn't sleep very much,' said Lily, shaking her head. 'Neither of us get much sleep.'

'It must be hard work,' said Henry, sitting opposite Lily. 'Doing all of this alone, without a father on the scene.'

'Yes, it is,' said Lily, frowning. 'Sometimes I can barely see straight for being tired.'

'Is there a problem with her?' said Henry. 'That's stopping her from sleeping?'

'No,' said Lily. 'Only that she's got into the habit of it, I think. And I'm too tired to break that habit. It's easier for everyone if I just go with what she wants…'

'Easy isn't always the best option,' said Henry, a little tersely.

When Lily lowered her eyes, feeling admonished, Henry tapped the table in front of her to get her attention. She looked up, her eyes flashing.

'But what do I know?' he said, with a quick smile. 'I'm sure you have no respect for my opinion.'

They were interrupted briefly by the waiter, and without even asking Lily, Henry ordered two Martini cocktails. When she'd first met him, Lily had liked his air of authority, but tonight she felt irritated. She decided, when it arrived, that she wouldn't drink the cocktail, in a show of resistance.

'I'd like to know why I'm – we're – here,' said Lily, faltering. 'When we first met, I looked up to you, Henry. You told me you had feelings for me and I believed you. When you told me about your wife-to-be, I felt stupid and ashamed. You didn't want anything to do with me, or the baby, but now you summon me to a fancy hotel for drinks. It doesn't make any sense. Is your wife here too, or in London?'

Henry leaned back in his chair and lit a cigarette. He took a few drags of it and then narrowed his eyes at her through the smoke, as if scrutinising her. She flapped her hand in front of her face to get the smoke away from Joy's face. Henry removed his hand holding the cigarette from the table.

'The truth is I did like you, Lily,' said Henry, leaning forward now and gently putting his left hand over hers. 'Very much. But I was in no position to have an affair with you—'

'I didn't want to have an affair,' interrupted Lily, removing her hand from under his. 'I didn't even know you were engaged. I thought we were both unattached…'

She blushed as the waiter arrived at the table's edge, the drinks on a shiny silver tray. He placed them down and Lily stopped talking completely. She felt silly mentioning their fling now that so much time had passed and that he was married. Deciding in fact that she needed a sip of something strong, she lifted her glass to her lips, her eyes watering as the alcohol slipped down her throat. Henry smiled at her in amusement, so she drank the rest of the drink down in one. He raised his eyebrows and leaned towards her.

'I know what you thought,' said Henry eventually. 'That was wrong of me to lead you to believe something untrue. But please, can we move on? There's something I want to discuss with you, something important. In my note I said I thought I could be of assistance, but first, I need to ask you a few questions.'

Fiddling with the elegant long stem of her empty glass with one hand, holding Joy balanced on her knee with the other, Lily felt vaguely dizzy from the Martini.

'What questions?' she asked. 'I can't imagine what you need to ask me, but go ahead.'

She was baffled by Henry's behaviour and had no idea what he was leading up to. In her heart of hearts, she hoped that he had seen the error of his ways and had decided to 'assist' her financially, because money was a big problem. It was the decent thing to do, wasn't it? If you'd stripped a girl of her ability to earn a living and knew how that would impact on your own flesh and blood, would any right-thinking man, as wealthy as Henry Bateman clearly was, begrudge parting with a few pounds?

'Are you positive that this baby is mine?' he asked.

Lily bristled and half laughed. His directness shocked her, but she took a deep breath and remained calm.

'I am one hundred per cent sure this baby is yours,' she said quietly but firmly. 'You are the only person I have ever—'

Embarrassed, her words trailed off and Henry nodded once, apparently in acceptance.

'You're living at the bakery with Audrey Barton?' said Henry. 'But her husband has joined the army?'

'That's right,' said Lily, frowning. 'What is this? I feel like I'm being interrogated.'

'I'm just trying to work out how difficult this is for you,' he said. 'I'm trying to work out the best way I can assist you.'

'It's very difficult,' she admitted, a thought of the day she'd foolishly left Joy on the beach flashing into her mind. 'I don't have a penny to my name. As you know, my father has rejected me because I'm unmarried, and I'm completely reliant on the generosity of Audrey, who has allowed me to stay on at the bakery. She has always wanted her own child, but unfortunately hasn't been able to have one, so I know she loves having Joy around. I work occasionally for her, but it's not always easy, with having a baby to think about.'

'What will you do as Joy grows?' said Henry. 'Where will you live?'

'I haven't thought that far ahead,' she said. 'At some point I will get a job. I'm sure Audrey will give me shifts at the bakery, but…'

'You can do better than that,' snapped Henry. 'You'll earn a pittance as a bakery hand. When you were at the Ministry, you showed real potential. If you're going to give Joy the best education, clothing, health and opportunities to travel and see the world, you'll need more than a bakery wage.'

Lily blanched at the irony of what he was saying. Yes, she had showed potential in a job she loved at the Ministry of Information, but Henry had taken all that away from her by getting her pregnant and then sacking her. Maybe that was why he was here; because he knew that and wanted to make up for it. Her legs jogged up and down under the table, wishing he'd hurry up and get to the point. This whole experience was like being interviewed for a job she didn't want.

'Travel!' she asked. 'Joy is just a few months old. There's a war on and the future's uncertain. I'm a lone mother. I'm not really thinking about travel, Henry.'

A possibility sprung into her head: was he going to offer to pay for these things?

'But obviously I want the best for her,' she added hurriedly.

Henry nodded sagely. He took one more drag of his cigarette before stubbing it out in the crystal cut-glass ashtray, then swallowed down the remainder of his drink in one gulp. He looked Lily directly in the eye, making her suck in her breath.

'My wife, Helen, was severely injured in a bomb blast in the Blitz,' said Henry, pausing to light a new cigarette. 'Great swathes of London have been completely destroyed, and unfortunately Helen was in the wrong place at the wrong time. A brick wall came down on her. She had to undergo lengthy and complicated surgery and lost the child, *our* child, that she was carrying. She is paralysed from the waist down and, as a result, the doctors say she won't ever be able to have another child. She is, how can I put it, inconsolable.'

Henry was choked, his eyes wet. He smiled sadly up at her through his floppy hair, pushing it back from his forehead. For a split second, Lily saw the Henry she had first been attracted to, and her heart went out to him. Her thoughts turned to Helen, his beautiful wife, now bound to a wheelchair for the rest of her life.

'I'm… sorry,' she stuttered. 'That's awful, just terrible. I'm so sorry for you both. I don't know what to say.'

'There's no need,' said Henry, holding his palm up, to stop her speaking. 'But I might as well get to the point and explain to you why I'm here. Helen is desperate to be a mother and, what with you being so young, and struggling with money and with being alone and not even having the support of your father, I think it might be a good idea if she and I were to take on and adopt Joy. We have a huge house in London and another in the Sussex countryside. Helen's family are very wealthy and would see to it that Joy would have the best schooling and prospects for the rest of her life. They would help to look after the child too, pay for a nanny, that kind of thing.'

Lily's mouth fell open. Joy let out a delighted gurgle.

'I would never have asked this question if I didn't know the truth – that you didn't ever want this child or to be a mother at such a young age,' he continued. 'She was an accident of ours. Mine. This was my mess, and so I feel I should clean it up. You were an innocent victim who made a mistake and I'm sure you'd agree that this would be a satisfactory solution for everyone concerned. Most importantly, Joy.'

'Did you tell Helen about me?' Lily said, incredulous.

Henry shook his head and sighed.

'Helen found out about our indiscretion, thanks to your stepmother,' he explained. 'She decided Helen should know.'

'Daphne?' said Lily, confused. 'She told Helen what happened? Why?'

'Yes,' said Henry. 'It was Daphne who came up with this idea and suggested it to Helen. I think your father, Victor, is finding things difficult without you, and Daphne thought this way you could return home and resume your previous life. My wife has been quite understanding about what happened between us, but on the proviso that we parent the child. It all makes perfect sense really. Of course, you will be financially rewarded too. I must make that clear.'

Lily was aghast. She struggled to digest what Henry was asking of her. Was he trying to *buy* Joy? Clutching the child close to her chest, she shook her head in dismay.

'How could you possibly think I would ever give her—' she started, her voice trembling and tears threatening to spill from her eyes. 'I'm sorry for Helen, the accident, I am sorry, but…'

Lily broke down in tears. Henry sighed deeply, closing his eyes briefly, before speaking to her very calmly.

'Spare me the histrionics,' he said. 'This is a grown-up arrangement that would suit everyone concerned. Joy would have every opportunity afforded to her, two parents and a big loving family. After the war, she would travel, go to the best schools, everything. How can you deny her that?'

Lily stood up and pushed back her chair so hard that it fell over, crashing onto the tiled floor. There was a sudden hush in the room as everyone turned to see what the commotion was, before Henry raised an apologetic hand and they resumed their conversations. Lily gripped hold of Joy, who was crying now, and glared at Henry, who was standing, holding out one of Joy's booties that had fallen off. Lily snatched it from him.

'Do we have an agreement?' said Henry. 'Lily…?'

She shook her head in defiance and shock. 'No, we do not have an agreement,' she hissed, before turning to leave. 'And we never will.'

Cupping her hand protectively around the back of Joy's head as she ran with her in her arms, Lily pushed past the uniformed men and ladies in their glad rags, through the hotel's grand entrance and into the street, where night had fallen, gulping in the fresh air, like water. With a trembling hand and pounding heart, she felt for her little torch in her pocket, pointed it downwards, as was required in blackout, and followed its shaky light towards the bus stop to get as far away from Henry as possible.

Chapter Eleven

Elsie suppressed a yawn in the sleeve of her bus conductress uniform. Her evening shift on the buses was almost over and she'd worked through rush hour at terrific speed, dashing about punching tickets and finding change, forcing herself to be cheerful as she wound the handle of her ticket machine hundreds of times over. There was no time to stop to have a yarn with the passengers and, instead, William's words played over on a loop in her head: *The engagement's off. You're free of me. Isn't that what you wanted?*

Now that darkness had fallen and because of the dreaded blackout, the bus crawled along the road at a snail's pace and she longed to deposit the takings at the bus depot, remove the distinctive bottle-green uniform she wore and climb into bed. With dull eyes, she stared through the darkness at the advertising posters on a billboard, as the driver approached a bus stop. 'Did you Maclean your teeth today?', one questioned, while another bore an image of a tin hat bearing the slogan: 'Keep it under your hat – careless talk costs lives', and another still: 'Housewives! Save waste fats for explosives!'

Elsie sighed, wondering if the war would ever end, and as the driver came to a halt to let people off, the unmistakable haunting wail of the air-raid siren sounded. The siren had sounded frequently in the last few months, but each time felt like the first, and fear and adrenalin shot through Elsie's body. As a bus conductress, it was her responsibility to lead the passengers to safety and direct them to the closest public shelter, which, in this instance, was signposted by a dimly lit arrow.

Standing tall and straight, she cupped her hands around her mouth in order to project her voice.

'Ladies and gentlemen,' she called out to the passengers, 'if you would like to follow me, I will lead you to the safety of the nearest public shelter.'

The passengers – servicemen and women, and locals, who had been dancing, or at the pictures, or who were on their way home from work – wearily did as they were instructed. The air raids were a constant interruption to life and everyone dreaded them lasting for hours on end, which they sometimes did, as dogfights and raids played out overhead.

Elsie led the group to the shelter in the Lower Gardens and prayed that the 'all-clear' siren would soon sound. A night in the shelter was the last thing she wanted, although at least Bournemouth Council had been ordered by the Ministry of Food to provide refreshments, so the electric boiler was already heating water, and cups of tea were being distributed by kindly volunteers. Others carried trays of apples and buns that they were selling, and there was a bottle-warming service for babies.

Elsie waited in the queue for a tea, her eyes resting on the engagement ring she wore. The tiny solitaire diamond twinkled in the dim light and, once more, she felt her heart sink into the pit of her stomach. Chewing the inside of her cheek until she tasted blood, she suddenly felt like whipping the ring off, running down to Bournemouth beach and throwing it into the ocean, where she imagined it sinking into the seabed, never to be seen again. She pulled it over her knuckle, then, after a moment's hesitation, pushed it back down. Tomorrow, if she could face it, she would return the ring to William.

'Elsie, you're here too!' said a voice from behind her, gently touching her elbow. 'You wouldn't believe what just happened to me!'

She turned on her heel to see Lily standing there, a shocked expression on her face, holding Joy wrapped in a pale-yellow blanket in her arms. Despite all the noise and the crowd, Joy was, amazingly, sleeping soundly. Lily's eyes were wet with tears and, instinctively, Elsie clutched Lily's hand in hers and squeezed.

'What is it?' she asked. 'Why are you out at this time? What are you doing here?'

'Let's get a cup of tea and find somewhere to sit,' said Lily. 'Otherwise we could be standing all night long!'

Sinking into two green and white striped deckchairs, requisitioned from the beach promenade where holidaymakers once sat to lick ice cream and soak up the sun, Lily recounted her evening with Henry. Elsie's eyes widened in disbelief as she listened, occasionally nodding and murmuring in astonishment. Her overriding feeling was one of anger – Henry needed a flea in his ear.

'What a fool I am for thinking Henry was going to try to make amends,' said Lily, rolling her eyes at herself. 'I should have known he was only interested in himself.'

'It sounds like his wife put him up to it,' said Elsie. 'She knows about his affair with you and wants to get something out of it, or at the very least make the two of you suffer. Henry has no backbone whatsoever. He's a weak man and I can only think you must despise him.'

Lily trembled, her eyes dropping to her hands in her lap. After letting out the story in a rush of words and emotions, she seemed to be all out of energy. Elsie grabbed her hand and squeezed it. Lily looked up at her, her blue eyes glassy and her copper hair tumbling over her shoulders.

'Do you think he's got a point?' asked Lily quietly.

'What do you mean?' asked Elsie.

'He said he could offer Joy things I never could,' she said. 'A good education, a house – actually, he said two houses – two parents, clothes, travel… He said she'd never know her grandparents, because my father won't have anything to do with me – and he's right. Maybe I was selfish to keep Joy. You know, there's a big part of me that wishes I could go out to work, while still have her.'

Elsie smiled kindly at Lily, her heart going out to her friend. Ever since she had arrived at the bakery out of the blue last year, carrying the secret of her unwanted and unplanned pregnancy, Lily had struggled with whether she was making the right decisions. She had been plunged into an unknown world in an unknown town, just like Mary the evacuee, with no support from her own father and no plan for the future – and she was still only just eighteen. The two of them had shared a room at the bakery for a while last year and had become close. Wondering how best to comfort Lily, Elsie remembered some words of wisdom her father had given her.

'Take each day as it comes,' she told her friend. 'Don't anguish about the past or worry about the future. In wartime especially, everything can change, and with all these new nurseries opening up to help mothers do war work, why shouldn't you work? Things can change at the drop of a hat, Lily. Look at me and William; I genuinely thought we would be together forever and that only death could part us, but I was wrong—'

Elsie's words stuck in her throat and her eyes pricked with hot tears. After taking a glug of her hot tea, she stared up at the ceiling of the shelter, listening to the sound of distant gunfire until she'd regained her composure. She smiled sadly at Lily, who was staring at her enquiringly.

'I don't understand,' said Lily. 'Why won't you and William be together? What's happened?'

'He's broken off our engagement,' said Elsie. 'It's over between us.' She shrugged and tried to look as if she wasn't that bothered.

'It never is!' Lily gasped, leaning forward in her deckchair. 'I don't believe it.'

'It's true,' she said. 'He said he thought it was what I wanted. How he worked that out, I do not know. I've been in love with him since the first day we met. Anyway, it's over and I'll move on with my life. What else can I do but keep on keeping on?'

An older gentleman who was sitting nearby, reading a newspaper, lowered his newspaper to his lap, and pulled off his glasses to address the girls. 'I've been listening to you girls talking and I'd like to knock the heads of this William and Henry together,' he said, reaching into his pocket for his hip flask. 'What you need is a nip of brandy and a sing-song. Please, allow me to liven up your cups of tea.'

Before he had time to unscrew the lid of his hip flask, Elsie and Lily willingly lifted their cups towards him.

'This is to make up for the mistakes of my fellow men,' he said, pouring them a nip each. 'How anybody can set out to upset two beautiful girls like you – and a wee pretty baby – I do not know. In my day, a man knew how to treat a woman; with dignity and respect. These modern ways shock me, I'll tell you that for free.'

*

When the air-raid siren sounded in Fisherman's Road, Audrey was swilling out the milk bottles to preserve the last drops of milk, and storing the remaining milk water to make pastry. Pleased with herself for the work she'd done in the bakehouse – knocking back the dough as best she could, before setting it to prove – she sighed at the sound of the siren and the ARP warden's call to 'take cover'.

'It never rains but it pours, eh?' she said, rubbing her forehead and trying to figure out what to do. She couldn't go into the Anderson shelter and leave the ovens, which needed stoking up, but she needed to get Mary to safety. Popping up to her bedroom to wake her, she found her already dressed, with her gas mask case over her shoulder and her doll firmly clasped in her hand.

'Well done, Mary,' Audrey said. 'I'm going to see if you can go into Old Reg's shelter. Come quickly.'

Calling for William as she passed his room, there was no answer, so she assumed he was already on fire-watch duty. Lily and Joy were nowhere to be seen either. Fear ripped through her as she prayed they were somewhere safe. That was one of the worst things about the siren going off; if you weren't with your loved ones, then you had no idea if they were safe, and no way of telling until they returned home.

With Mary's small hand in hers, she rushed out into the courtyard and, standing on an upside-down apple crate near the wall, she called over to her neighbour, Old Reg and his wife, Clara.

'Can you take Mary into your shelter please, Reg?' asked Audrey. 'John's been taken poorly and I've got to stay in the bakehouse. I don't want to leave her alone in our shelter.'

Audrey leaned over the wall, glancing up as the searchlights criss-crossed the sky and the sound of aircraft and guns firing in the distance, as Reg and Clara headed towards their Anderson shelter, with a couple of blankets in their hands in case they were in there all night. A sudden boom, boom sent Mary's little hands flying up to cover her ears.

'Course we can,' he said, holding up his arms. 'Pass her over. Come on, Mary, love, quickly does it. We'll play a game of cards, shall we? I've a bag of Midget Gems needs eating up too. These air-raid sirens are actually an excuse to have a bit of an adventure and a midnight feast, aren't they, love?'

Audrey's head and heart melted with appreciation. She smiled gratefully at Old Reg, thinking she must take him a jar of jam or some fruit buns with part of her butter ration in the morning to thank him for being such a generous old soul. Lifting Mary and her doll over the brick wall – she was as light as cotton wool – Audrey's head whirred. She had to stay in the bakehouse to make sure the bread would be ready in time for the morning. There was a strong kitchen table in there – she would have to take shelter under that.

'You take care, Audrey dear,' said Old Reg, as she rushed back to the bakehouse. 'Keep safe.'

Hearing Mary whimper when she dashed off, Audrey froze, not knowing whether to rush back to give her words of comfort, or to continue to the bakehouse, but then gave herself a talking-to. Not once, in a year and a half of air-raid sirens and attacks, had Charlie or John failed to get the bread out. Tonight the responsibility lay on her shoulders – and she would not give up.

*

Hours later, her arms and back aching like never before, the loaves were ready for the oven, and Audrey thought she might collapse with tiredness. She'd had no sleep for almost twenty-four hours and her eyes felt as though they were spinning balls in her head.

Collapsing into a heap under the table, she folded up a hessian sack on which to rest her head, just for ten minutes, while the loaves were baking. Tucking her knees up to her chest and sliding her hands under her face, it was then she noticed her wedding ring was missing. Sitting bolt upright, she felt around on the dimly lit floor for her ring. She tried to control the panic rising up within. Her wedding ring was her tangible bond to Charlie, her most precious and beloved possession. She dredged her mind for what she'd done earlier in the day.

Sometimes she took it off when she washed up, or collected the anthracite – popping it into her apron pocket. But she always put it back on, didn't she? Checking her apron pocket, only to find it empty, she rested her hot cheeks in her palms, feeling tearful. Where on earth could it be?

A terrible thought occurred to her: Maggie. Could Maggie have taken her ring? Was she capable of such a thing? Groaning in disbelief, Audrey laid her head back down on the hessian sack in despair, and closed her eyes. In a moment, she was in a blank, deep sleep.

Chapter Twelve

The 'all-clear' siren sounded at dawn and, after a sleepless night, Elsie and Lily emerged from the public shelter, bleary-eyed and pale. Mercifully, despite the noise, singing and conversation, Joy had mostly slept through the night in Lily's arms, but now she was hungry. To give Lily's arms a rest, Elsie was holding her.

'You'd think that guttersnipe Hitler had enough to do with turning the Soviet Union upside down,' said the old man who had given them a nip of his brandy before bidding the girls goodbye. 'Word is that the Northeast got it last night. Poor blighters! If I could get my hands on that man, I'd have his guts for garters!'

Lily and Elsie made their way back to Southbourne by bus, too tired to talk, arriving at the bakery as dawn broke. Elsie couldn't face the thought of seeing William – but she promised to help Lily carry Joy home, before she headed off back to Violet and the twins. At the same moment they arrived, and when Elsie was handing Joy back to Lily, Old Reg, Clara and Mary emerged from their Anderson shelter and waved.

'Long one last night,' said Old Reg. 'I'm ready for bed, but the working day's about to begin! I sometimes wonder if it's a tactic to make us surrender. The more tired we get, the less fight we have left in us. Have you seen Audrey yet?' He explained that Audrey had asked them to have Mary in the shelter with them when the siren sounded, while she tended the ovens, as Uncle John had been taken to hospital in an ambulance.

'Gracious me!' said Elsie, sharing a concerned glance with Lily, before lifting Mary back over the wall. 'We better check on her.'

Though Elsie's heartbeat quickened and her legs turned to jelly as she dreaded the thought of having to see William, she followed Lily into the bakery to look for Audrey. Entering the warm bakehouse building, the wonderful smell of freshly baked bread enveloping them, the girls saw Audrey hard at work. Standing near the ovens and next to the table which was covered in golden crusted loaves, she was using the long wooden peel to take the baked loaves out of the oven. Her hair sticking to her damp forehead, face pink from the exertion, she looked more exhausted than Elsie had ever seen her, but managed a smile for little Mary.

'Hello, everyone,' Audrey said, putting down the peel to embrace Mary. 'Did you get some sleep, Mary? I heard several distant explosions last night – along the coast, I think.'

Mary wrapped her arms around Audrey's waist, pushing her face into her apron. Elsie was suddenly struck by how Audrey had pretty much become a mother to Mary this last year and wondered how difficult it would be for the little evacuee to return home to her father when the war ended. The word 'if' crept into her mind, but she pushed it away.

'Have you done all this alone?' asked Elsie, her eyes running over the bread before exchanging incredulous glances with Lily. 'Have you not slept? Your energy knows no bounds, Audrey Barton!'

'I took ten minutes to nap,' said Audrey. 'But I had to get the bread out. Can you imagine what Flo and Elizabeth and Mrs Cook and all the housewives would say if their bread wasn't ready? My life wouldn't be worth living! Could someone please make me a brew? I'm gasping and I must get the counter goods ready, then open up shop. I'm not convinced Maggie will be in today.'

'Why not?' said Elsie distractedly, still amazed by the work Audrey had done all on her own. Not wanting to think about William, he popped into her thoughts. *Why wasn't he down here, helping his sister?*

'I'll explain another time,' said Audrey, not looking Elsie in the eye. 'You haven't seen my wedding ring, have you? I think I put it down somewhere and—'

Lily and Elsie shook their heads and Audrey chewed her bottom lip, confused.

'Well, you can't be expected to do all this on your own,' said Elsie, feeling an increasing sense of injustice on her behalf. 'Where's William?'

'In his bed, I suspect,' said Audrey. 'He had his fire-watching duties last night, then I suppose he must have turned in, while I was working in here. It's a big responsibility, being a fire-watcher. Tiring. Especially with his injuries, I'm sure.'

Elsie sighed deeply. She found that she was trembling with anger. William might not want to marry her anymore, but the old William would never have let Audrey spend the entire night alone and sleepless, trying to get the bread order out. It was time he got his act together. Fine, if he didn't love her, but he needed to hear the difficult truth: it was time for him to get on with his life.

Elsie didn't even knock. She opened the door to William's bedroom door and flung open the blackout blind, before standing by his bed, her arms folded.

'What the heck are you doing?' said William, blinking in the daylight, pulling himself up into a sitting position in bed. The injured side of his face was towards Elsie and on the bedside table was a bottle of Milk of Magnesia, which she knew he took for the nervous acid in his stomach and, for a moment, her resolve weakened. But then she remembered Audrey, battling away all night alone in the bakery, exhausting herself both physically and mentally.

'When I first met you, William, you had integrity,' she said quietly. 'You worked hard in the bakery, you smiled and laughed and looked towards the sun. You loved fresh air, the dunes and the beaches and the sea. You loved music and playing your mouth harp. Most of all, you loved your sister and you looked out for her. Audrey, you once told me, was all the family you had that mattered – and that when you left London, she protected you and found you somewhere to live, food to eat and a job to go to. Do you have any idea what she's doing at the moment?'

William shook his head, his eyes widening.

'She hasn't slept,' Elsie said. 'She's spent the whole night getting the bread ready, alone, because John was taken to hospital before the air-raid siren went off. The bread is baked, but she's exhausted, and now she has to open the shop. She needs help. I think it's about time you got up and came back to life. You're creeping about at night looking for fire, like some kind of bat, but in the daytime you're hiding away and ignoring the people who love you the most. That's not the William I knew and loved.'

She paused, her gaze falling to the wooden floorboards.

'You might not love me anymore,' she said, softly, 'but I know you love Audrey and she needs you.'

William sat up and grabbed Elsie's hand. He pulled her gently towards the bed, where she sat down on the edge of the mattress. His face was written over with anguish.

'You're right,' he said, his eyes filling with tears. 'I have changed, but it's because I feel like I've lost everything.'

'But you haven't,' Elsie pointed out. 'I know you were injured, but you're still alive.'

'I've lost you,' he said, his lip trembling. 'To another.' His gaze slipped to the floor where, under the bed, she saw the letter and photograph that Pilot Officer Jimmy Browne had sent her months earlier.

Confused, she bent down and lifted it up, holding it in her shaking hands. Blinking away the tears blurring her eyes, she looked at the photograph as if she was looking at strangers. Was this the reason he'd ended their courtship? Anger coursed through her veins.

'Is this what the problem is?' she said, standing and waving the letter around. 'Is this why you called off our engagement? I don't believe it!'

Elsie's face was bright pink. She felt ready to explode. That letter had arrived months before, in January, and she had thought nothing more of it other than to hope Jimmy was safe as she knew he had been posted overseas. She'd had no idea that William had found it and read it – he hadn't even talked to her about it. He'd made a decision, without even consulting her.

'Why didn't you tell me about him?' he said, his voice and lips quivering.

'There was nothing to tell!' said Elsie. 'There's no denying he was lonely, and that he needed a friend to take to the dance, but he knew I was engaged! I told him often enough! I hadn't heard from you in months. All I did was to go to a dance with a friend who was about to be posted overseas. I was never disloyal. It was innocent – you have to accept that. If you can't, then you don't know me very well.'

She watched various emotions pass over William's face as he processed everything she said. In some ways his jealousy should be comforting to her, but in essence, it just served as another insight into his lost confidence, which saddened her greatly. Saddened her, but also infuriated her.

'I'm sorr—' he began, but Elsie interrupted by lifting her palm to silence him.

'They're just words,' she said. 'Show me you're still the William I fell in love with. The future is in your hands.'

'But that's the thing,' he said. 'I feel like I have no control over the future at all, none of us do… you just have to read the paper to know that.'

'You can give up,' said Elsie, her voice cracking. 'Or you can get on with it.'

She smiled a sad smile and left the room, quietly closing the door behind her. It wasn't up to her to persuade William that he had a life to lead, he needed to realise that for himself. With a deep breath, she made her way down the stairs, turning the ring on her finger as she moved.

Chapter Thirteen

Revived by a cup of tea and forty winks, but with underlying exhaustion and red sore eyes that no eye drops could relieve, Audrey set to work in the shop, stacking up loaves in the window. Moving behind the counter to switch on the wireless in preparation for *The Kitchen Front*, a broadcast that all the customers loved to listen to, she wondered if Maggie would show her face – and doubted it. What a shame she'd been pilfering. Maggie had been so excited about her marriage proposal, Audrey would have loved to be a part of organising the wedding food, but was now uncertain what the future held. Determined not to give up on her though, Audrey decided if she didn't come into work, she would go and visit her at home. There was no point burying your head in the sand and, on a practical note, she *needed* Maggie.

Pausing for a moment, her hands on her hips, she gazed out of the window, struggling to imagine how she would get through the day without Maggie and Uncle John. If she was going to get tomorrow's bread order out, she would need to factor in some proper sleep at some point and cut down on counter goods. The carrot cake, though popular, would have to wait and the eggless sponge cake, which was quick to make but tasted more like a scone than a cake, would have to do in its place. Oh, there was so much to do, there really wasn't time to sleep!

'Where are you when I need you?' she muttered, thinking of Charlie, who had put his sense of duty to defend his country over the responsibility of being Barton's head baker. Suddenly weary beyond words, she longed for him to be by her side. Interrupting her thoughts, there was a noise from behind her, as William moved into the shop, leaning on his crutch.

'I'm here,' he said, in answer to her question to Charlie. 'What can I do to help? I hear you had a tricky time last night? Elsie left me in no uncertain terms that I have let you down. You should have beckoned me.'

Audrey's first instinct was to protect and shield William, wanting him to focus on his recuperation, not be worrying about her or the bakery. He was her younger brother, after all, and ever since their father died, she felt she'd been watching his back, though over the last few months, she didn't know how best to help him.

'I'm fine—,' she said. 'I was taken off guard with John falling ill, so I had to cover for him. And today, well, I might be a shop girl down, so… it never rains but it pours, eh? But don't you worry. Take yourself upstairs, or outside for some fresh air if you prefer, I can bring you some breakfast…'

'Will you listen to yourself?' snapped Elsie, darting into the shop behind William. 'You're your own worst enemy, Audrey, let alone Hitler! Stop for a moment, will you, and ask for some help from your own flesh and blood. You'll be no good to anyone if you're on the floor by the end of the week, and the bakery will suffer. I have to go and get the twins to school now and then I have a shift on the buses, but I can help in the shop tomorrow if you need me. William, you'll just have to put up with me being here, if Audrey needs my help. We all need to put our feelings aside and make ourselves useful.'

Elsie walked through the shop and out the door, the bell jingling its merry tune as she went. Audrey and William watched in stunned silence, then looked at one another in surprise. William's face was caught in sunlight and the skin over one side was mottled, severe scarring across a large area, his eyelid swollen and without lashes, which had never grown back. Audrey knew that he felt ashamed by Elsie's reprimand and again wanted to compensate for that. She longed for him to come through this all, with his head held high, but before she could console him, he spoke up.

'Before I went to war I was apprentice baker here,' he said. 'I don't see why I can't take up that duty again. As long as I can lean my weight on a high stool while I work, I should be fine.'

'William,' said Audrey, 'why did you break up with Elsie? She really never did anything disloyal, I promise you.'

He looked desperately sad and leaned against the shop counter. For a while he said nothing.

'I'm not the man I was,' he croaked eventually. 'That's all I can say about it.'

Audrey's heart contracted. She wished she could rewind the months and stop him from ever joining up in the first place. Thinking of that day made her remember the threepenny coin she'd given him, for good luck, and the engagement ring he'd handed to her to give to Elsie. He had seemed so passionate then – if only she could reignite that passion in him.

'Can you remember when I gave you the threepenny bit that Mother used to put in the Christmas pudding for luck?' she said. 'That day at the railway station when you first left? Do you still have it?'

William froze, closed his eyes for a long moment, then slowly shook his head.

'I gave it to someone,' he said, faltering.

'Oh,' said Audrey, confused. 'I thought you would keep it, but never mind, I…'

Her attention was diverted to the customers, who were beginning to arrive for their bread. She knew the ladies would want to talk to William and she thought it would do him good to feel their concern, but he scuttled away, wanting to hide elsewhere.

'She loves you, you know,' said Audrey, calling after him. 'But if you're willing to lose her, then that's what will happen.'

*

The sound of gossip and laughter drifting from the shop, William limped through to the bakehouse, trying with all his might not to break down and cry. Once in the bakehouse, he closed the door behind him and leaned against the wall, his forehead pressing against the warm bricks. He squeezed shut his eyes and gritted his teeth, wanting to pummel the walls with his fists. Nobody had prepared him for this. Nobody had prepared him for *after* the fight. Oh, it was all very well when he joined up; the camaraderie was immense. The boys sang together, with him accompanying on the mouth harp; together they faced the prospect of stamping out the evil that Hitler was inflicting on the world with huge determination. Their morale was high. And then: the front line. There were no words to describe the horrors he'd witnessed, no song on the mouth harp that could take away the pain. There was nothing he could do to lessen the guilt he carried, since the dreadful day he'd made the wrong, split-second decision. A decision that had cost his dear friend, David, his life. How could he ever admit to Elsie that he was a coward and that his weakness had resulted in David's death?

The scene ran through his head on repeat. He had come face-to-face with a young German soldier and though he should have shot him there and then, there was something in the soldier's eyes that stopped him from doing so. What was it? he questioned himself. Fear? Kindness? Youth? The German soldier had run for his life – and William had let him go – only to find that moments later, the same soldier turned around and shot William's friend David in the stomach. He could recall the thud of his friend's body landing on the earth and the feeling of the soil beneath his fingers when he kneeled next to David, as he lay dying in agony. It was William's fault. His ineptitude meant that he was still here, while David wasn't.

'Forgive me,' he whispered into the empty bakery, but nobody replied. This was a burden he would carry alone, for the rest of his life, and that prospect was overwhelming.

Eyes wide open now, he steadied himself with his hand on the strong wooden bakery table. Elsie and Audrey thought his struggle was because of the loss of his foot and the awful scars on his face. That wasn't the case. His injuries were a warped, indirect kind of punishment for his actions, weren't they? If only the girls knew the truth about him; that he was responsible for his friend's death, that guilt plagued his thoughts and his dreams, like crawling insects. An image of the threepenny bit that Audrey had given him on the day he left Bournemouth flashed into his mind. How preposterous it was that he'd left the coin in David's palm. How illogical and brainless. Suddenly furious with himself, he knocked his forehead against the wall.

'William?' Audrey said, suddenly standing at the doorway to the bakehouse, the sound of a customer's voice calling 'Anyone home?' coming from the unattended shop. 'If this is too much for you, I understand. I can see how you're suffering and I don't want to make it worse, no matter what Elsie or anyone else thinks—'

Gulping, William quickly wiped his eyes with his forearm. He turned to Audrey and tried to offer a reassuring smile. She approached him, concern etched across her face. Sometimes she reminded him of their father, Don – he'd had a huge heart and endless patience too.

'I'm okay,' he forced out, but when Audrey gently put her arms around her brother, soothing him with gentle and kind words, he rested his forehead on his sister's shoulder and could no longer hold in his pent-up feelings of loss and shame. 'I'm sorry,' he wept. 'I'm so sorry! Forgive me.'

Chapter Fourteen

Audrey stood in the entrance to Maggie's house, trying not to judge Maggie's grandmother, Gwendolen, as she staggered across the room, knocking a glass of dark yellow liquid to the floor, before she slumped into a chair. The fire had gone out in the damp room and, by the look of the empty saucepans, there wasn't much on offer in the way of dinner, besides a potato and two carrots that had clearly seen better days plus the crust of a stale loaf Audrey recognised as one of Barton's. Newly washed tea towels were strung across the hearth – a small attempt at domesticity, at least – and a few pieces of crockery were piled up on a shelf above the sink, but apart from that the room was quite bare. It appeared that Gwendolen barely had two pennies to rub together – and what she did have, she probably spent on tobacco or alcohol.

'Gracious me!' muttered Audrey to herself. She'd had no idea that Maggie was living in such austere conditions, only that she lived with her two sisters and her grandmother since her parents were dead. Feeling desperately guilty for not knowing more about her friend's home life, the penny suddenly dropped. Was this the reason Maggie had been taking ingredients from the bakery? Had she been stealing in order to help her family eat? The first thing she would do when she got back to the bakery was to put together a food parcel and drop it to the family anonymously. A few pots of jam and bottled fruit she'd prepared in the winter would be a good start. She still needed to talk to Maggie, of course. Stealing was wrong, but it seemed she probably had an explanation. 'What a sorry state,' Audrey whispered to herself, before increasing her volume: 'I've come to see your granddaughter, Maggie.'

'Taken to her bed, 'asn't she?' slurred Gwendolen. 'Expect it's about a fella. She puts it around a bit, or so I've 'eard. Always hangin' around in them alleyways, like an alley cat she is, catching men like mice and playing around with them in her paws. Or claws, I should say.'

'That doesn't sound like the Maggie I know,' said Audrey, frowning. 'She's a delightful girl, always smiling and polite, or singing. The customers love her. I missed her at work today and wanted to check she's in good health and will be returning tomorrow.'

Gwendolen shrugged and pushed herself up once again from the chair. Smacking her lips together and rolling her tongue around her mouth, she pulled a disgruntled expression.

'Smoker's fur, ain't it?' she said, pointing to her mouth. 'Can't afford the mouth rinse though, can I?'

Audrey tried to hide her pity as Gwendolen limped across the floor in her threadbare apron, which looked like it hadn't been washed in a decade, and shouted up the narrow staircase, before breaking into a hacking cough. It reminded her of Uncle John's cough, which sounded like it might literally crack open his ribs at any moment. The woman clearly needed medical attention.

'Maggie!' she cried, wiping her mouth with the back of her hand. 'You've a visitor. Get down 'ere now!'

The shouting and coughing was greeted with silence from Maggie, but moments later, she was at the top of the stairs, poking her head around the bedroom door. With her hairdo flat and unpinned, and without her usual make-up, Maggie looked pale and drawn – not at all like herself. On seeing Audrey, her cheeks flushed pink.

'I know I'm in trouble,' she said, sulkily. 'I know what you've come to say.'

'Hear me out,' said Audrey. 'Why don't you come outside for a walk with me and we can talk? I'll wait on the pavement.'

Audrey let herself out of the tiny terraced house, bidding farewell to Gwendolen, as the old woman resettled into her chair and stared into space.

'You don't know a thing about me, y' judgemental witch,' Gwendolen barked, her sharp words sticking into Audrey's back like darts.

'I'm not judging you, Gwendolen,' she retorted. 'Who am I to judge?'

Closing the door behind her and stung by Gwendolen's harsh words, Audrey took a gulp of fresh air and, while waiting for Maggie, paced the street in front of the house, her gaze sliding over to the wall opposite, where a police officer was painting an arrow and the wording: Public Shelters in Vaults Under Pavements In This Street.

Tutting, Audrey wished for the millionth time that the war was over. At the moment, life felt like it was being held together by a thread and war was impacting on everything. Connections she had previously thought were strong and unbreakable were dissolving before her eyes. Take William and Elsie; she never could have anticipated that William would break off their engagement. His outburst earlier had shocked and surprised her and made her realise that his mental state was even more fragile than she'd thought. She didn't believe for a second that he really wanted to split from his true love – there was something else going on. She had to get them back together, somehow. And Maggie, who she would never have expected to steal from her, had done so, probably because she was struggling at home.

Distracted by the sight of a young girl, no more than sixteen, approaching and obviously in tears, she stopped still.

'Excuse me,' Audrey said. 'Are you okay?'

The girl stopped and wiped her eyes on her sleeve. Her eyes and nose were bright red from crying. When she faced Audrey, she could see Maggie's features staring back: the girl must be one of her sisters.

'Who are you?' the girl asked, wiping her eyes on her sleeve. 'Why are you outside my house?'

'I'm visiting Maggie,' she said. 'Are you… her sister?'

'Yes,' she replied. 'I'm Isabel.'

'I'm Audrey,' she said. 'I work with Maggie at the bakery. Why are you crying, sweetheart?'

'Oh, I've been "let go" for working too slow,' she sighed. 'It's because my hands are so sore.'

Isabel held up her red-raw hands for her to inspect. Audrey gasped and took the young girl's hands in her own, frowning at the blistered skin. Isabel needed a warm bath, camomile lotion on those hands and, from the look of her ribs sticking through her dress, a decent meal.

Audrey opened her mouth to give the girl some advice, but the door to Maggie's house flew open, then slammed shut and then Maggie appeared beside them, and threw her arms around her sister.

'Oh gosh, Isabel, whatever's happened?' she said. 'You've lost your job, haven't you?'

Audrey watched as Maggie, who had applied make-up, fluffed up her hair and pulled on a cardigan, hugged her sister and patted her back while she cried on her shoulder. Feeling suddenly guilty for being there when Maggie had plenty to deal with, Audrey thought she should come back later.

'Maggie, I should leave you to deal with your sister…' she started.

'No,' said Maggie. 'Wait, we need to talk. Isabel, go inside and put your feet up. We will talk later, and don't worry, I'll help you find more work. You're better off away from that dreadful place! Just don't tell grandmother yet, I'll break it to her later.'

Audrey's heart contracted as the sisters hugged one another. Maggie was always cheerful, no matter what was happening – and she loved that about her. Walking along in silence, Audrey struggled to find the right words, passing a corner shop where the shopkeeper had chalked up a sign that read: 'Fags and Beer, We Are All Here' and hung out a Union Jack flag, which flapped in the wind.

'Maggie, I—' she started, but Maggie laid a hand on her arm, to interrupt.

'I'm sorry,' said Maggie quietly. 'I've taken sugar and dried fruit from the bakery and swapped it for clothing coupons. I know I've done wrong.'

'Clothing coupons?' Audrey asked, frowning. 'I thought food perhaps, for your family, but clothing coupons… now I'm confused.'

Maggie stopped walking. She crossed her arms over her chest and sighed.

'You've seen what my life is like,' she said, gesturing towards her home. 'Between us we bring in just about enough money to pay the rent and put a meal on the table, but you know how much prices have gone up.'

Audrey nodded. It was true – some non-rationed items had rocketed.

'You have your rations and the price of bread has stayed the same because it's subsidised,' said Audrey. 'I'd never see you go without, Maggie.'

Maggie smiled in acknowledgement before carrying on.

'We also pay for my grandmother's bad habits,' she said. 'And we have to pay off her debt – she got into a bit of trouble a few years back and borrowed money off some lowlife around here. We have to help her out if we want to keep the roof over our heads. It's that simple.' She shrugged and pushed her hands into her dress pockets.

'Yes,' said Audrey. 'I can see it's not easy… your grandmother clearly has problems.'

'I want a way out of this for me and my sisters,' said Maggie. 'And what have I got going for me? I don't have brains, but I do have fair looks. People always comment on how well I look after myself. I've been spending the clothing coupons on good clothes, so that when I go out with George Meadows, he likes what he sees and thinks of me as a better class of girl. Then, when he asked me to marry him, I thought, "How on earth will I buy a dress?" It sounds daft, I know it does, but I took the sugar, thinking you wouldn't miss it. I thought one day I'd pay you back somehow. I know it's selfish of me, but I didn't know what else to do.'

Audrey's heart went out to Maggie. She pulled her in for a hug and squeezed her tight. Then she remembered her wedding ring.

'I need to ask you another question,' she said, unable to meet Maggie's eye. 'Did you take my wedding ring?'

Maggie shook her head emphatically. 'No!' she cried. 'I'd never do such a thing. I swear, Audrey, I swear to you, I wouldn't take something so precious. I should never have taken the sugar. I'm sorry.'

She wept into her hanky and Audrey gently patted her back. She could easily see and understand why Maggie had done what she'd done – desperate people did desperate things.

'If you'll permit me, I'll work some shifts for free,' offered Maggie. 'To make up for my wrongdoing.'

'Listen, I've got some dresses I never get the chance to wear,' Audrey told her. 'Why don't you have a look at them for you and your sisters? Pat could take them in for you, if they're too big. As for a wedding dress, they're doing the rounds at the moment – people borrowing from each other, and buying them second-hand or making them from scratch. I'll help you find something lovely, if you promise not to go behind my back again? If you're in trouble, just come to me.'

Maggie sniffed, nodded and squeezed Audrey's hand. 'Thank you,' she said. 'You're so kind.'

'I know a good shop girl when I see one,' said Audrey, with a wink. 'And everyone deserves a second chance.'

'You've done *what*?' said John, when she visited him in hospital a few days later and told him the whole story. 'How can you give the girl her job back when she's stolen from you? You must have taken leave of your senses!'

He hoisted himself up to sitting and burst into a coughing fit. Audrey passed him a cup of water, which he sipped, his eyes watering. His nurse popped her head in around the door and Audrey waved, to say he was okay.

'I've decided to forgive her,' she said when he'd calmed down again. 'She knows the bakery inside out and the customers love her. She doesn't have it easy, John, not at all. If I'm wrong, then on my own head be it. She's got a wedding coming up and, to be frank, I think we could all do with enjoying a knees-up. I don't want it all ruined just because she did something wrong.'

But John shook his head. He twisted around in the bed and slammed the glass of water down on the bedside table, where Audrey could see traces of a visit from his sister Pat. There was a jigsaw puzzle, a bar of Plain York Chocolate and a slice of gooseberry pie – Bournemouth was awash with dessert gooseberries since a consignment had arrived from Devonshire.

'You want your head examining,' said John, picking up the chocolate and offering her a piece. 'And what about the old bakehouse? Is William helping? I can't stand being stuck in here when I should be there!'

Audrey broke off a piece of chocolate and put it on her tongue. The sweetness was such a treat. Even though it hadn't yet been rationed, the ingredients it was made with were scarce, so chocolate was becoming increasingly expensive and hard to come by. Some bars, such as KitKat, would not be made again until after the war.

'Yes, he's helping, thank goodness,' Audrey said. 'It's hard for him, but he's doing a grand job. I think it's helping settle his mind too, but then again—'

Her gaze drifted to the window, where rain beat against the glass.

'Then again, I wish I knew how to get him and Elsie back together,' she continued. 'They should be together.'

'Send the lad in 'ere to see me,' said John, reaching for the last of the chocolate. 'I'll have a word with 'im and knock some sense into 'im – it's the least I can do.'

Chapter Fifteen

William hobbled into the hospital on his crutches, receiving sympathetic glances from the nursing staff. He was shown in to see John, who was sitting on the bed in his pyjamas and dressing gown, with his back towards William, as he stared out of the window at the grounds, where giant foxgloves in the borders swayed in the breeze. The sky, through the glass, was bright blue and cloudless. William tapped gently on the door and walked in.

'You got your summons then?' said John, turning around to greet him.

'Yes,' said William. 'Are you going to tell me I'm getting something wrong with the baking? The yeast has been tricky to handle in this hot weather and—'

'Here's the thing,' interrupted John. 'I've realised I'm pretty much the closest thing to a father you have. I know that after your dad died, you and Audrey fell out with your stepfather, Victor. By all accounts he sounds like a bad egg and you're better off without him. But since you started work as a delivery boy at the bakery all them years back, I've watched you learn and grow. I've been proud of you, William. You're a good lad. How old are you now?'

'Twenty-two,' said William. 'Twenty-three next month.'

John nodded sagely. 'I've heard you've called off your engagement to Elsie,' he said. 'You might think it's none of my damn business, lad, but why?'

William shrugged and, using his crutches, walked over to the window to look out at the sky. There was a protracted silence, before he offered an explanation.

'I think she's better off with someone else,' he said.

'But she don't want any bugger else,' said John, exasperated. 'That's what I don't get. I think there's summat else, lad, ain't there?'

William thought of the images running through his head that nobody else in the bakery had seen: indiscriminate violence, the thunderous roar of heaving shelling and fire bombs, hiding from the enemy like rats. The German soldier running away from him. Dear David, twisting and turning in the soil, breathing his last breath. William swallowed.

'While I was away,' he started, 'things happened… I did something… made a poor decision. I'm not the person Elsie fell in love with. Before I went, I was naive and believed I was a stronger man than I am. War has changed me. She's better off with another man.'

He blinked, waiting for John to respond, but the old man's face was expressionless.

'That's guilt talking,' said John, his voice serious. 'Guilt can kill strong men, but you've got to own it and fight it. Nothing prepares you for war. *Nothing*. I fought in the Great War and I know what you've witnessed, but now that you're home, you have a choice. You could let this affect you for the rest of your life, or you could put it behind you and never look back. I don't want to know what your burden is, that's your business, but we all have a cross to bear. If you want my advice, do good for those who love you, or else turn inwards and let guilt rot you from the inside out like a bad apple. What's it to be, William?'

William frowned and stared out of the window at the cloudless sky: a blank canvas.

Chapter Sixteen

Lily had not been able to get Henry's proposition out of her head. Though she had told Audrey that he wanted to adopt Joy, she hadn't told her the other part of the story: that it was Audrey's mother, Daphne, who had told Helen about Lily in the first place, apparently because Victor was so unhappy about not having Lily in his life. On hearing that news, Lily had immediately written to Victor, asking him to meet her in the Lyons Corner House, a tea room in London's Piccadilly. She had said, in her letter, that she would come alone, but actually, she had brought Joy with her. It might be the case that Victor didn't want Lily and Joy in his own home but this was a public place. He would have to behave civilly.

Sitting at a table by the window in the tea room, she watched the Londoners go by. Amongst the buildings devastated by the horrendous Blitz bombing, people carried on with their lives as best they could. A small typing pool of smart young women worked on desks in the courtyard of their bombed-out office building opposite the café, the office presumably too dangerous to work in.

'What do they do in the rain?' Lily asked the waitress, gesturing towards the typists.

'Umbrellas,' she replied with a shrug. 'Or sometimes they sit in cars with their typewriters on their knees. It's a solicitor's firm, so I suppose they can't very well pack up and go home just because their office has been bombed.'

Lily smiled as her eyes were drawn to another shop window where women were having their legs painted by a man with a paintbrush, near a notice declaring 'no more ladders'. Further along the street, people browsed the plants and flowers at a flower stall while buses rumbled past, taking people to work, carrying on with life as normal.

'What can I get you, love?' said the waitress.

'Tea, please,' Lily said. 'Tea for two.'

'Coming up!' she replied, then lowering her voice, 'If I were you, I'd take it sweet while you can. You know Lord Woolton says there's going to be a complete sugar ban in cafés soon? May as well drink dishwater!'

The waitress laughed and walked away, leaving Lily to look around the tea room. It was packed full of people of all ages being served by the waitresses in their smart black and white uniforms. There was a bakery counter at the front and an atmosphere of conviviality, despite evidence of the war playing out all around. She spotted her father, Victor, before he saw her and having not seen him for almost a year, her mouth went dry and her heart pounded in her chest. Standing to wave, she could barely conceal her excitement.

'Father!' she called. 'Over here!'

As she watched Victor walk towards her, dressed in a smart suit despite the hot weather, Lily felt overwhelmed. Seeing him like this made her realise just how much she had missed him over the last months – and she felt angry, upset and happy all at once.

'Lily,' he said, greeting her with wet eyes. 'How are you? I—'

Lily studied Victor's expression as his eyes slipped from her face to Joy's. He seemed to be frozen to the spot, and even when the waitress brought over their pot of tea, he didn't move. She panicked, wondering suddenly if he might just turn around and leave the café.

'I know I said I wouldn't bring her, and that I'd come alone,' said Lily hurriedly. 'But I wanted to show you that she's the innocent one in all of this. I want you to understand why I can't give her to Henry and Helen, even if it means she'd have a more privileged life. That she's my child and a part of our family, of *your* family. I wanted her to meet her grandfather and know that I love you.'

She lifted Joy up, sat down and perched her on her knee, silently praying that she wouldn't cry. Victor, continuing to stare at Joy, sat down slowly on the seat opposite. Lily watched emotions flicker across his face.

'She's exactly like you,' he said quietly. 'It's taking me back to when you were a baby. I feel – I'm disorientated, Lily.'

He leaned back in his chair and shook his head, muttering, as if in conversation with himself.

'When your mother and I had you,' he started, 'I was a good father. I loved you and your red hair and your bonny face. Your mother too, I loved with all my heart. When she fell pregnant with your brother, I was the happiest man in London – life was going just fine. But then, when your mother and brother died in childbirth, it was as if a black veil had been pulled over our lives. You, just four years old at the time, missed your mother so much, it broke my heart. I couldn't replace her, and I wasn't good enough for you—'

'But you were,' said Lily, her voice trembling. 'You were always enough.'

Victor's lip wobbled as he struggled to contain his emotions. Lily had never, ever seen him like this, and she wished she knew how to console him.

'I tried to be a good father to you,' he continued. 'It was just you and I, and as you know, I'm a rather old-fashioned man. My own father barely spoke to his children. I didn't want to be like him, but I became more like him as the years went on and, well, when this happened, when you fell pregnant, I didn't know what to do. It took me by surprise.'

Victor stopped talking and regained his composure, pouring himself and Lily a cup of tea. Words rushed into her mouth and sensing this meeting would be short, she blurted them out.

'Father,' she said, 'I know I've let you down and brought shame to your doorstep. I know I made a terrible mistake and that I acted carelessly and selfishly and that people can be very cruel about girls like me. But I have to move on from that and look to the future. Henry approaching me about adoption made me realise that I need to make sure Joy has security in her life. I want to get a job, to help with the war effort, and earn some money so I can save up. I want Joy to know her family. I don't want us to be strangers. I miss you terribly and have so many things I want to talk to you about. I love Audrey and the people at the bakery, but I miss you.' Flicking her gaze up to his, she smiled. 'Would you like to hold her?' she said.

Lifting Joy over to Victor's knee, Lily held her breath as he awkwardly supported her small, squidgy frame. Joy giggled and wound her fingers around his finger, her cheeks pink and her eyes on everyone and everything in the tea room, blissfully unaware of the significance of this meeting. Relief washed over Lily when a small smile crept onto Victor's face.

'I know you don't want me to live at home,' said Lily. 'And anyway, it's not safe in London. But I would like you to come and see me in Bournemouth if travel is permitted. I know Audrey and William would like that too.'

'I don't know about that,' her father said. 'William and I parted on very unfriendly terms.'

Lily recalled the night William and Audrey had suddenly left the family home, seven years earlier. It had happened after an argument when Victor told Audrey and William that they were no longer permitted to mention their dead father's name, Don, in the house. William had objected to that and had argued with Victor – and Daphne, who sided with Victor. The whole thing had got out of hand, terrible, unsayable things were said and punches were thrown. Victor had thrown Audrey and William out of the house – and they had fled to Bournemouth.

'Why did you dislike Don so much?' Lily asked gently.

'I didn't dislike him,' said Victor, looking uncomfortable. 'I felt, oh, I don't know, I felt that Daphne would always love him more than me. William and Audrey, my stepchildren, idolised him. I didn't want to be second best. It was complicated. I've been very foolish.'

Admitting that he was wrong was clearly difficult for Victor and his expression darkened. He handed Joy back to Lily, standing from his chair, making to leave. He seemed terribly ill at ease, as if he had said too much. Gathering himself together, he buttoned up his coat – and his emotions.

'But you've only just got here,' said Lily, feeling choked.

Victor checked his pocket watch, opened his mouth to reply but, saying nothing, leant down to kiss Lily briefly on the cheek. She smiled up at him, trying to communicate how much she loved him in that one smile.

'I need some time to think this all through,' he said. 'Goodbye, Lily – and thank you for coming here.'

'Goodbye, Father,' she said, cuddling Joy, who was tugging at escaped tendrils of Lily's hair and trying to stand on her lap, strengthening her chubby little legs.

Lily kept her eyes on her father until he'd left the café. She longed for him to look back and wave at her, but he didn't, until he was almost out of sight – and then he turned and raised a hand. Lily beamed and waved frantically through the window. 'I love you,' she mouthed. And then he was gone.

*

Elsie was in bed when she heard the music. After a long shift on the buses, her limbs felt like dead weights, yet she was unable to sleep with thoughts rushing through her head. The entire day had been filled with passengers talking of the previous night's raid on Southampton, when the Luftwaffe had carried out a short but intense attack late at night, destroying churches, schools, public houses and dwelling houses, killing men, women and children.

'A baby girl, just one month old, was killed,' one passenger had told her. 'She'd only just been christened, bless her soul. And a stables was hit, with most of the horses dead. The RAF have hit back, of course, but where will it all end?'

Where will it all end? echoed in her thoughts. Elsie turned over in bed and blinked in the darkness, straining to hear the music coming from outside. At first she thought it was from a dance hall – they had been packed earlier that evening with young people grabbing hold of life like it was a balloon about to float away on a high wind, but while other young people enjoyed what they could of life, Elsie was set on working as hard as she could. She'd made a decision: every waking hour she would work, until the thought of William had faded from her head and heart. As the music grew louder and more familiar, she sat up in bed.

'William?' she whispered. The music, she now knew, was William. She would be able to recognise it anywhere; the tuneful rhythm of his song. He must be outside in the street!

Pushing the covers off her bed, without disturbing her sisters, she tiptoed over to the window. A smile breaking out over her lips, she moved the blackout blind out of the way and opened the window, peering out into the night. The air was warm on her skin, and the moonlight bright. Casting her gaze to the garden, there in the shadows she saw William's outline. He was leaning against the garden wall, his mouth harp to his lips, playing one of Elsie's favourite songs, 'Goodnight Sweetheart'. His eyes met hers.

'What are you doing here?' Elsie said, quietly, trying to suppress a giggle.

William stopped playing and moved over to under the window, his face upturned.

'Can you come down?' he whispered. 'I need to talk to you.'

'Wait there,' she said, letting the blind drop down again, her heart racing in her chest. Pushing her feet into her shoes, she froze when her sisters stirred in their beds – June was sitting up, her eyes wide open.

'Go back to sleep,' said Elsie, gently, and luckily her sister did as she was told.

Pulling on her mackintosh, Elsie crept down the stairs, past her mother's bedroom and unlocked the front door as quietly as she could. In the darkness, William was there, waiting for her. Suppressing the urge to throw herself at him, she folded her arms across her chest and smiled.

'Let's walk,' he whispered. 'I'll hop.'

They walked slowly together towards the clifftop, in the moonlight, and though Elsie desperately wanted to talk, she stayed quiet, wanting to hear what William had to say. He had, after all, come to see her in the middle of the night – he must have something important to get off his chest. She hoped he'd had a change of heart.

'Shall we sit here?' he said. They sat on a patch of grass on the clifftop, which had been carefully trimmed, cared for even in wartime. Searchlights shone across the sky in the distance and the sea glittered.

'I want to say I'm sorry,' he said. 'I'm sorry for being how I have been and for calling our engagement off. I want to change. It's just, Elsie, I saw things, I did things… unforgivable things… I… over there, I saw… all these families, people with their possessions in handcarts, leaving their homes in bare feet, being dive-bombed by Hitler's army, chased by soldiers with guns. Their worlds were turned upside down.'

His words caught in his throat and his eyes filled. Elsie lifted her hand and carefully wiped away a tear that had escaped his eye and was running down his cheek.

'But it's separate to this. I love you,' he croaked. 'I love you so much.'

Elsie felt relief wash over her. Though she knew William was suffering, she was delighted that his feelings for her hadn't changed. Since he'd called off their engagement she'd wondered if she would ever get over him.

'I love you too,' she said, quietly. 'I always have and I always will.'

They embraced one another, enjoying the warmth of their bodies.

'Would you marry me?' he said. 'I think we should get married and do it properly this time. A big wedding, with all our friends and—'

'No,' said Elsie, then laughed affectionately when she saw William's disappointed face. 'I mean, yes, of course I will marry you, but let's keep it small. Just us and our closest family, a cake and a barrel of beer, and some music. Let's keep it simple. Life's complicated enough as it is at the moment. Besides, my father is away and, without him to give me away, I would want to keep the wedding a modest affair.'

William nodded and smiled in understanding. He looked into Elsie's eyes and tucked her hair behind her ears. She sensed he had more he wanted to say, but instead of speaking, he moved his head closer to hers and they kissed in the moonlight, finding comfort and relief in one another's lips.

Chapter Seventeen

'How about this one?' said Audrey, opening up a tiny cardboard box and holding up a cake topper consisting of two clasping hands, made of wax. 'It's really old, probably an antique. Or, oh, I do love this one!'

She smiled as she rummaged through her modest collection of carefully selected cake toppers and placed one down on the shop counter in front of Maggie and Mary. This one was an intricate white and silver model of a bride and groom seated together on the curve of a crescent moon. The moon had features carefully hand-painted on it, and a cluster of tiny stars attached to one end. All three of them smiled at one another.

'I love that,' said Maggie, carefully picking it up and holding it up to the sunlight pouring in through the shop window. 'It's perfect, isn't it?'

It was an unusually quiet Saturday afternoon in the shop and almost time to close. The morning had been busy as always, with people buying their bread, currant buns, carrot and Madeira cakes, but now there was little left on the shelves, and, with the stales bagged up and sold, Audrey, Maggie and Mary were discussing Maggie's wedding, which she and George were arranging before he was posted overseas. Audrey now knew how hard up Maggie was, and had offered to make her a cake and put on the food, as a contribution. Charlie's mother Pat was going to make a posy out of artificial flowers, and instead of trying to buy a new one, Maggie was borrowing a delphinium blue dress from Fran, Audrey's sister-in-law. It was a very pretty frock, but whatever Maggie wore, even if it was a flour sack, she'd look beautiful.

'Afternoon, ladies,' said George, entering the shop and kissing Maggie's hand. The three 'ladies' looked up and beamed. He was the kind of twinkly man it was difficult not to smile at. 'What are you three plotting?'

Audrey explained to George that now Mr Woolton had banned icing on wedding cakes, because it was considered a too-indulgent use of a rationed food, she was having to think around the problem and be creative.

'Some folk are using painted cardboard over the top of a stack of tiny squares of cake that the guests can take home with them,' she explained. 'Others have a standard cake, fruit or sponge, and ice it with chocolate icing, or have a decorated plaster of Paris mould over the top. I've got a few moulds that I'm using now. Of course, there's nothing that compares to the taste of the sugar icing, or the marzipan, but a cover will look good on the photographs and I'll make sure the cake is delicious.'

'If it wasn't wartime I'd want you to have a cake that was five tiers high,' George told Maggie.

'And pink!' she said, beaming at him, a blush creeping up her cheeks.

'Five tiers?' said Audrey, shaking her head. 'You might have to find another baker! I'm good, but I'm not *that* good!'

George laughed but was interrupted by the heavy step and explosive cough of Uncle John, who had come into the shop, stopping in the doorway to cling to the door frame with both hands. He was breathing heavily as an old dog.

'John!' said Audrey. 'What on earth are you doing here? I had no idea you were going to be discharged from hospital today. I would have come to get you.'

'I discharged m'self,' he said. 'I couldn't stand another bleedin' day in bed. I need to get back to m' bread. I've been thinkin' about that wheatmeal bread the Ministry of Food are trying to bring in, the one that's supposed to be good for us all. I need to try it out.'

'The National Loaf?' said Audrey. 'Yes, we've had more letters from the Ministry about it and the Bournemouth Food Control Office told me the grand plan is that all the bakeries will have to start baking it.'

She felt for some advertising leaflets under the counter, then put them on the countertop for John and Maggie to see. The Ministry of Food were trying to popularise a wheatmeal loaf which had extra vitamin content, but so far Barton's had stuck to white bread, beloved by its customers.

'Apparently the wheatmeal loaf, or the National Loaf, I should say, is going on trial at the Isolation Hospital and the Linford Sanitorium,' said Audrey. 'To see if it makes any difference to the patients' health. We're to get wheatmeal flour from the miller soon.'

'That'll be a bugger to work with! And how are the patients in the Isolation Hospital going to tell anyone what they think?' laughed John. 'The Bournemouth Food Control Office ain't thought that one through properly, 'ave they? Ha!'

Audrey laughed, glad to see John in better spirits, but concerned that he wasn't yet fit enough to be back at work. Walking out from behind the counter to greet him properly, she scolded him under her breath, taking his arm to help him walk. He batted her off with a playful slap, but when he reached Maggie, his mood changed.

'I've heard about what you've been up to, young lady, and I do not approve,' he said. 'When did you ever think it was okay to bite the 'and that feeds you?'

Maggie's face flamed red and she quickly busied herself with wrapping up the cake toppers in tissue paper and carefully putting them back in the cardboard box. George looked quizzically at her, but she said nothing. Audrey sighed and chewed the inside of her cheek. Maggie had worked really hard to make amends for what she'd done, but John wasn't one to let things go so easily.

'What's this about, sir?' George said, confused. 'Are you okay, Maggie? You seem flustered.'

'No wonder she's flustered,' said John, leaning his elbow on the counter to take a breather, 'she's been caught pilfering, ain't she? I'm disappointed in you, young Maggie. I've always been fond of you, girl, and thought you had your head screwed on.'

Audrey sighed as Maggie's face grew redder still and her bottom lip wobbled. Without saying a word, Maggie pulled off her apron and threw it onto the shop counter, before running out of the bakery and into the street. George stood, open-mouthed, in the bakery, looking from John to Audrey in confusion.

'For goodness' sake, John!' Audrey cried. 'If you've nothing useful to say then why speak? I'll not have you talking like that to Maggie. Now, go on with you and make yourself useful or get out from under my feet. Honest to goodness!'

Grumbling, John left the room and went upstairs to the kitchen. Mary, who hated any confrontation, slipped her hand into Audrey's for protection.

George pointed over his shoulder to the door. 'I should go after Maggie,' he said, but Audrey quickly grabbed his arm.

'Wait,' she said. 'I want to explain what's happened, so you know.'

Haltingly, Audrey told George that because Maggie had been so keen on him, ever since they first met, she'd taken a bit of sugar to swap for clothing vouchers. She'd always intended to give it back. Audrey also explained that Maggie had a difficult grandmother, who was a drunk, and who was in debt.

'She didn't mean any harm by it,' said Audrey. 'I've known that girl for years and she's got a good heart. She just thinks you will be disappointed in where she's from. She made a mistake, that's all. How does that make you feel about her?'

Audrey sucked in her breath, hardly daring to wait for his opinion. If what she'd told him had changed his feelings for Maggie, she'd never forgive herself for meddling. Mary's hand squeezed tighter around her fingers.

George concentrated as he formulated his answer, and then he broke into a smile. Running his hand through his hair, he let out a big sigh.

'It's not right, what she did, but I understand why,' he said. 'I love that girl. She's got me hooked.'

Audrey's shoulders dropped in relief. She looked down at Mary, who smiled up at her. They both took a deep breath.

'That's that then,' said Audrey. 'Now you better get on after her. She'll be on the Overcliff. There's a bench there, where before the war, people used to sit and enjoy the view. It's where we all go when things are getting on top of us.'

*

'Stupid old fool,' Maggie muttered as she sat on the bench, hugging her knees. She stared out to sea, thinking she'd like to wring Uncle John's neck, for ruining everything for her, when there was a tap on her shoulder. Quickly wiping her eyes with her hanky, she turned to see George smiling down at her. The skin around his eyes crinkled into tiny smiles, making his face light up. Despite her embarrassment, she couldn't help return his smile.

'May I?' he said, taking a seat next to her on the bench. They looked at one another and he reached over, lifted her hand and held it in his. 'Maggie, I love you, no matter what,' he said. 'Audrey explained about what's happened. Why don't you start from the beginning and tell me everything? You know I'll be posted overseas as soon as we're married and I don't want there to be secrets between us.'

'I just didn't want to mess it up,' she said, her voice barely audible. 'I wanted to be a girl you couldn't resist. I would love to be your wife, but I didn't think you'd be interested in me once you saw where I was really from. We… we… don't have a penny to our names. My grandmother lives for fags and any booze she can get her hands on, and I'm, well, I'm just a shop girl.'

'You're not "just" anything,' he said. 'You're Maggie Rose, the girl of my dreams, my wife-to-be. It's not your fault that your grandmother is a ruin.'

'I know what I did was wrong,' she said. 'Audrey is so kind, she has been so kind to me. I don't know what I'd do without her.'

'She's a big-hearted lady,' said George. 'In wartime, that's refreshing. Anyway, there's something I need to tell you too. I haven't been entirely honest with you either…'

'What?' said Maggie, suddenly stricken by an all-consuming fear that George was going to tell her something dreadful, like that he was already engaged.

'I'm to be involved in a dangerous mission, with an elite group of pilots,' he said in a serious, quiet voice. 'You mustn't talk to anyone about this, but after we're married, that's what I'll be doing. I'm fearful for my life, Maggie. I must be honest.'

Maggie felt as if she could hardly breathe. The prospect of losing George, just as soon as she had met him, filled her with unspeakable dread. But, in her usual fashion, she knew she must remain upbeat, positive and hopeful. Perhaps he would be lucky, perhaps he would escape whatever this mission was, unscathed. She knew not to dismiss his fears or pretend that he wasn't facing danger, but instead squeezed his hand, trying to transmit all her love to him through her hot palm.

In the warm sunshine they sat there together, looking out to sea, not knowing what was waiting around the corner, or whether they would have the luxury of a future together. For now, they were together and for that she was grateful.

Chapter Eighteen

It was mid-August and preparations for Maggie and George's wedding were well under way. Audrey had organised the food and planned to make small 'finger' sandwiches with three different fillings: fish paste, mock crab (reconstituted dried eggs, a tiny bit of cheese, salad dressing and a few drops of vinegar) and carrot (grated carrot and cabbage bound with sweet pickle and a dash of vinegar), as well as savoury splits (scones stuffed with diced beetroot and horseradish), spice cake, carrot cookies and rosehip jellies. There would be home-made lemonade to drink and glasses of sherry. The men would want beer, of course, but there was such a beer shortage at the moment, they'd have to go without. Even the public houses were having to shut up shop, though the Carpenter's Arms seemed to keep going! Wasn't much of a wedding feast, she knew that, but rationing meant feasts just weren't possible. With even potatoes hard to get hold of, putting a meal on the table was difficult; just last week when a greengrocer advertised he'd sell potatoes at 9.30 a.m., women started queuing at 7.30 – four of the older ladies fainting in the street.

'Poor old dears,' said Audrey, thinking of those women who were just trying to feed their families. She had planned to ask Sid the butcher for any ham offcuts he might have for Maggie's big day, but he'd gone on such a rant before she'd even opened her mouth, complaining 'them that try to wangle an extra bit to the ration are downright selfish and downright unpatriotic', she'd stopped before she started. What she had planned would have to do.

'Maggie, love,' she said, at the end of a busy day in the bakery. 'Will you close up the shop for me while I check the takings?'

Maggie nodded and went to turn the shop sign to closed when a uniformed man came in. He was in his late twenties, with cropped dark hair, electric blue eyes and a lovely smile, with deep dimples each side of his mouth. Audrey smoothed down her apron and, when he fixed her with his blue eyes, was horrified to feel herself blush. She held a hand up to her cheek and wondered what on earth was wrong with herself.

'Can I help you, sir?' she said. 'We're just about to close up. There's nothing left on the shelves now. We'll be open first thing with fresh bread, rolls and all the counter goods we can manage in rationing.'

'Could you tell me who runs this bakery, please?' he asked. 'I've got a complaint.'

'I do,' she replied, her heart hammering – there had never been a complaint before and her mind trailed through everything she might have done wrong. 'Oh, my goodness, what's the complaint?'

'Well, I was biting into a slice of bread this morning,' he said, 'when I bit into this.'

He held up Audrey's wedding ring. She slapped her hand over her mouth and rushed out from behind the counter.

'Oh!' she said, taking the ring and pushing it straight onto her finger. 'I am *so* happy, I mean, I'm *so* sorry!'

She threw her arms around the stranger and gave him a quick hug.

'Thank you, thank you, thank you,' she said. 'I thought it was gone forever.'

'My teeth were nearly gone forever,' he said. 'But the ring is fine.'

'Audrey!' said Pat from the doorway. 'What on earth is going on here? Why are you draped all over this poor man?'

Audrey turned to see her mother-in-law and noted the disapproving expression on her face. Quickly moving away from the man, she clasped her hands in sudden embarrassment.

'I'm *not* draped all over him!' Audrey said. 'I lost my ring. My wedding ring – and this gentleman, he just came in and said he'd found it in one of our loaves. I lost it the evening John went into hospital and I worked on the dough.

'I don't know how to thank you. I don't even know your name,' she added, turning to him.

'It's fine,' he said, holding out his hand. 'I'm Arthur. Your bread is really very good, apart from the gold content.'

'Well, I never,' said Pat, tutting. 'Thank goodness you didn't choke on it!'

'Why don't you come in for your dinner?' Audrey said. 'We're just about to shut up shop and eat. Maggie, Pat, why don't you come in for your dinner too? Mary, can you set the table and set places for eight of us?'

'Eight?' said Arthur. 'Sounds like you already have your hands full. There's no need—'

'There's always room at my table,' Audrey interrupted. 'It would be a pleasure. A way to thank you for returning my ring.'

Audrey placed a steaming dish of Lancashire hotpot down on the table, and when she ladled the meat, carrots, onions and potato onto the plates, accompanied by a thick slice of bread to mop up the gravy, everyone made appreciative noises.

'You always do us proud,' said Uncle John, tucking his napkin into the collar of his shirt. 'Even in rationing you manage to serve up a lovely supper. It's like a magic trick.'

Pat cleared her throat before picking up her cutlery and getting stuck in. 'It's not magic,' she said. 'It's careful planning and making what you have got last. Us women are good at that – we have to be, mind.'

'Oh, I might have known you'd have an answer!' laughed Uncle John.

Pat glared at him and Audrey smiled at Arthur, in apology.

'There's Prune Roly for afters,' Audrey said, quickly interjecting. 'Bit of an experiment, mind, since I'm almost out of prunes and I've no idea when a new consignment will make it through.'

'Merchant Navy's suffering an awful battering,' said John. 'It's no surprise stocks aren't making it through.'

For a moment, everyone ate in silence, reflecting on the strategy Hitler and his army were trying to put into place, to sink ships transporting food into the country and starve Britain into surrender. That's why everyone was 'digging for victory', turning every piece of available land into allotments, and why nothing was allowed to go to waste. Even the fat that collected in the bottom of the bakery ovens when they cooked the neighbours' roast dinners on a Sunday morning could be scraped up and kept for cooking. Today's scraps were tomorrow's savouries.

'Anyway, Arthur, what brought you to Bournemouth? I don't believe you're local?' said Audrey, breaking the silence. 'I don't recognise your face.'

'I'm an engineer, originally from Norfolk. I'm involved with the radar station that's been set up near here,' he explained. 'The radar helps to detect and track aircraft.'

'Interesting work,' said Pat. 'And where are you staying? I have a spare room if you need a billet – I make a very good stew.'

'I'm staying in a local hotel at the moment, but thank you for the offer,' Arthur said. 'Bournemouth seems to be a fine town, with generous people. I'm staying near to Swanmore Gardens. Have you seen the roses there? They're quite spectacular.'

Audrey smiled, thinking of the roses of Swanmore that she and Charlie used to visit once a year. The fragrance of those flowers was like nothing she'd ever known. It heartened her to think they were still blooming, despite the war.

'Haven't got time for roses, there's a war on!' laughed John, raising his cup of tea. 'I'm just jokin', young man, but I believe you found Audrey's ring in the bread? That'll be a first. Don't go tellin' the regulars, or they'll all be wantin' one!'

He laughed again and then broke down into yet another coughing fit, though it didn't last too long. Audrey fetched him a glass of water and patted his back, before returning to her seat and smiling at Arthur.

'Yes, thank you for bringing it back to me,' she said. Picking up her mug, she said. 'Here's to Arthur, and to our absent friends and loved ones.'

She glanced at her ring and smiled sadly, her thoughts going out to Charlie, wherever he was. Then William banged the side of his cup with a fork.

'I've got an announcement to make,' he said. 'It's not been easy lately, with my leg and all, and the way I've been carrying on… But I've seen sense and I've asked Elsie to marry me. Again.'

'Hurrah!' said John, with another laugh. 'Good for you, lad, good for you.'

'Thank you,' he replied. 'Elsie wants to keep it small, but as long as we're married, properly this time, I don't mind.'

Audrey pushed back her chair and hugged her brother. 'That's wonderful news,' she said. 'Two weddings! Mary, we better sort through those cake toppers, hadn't we, love?'

When dinner was over and the dishes were washed, Arthur thanked Audrey once again, gently taking her hand and kissing it lightly.

'Thank you,' he said. 'You should visit those rose gardens near me, they're truly special, as I can see you are too.'

'Get away with you!' said Audrey, feeling her cheeks flame. 'As John said, there's no time for rose gardens, but it heartens me to hear they're in bloom, offering some beauty in these dark times.'

Arthur winked at her and walked away into the street, leaving her standing in the doorway, her arms folded, a warm sensation in her heart.

Chapter Nineteen

The billeting officer for child evacuees, Margaret Peak, called when Mary was at school and the queue for morning bread was trailing down Fisherman's Road. For a second Audrey wondered if she was there to scold her, as Mary had forgotten to take her gas mask to school twice last week. It was only when the schoolteacher told Mary she wouldn't be able to attend the victory party when the war was over that the little girl made sure to take it. Audrey appreciated the schoolteacher's optimism and sent her in two rock cakes.

'Can't it wait, Margaret?' asked Audrey. 'You can see how busy we are.'

Margaret was a friend of Pat's and very much cut from the same cloth. Sturdy, resilient and with a manner of someone who had 'seen it all', she shook her head, unperturbed by the queue.

'Not really,' she said. 'It will only take a minute, if I can talk to you in private, please.'

Rubbing her forehead, Audrey sighed and asked Maggie to hold the fort, then she ushered Margaret into the back room, where the day's scones and cakes were cooling.

'If you're here to ask me to take on another littl'un,' said Audrey, 'I don't know where I'd put her or him. But, of course, I will try. If there's a little evacuee that needs a home, I will find space.'

The billeting officer smiled gratefully, but shook her head, her lips pursed together. 'No, Mrs Barton,' she said. 'It's more delicate than that, I'm afraid. How is Mary doing here?'

Audrey smiled, pushing her hands into her apron pockets as she thought about the girl she had grown to love as if she were her own. Happiest when cuddling her pet rabbit, or engrossed in a jigsaw puzzle while Audrey worked in the kitchen, she had grown in confidence and happiness. Mary was a good little helper too and relished helping with the baking, or in the shop.

'She's a lovely girl,' said Audrey. 'She's quiet and a thinker, but she's come on leaps and bounds since she first arrived. You know she'd never seen the sea or the sea birds, or a lamb or cow, so she's learned a great deal about nature, I think. She never used to say a word, but now she does talk. She loves baking with me. In fact, she's become like my little shadow – my companion. I care for her deeply, I really do.'

Margaret nodded and took a letter from her coat pocket. She handed it to Audrey, who unfolded it and quickly scanned the words, the weight of them pressing down on her shoulders. Her hand flying to her mouth, she handed it back to Margaret.

'Oh dear God, no!' said Audrey, a deep frown creasing her brow.

'Her father was killed in action,' Margaret said quietly. 'She'll need to be told, of course. Are you willing to break the news to her, Audrey?'

Audrey blinked before taking a deep breath and nodding.

'Of course,' she said. 'I told her about her mother at Christmas. I don't know how the poor thing will take this, though. How dreadful!'

Margaret murmured in agreement, and shook her head sadly. 'Unfortunately this isn't the first time I've had to make one of these visits to an evacuee. Luckily, Mary has you for support.'

Audrey smiled at the kind comment, then rubbed her forehead, aware of the enormity of the awful task ahead.

'And for the time being, are you happy to keep Mary with you at the bakery?' Margaret asked. 'Mary has an ageing aunt in Scotland who's in no fit state to look after a child, so I expect she'll have to go into a children's home.'

Audrey didn't hesitate for a moment. There was no way Mary was going to suffer more disruption and go into a children's home with nobody there who knew her or cared about her.

'Never,' said Audrey. 'She's part of the family. I'll do whatever I need to do, Margaret. Perhaps I can write to her aunt and ask for her permission? Mary must stay here with me – she's family.'

Margaret nodded briskly and held out her hand for Audrey to shake.

'Very well,' she said. 'I'll look into it for you, Audrey. Mary is lucky to have you looking out for her. Very lucky indeed.'

Audrey's thoughts went to the numerous disappointments she'd had when trying and failing to fall pregnant. She smiled at Margaret and said: 'We're lucky to have each other.'

Audrey reached up to the top of the kitchen dresser and pulled down the *Peter Rabbit* sweet tin that held a few remaining barley sugar twists inside. She offered one to Mary, who, after a hasty 'thank you', quickly took one of the sticky orange twists, popping it in her mouth and tucking it safely into her cheek, a smile breaking out over her lips.

'Is it m' birthday?' Mary said, her eyes twinkling. Usually the barley sugar tin only came out in the air-raid shelter if they had a particularly long sit, waiting for the 'all-clear' to sound.

'No, love, else there'd be musical bumps, jellies and party hats,' said Audrey, smiling, but feeling thoroughly wretched at the thought of the news she had to break. 'I thought we could go for a walk together in a minute, to the sea cliffs – see if the sand martins have flocked yet, ready to follow the swifts overseas. What do you think? I sometimes wonder if all those Spitfires and Hurricanes worry the birds and put them off their journeys…'

Mary shrugged and Audrey stopped talking, realising that nerves were making her witter on. It was the end of a busy day and Audrey had spent every moment of it worrying about how to tell Mary about her father's death. The child had already endured so much sadness: her brother's death, her mother's death – and now this. Was there a point when she could not withstand any more tragedy?

Walking out to the sea cliffs beyond the Overcliff, where there was a small area civilians could still access, Mary and Audrey sat down on a mound of grass and looked out over the sea. Pointing to a flock of small, dark and pale brown birds flying near small tunnels they'd excavated in the cliffs, they watched them swoop and dip through the sky, flying with natural agility, their excited twittering carrying through the air.

'Oh no!' said Mary, glancing up at Audrey. 'There's one there on the ground that's injured. It looks like its wing isn't working properly.'

Audrey strained to see the bird Mary was referring to.

'Perhaps it's having a rest,' she said, nudging her shoulder into Mary's. 'It's gathering strength because they'll all fly off to Africa for the winter, where it's warm, then they'll come back again next year. You can tell the seasons by the birds – and whether the harvest will be late or early. Charlie told me that.'

Then, after a long pause while they sat watching the birds, Audrey picked up Mary's hand and held it tightly. 'There's something I need to tell you,' she said, her heart hammering in her chest. 'It's sad news, I'm afraid, Mary.'

Mary picked up a pebble from the ground and turned it over in her hand. She stared up at Audrey, her big brown eyes like pools, her cheeks bright. 'Is it Daddy?' she said in a tiny voice.

Audrey nodded and swallowed hard. She had to remain composed, despite how she really felt.

'I'm afraid so, Mary,' she said. 'There was a letter from the military, to inform his family that he has died. The letter came to me. Your father was killed in combat, fighting in the war.'

'Why was he fighting?' Mary immediately asked. 'He used to tell me off for fighting with my brother.'

Audrey's throat ached with emotion, but continuing to hold Mary's hand, she quickly tried to work out how best to explain the inexplicable. The little girl's eyes were burning into Audrey's face, waiting for an answer.

'The war is complicated,' she said. 'Your father was fighting to try to help end the war.'

'But why was he fighting?' Mary insisted. 'I don't understand why he was fighting.'

Audrey could see that Mary was agitated. Her mouth was contorting as she spoke and she battled to hold in her tears. Her shoulders had stiffened and she held her hands on her lap in fists.

'Because…' Audrey started, her eyes darting around her as she struggled to formulate an answer. 'Because when one person starts fighting, it's difficult not to fight back.'

'But it's wrong to fight,' Mary said again, her voice hoarse. 'I would never, ever fight anyone. At school when you fight you are sent to the head teacher and made to write lines or stand in the corner and face the wall. It's stupid and wrong and naughty. NAUGHTY DADDY!'

She threw the pebble as hard as her little arm could throw, then threw herself flat onto the ground, sobbing so hard her body convulsed.

Audrey crouched down on the soil next to her, resting her hand on Mary's back, which was hot and clammy through her dress. Though Audrey tried desperately to remain calm, tears dripped down her face.

'He wasn't naughty,' she said softly. 'He was doing his duty and, very sadly, he lost his life. We must be kind to his memory.'

Mary kneeled upright, her face red and wet from crying. Her body was taut with anger. 'I don't want memories!' she screeched. 'I want my daddy, my mummy and my brother back! Why have they all left me? They didn't care about me!'

'I'm sorry,' Audrey said, gently taking her little frame and holding her in her arms, tightly, until the sobbing relented into hiccups and the collar of her dress was sodden with Mary's tears. 'I'm sorry, Mary. I'm *so* sorry.'

After a long time, with the light fading and the sand martins now black dots and dashes against the sky, like Morse code, Audrey asked Mary if she was ready to go home. Mary seemed empty and withdrawn and it felt to Audrey as if she had retreated within herself again, somewhere impossible to reach.

As they stood up from their spot on the grass, Mary looked back at where the injured bird had been rooted to the spot the entire time. Audrey willed it, with all her might, to take flight and, as if the universe had heard her wish, the bird lifted its fragile wings and took to the sky, where it joined a small flock of birds preparing to migrate, and was, thank goodness, no longer alone.

'Come on, Mary dear,' Audrey said. 'Let's get you home.'

Chapter Twenty

Over the coming days, following the news of Mary's father's death, everyone in the bakery did all they could to keep up the little girl's spirits. Encouraged to help out in the bakery, she was also given more responsibility in the kitchen, including getting the breakfast on the table. Now, Mary was spreading margarine (made to go further by whipping it with milk and flour) on toast for herself and sitting with Lily and Joy at the kitchen table, while Audrey served customers in the shop. Popping upstairs with a letter for Lily, Audrey stroked Mary's hair, gave her a quick kiss on the cheek and smiled at her. Lily smiled at her stepsister in admiration – she was doing all she could to help Mary feel loved and cared for at all times.

'Letter for you,' said Audrey to Lily, then turning to Mary, 'Are you ready to help Maggie in the shop after breakfast?'

Mary nodded and Lily thought it was a good thing there was so much for her to do because when you were grieving so deeply, it helped to be busy.

'I'm not sure what this is, Audrey,' said Lily, distractedly taking the letter. 'How do I look? Smart enough? I'm nervous.'

Lily looked down at the simple, but smart navy dress that Audrey had lent her for her informal interview at the library. After meeting Victor in London, Lily had made the decision to find some work to aid the war effort, and she'd seen an advertisement calling for someone to help at the language centre at the local library, helping refugees of different nationalities – including German Jews, Austrians, Czechoslovakians and Polish, who were certified as refugees from Nazi oppression and given permission to remain in England – with their spoken English. There was a crèche facility at the library, which meant she could take Joy with her too.

'You look perfect,' said Audrey, as Lily started to open the letter. 'Doesn't she, Mary? Your red hair sets that navy dress off a treat. Good luck today.'

Lily opened the letter and quickly scanned it, then read it again to make sure she'd understood it properly – she put it down on the kitchen table, sat down and rested her hands on her lap. 'Gracious me,' she said. 'I can't quite believe it.'

Audrey, who was halfway out of the door, heading back down to the shop to serve the customers, turned back.

'What can't you believe?' she asked. 'You look like you've seen a ghost.'

'It's Father and your mother,' said Lily, her eyes wide open. 'You won't believe it, but they're coming to visit.'

Audrey's mouth fell open and, slowly, she came back into the kitchen. Twiddling her wedding ring round on her finger, all the colour drained from her face as she read the letter for herself. From downstairs Maggie called up for Audrey's help: 'The queue's halfway down the road!' but Audrey seemed not to hear her.

'Well,' she said, sinking into a chair. 'I never, in a million years, thought this would happen. What will William say? He hasn't seen them for years! I don't even know if he'll want to see them after what happened. Are they coming to see Joy, really?'

Lily, equally bemused, shrugged her shoulders, but slowly, realising that what she'd said in London that day must have changed Victor's mind, a smile crept onto her face.

'It must have been something I said when we met,' she replied. 'They're coming next Sunday.'

'Good Lord,' said Audrey. 'My mother is actually coming here? This will be the first time in seven years and she chooses now, during wartime, when Charlie's not even here. I can hardly believe it, Lily.'

'Audrey?' Maggie called from downstairs, louder now. 'I need a hand if you can?'

'Coming!' called Audrey, leaving Lily, Joy and Mary in the kitchen.

Lily thought that it was exactly because it was wartime that Victor and Daphne were visiting. Perhaps it had taken the realisation that life was short and the future uncertain for them to reconsider their attitude. She felt excited by the prospect – more than anything she would love for Victor to be a part of Joy's life and she was pleased they were coming after she'd had her interview at the library. That way she could show her father that the good education he'd provided her was not going to waste just because she had a baby daughter.

Glancing at the carriage clock on the mantelpiece, Lily gasped. 'Oh, Mary, I'll be late!' she said. 'Can you hold Joy for me while I sort out these plates, please? Give her one of those jigsaw pieces to chew, she loves them on her gums.'

In Mary's arms, Joy wriggled into position and tugged gently on Mary's fringe with one hand, a piece of the jigsaw puzzle in the other. Despite everything she was going through, Mary giggled, which made Joy giggle too. Lily paused from rushing around the kitchen to smile at the girls, warmed by their innocence, and was filled with sudden hope for the future.

Chapter Twenty-One

Sunday arrived in a blink. The week's work done, there was a short pause, a brief moment to take a breath, while the fierce heat of the ovens diminished and the tins were scrubbed and cleaned, the flour sacks heaved into position for the next week's bread – and it was during this quick breath that Daphne and Victor were due to visit.

'Does it look clean to you?' Audrey asked Lily, as she sprinkled a few drops of paraffin onto a lintless duster and polished the wooden countertop in the shop. She placed the bottle of paraffin down and paused to scrutinise her work, rubbing her lower back with her fingertips.

'It's spotless,' Lily said, smoothing down her floral-print day dress and correcting her hair as she spoke. 'The whole place looks immaculate.'

Standing with her hands on her hips, Audrey slowly ran her eyes over the bakery shop. It was small and simple, yes, but cosy and charming, and each of the teapots in the collection she had displayed on a shelf above the counter as decoration had been carefully dusted. Moving towards the window, she breathed on a small smudge on the glass and rubbed it with a hanky until it squeaked. There was little more she could do.

'Right,' she said, checking her pocket watch. 'Better check the food and tidy myself up. They'll be here in no time at all.'

When the knock on the door finally came, just before midday, Audrey almost collapsed on the floor with nerves. William's reaction to Daphne and Victor visiting hadn't been what she'd expected.

She'd anticipated anger that it had taken this long for Daphne to show she cared, but he seemed to take it in his stride.

'Come on, we can do it,' said Lily, who was hanging behind Audrey in the corridor as she went to open the door. 'They're only our parents, Audrey! It's not as if it's Hitler coming to get us!'

'Don't speak too soon,' said Audrey, thinking that it felt almost as bad. She let out a small nervous laugh and opened the door, plastering a big welcoming smile on her face.

On the step stood Victor and her mother, Daphne, looking just as nervous as Audrey felt. As well as her gas-mask box, Daphne held a small bunch of roses, which she offered up to Audrey, and Victor hurriedly took off his hat and held it under his arm.

Ushering them into the bakery, taking their smart city coats, enquiring after their train journey, and giving them a quick tour of the premises, she kept checking her mother's expression to see if she could fathom her opinion of Audrey's life in Bournemouth. Though she wouldn't admit it to herself out loud, deep down she longed for approval – and desperately wanted Daphne to be impressed, and to appreciate the life Audrey had built for herself with Charlie. When Audrey and William's father Don had been alive, Daphne had been a different character – warm and loving – it was only since marrying Victor that she had seemed to withdraw and close up, like a clam. But no matter how hard she scrutinised Daphne's expression, Audrey still couldn't tell what her mother was thinking. It was only the presence of Joy and Mary, really, that managed to break the ice, in the way only babies and children can – and, eventually, after an awkward, tense few minutes, the couple seemed more relaxed.

'If you'd like to come up to the dining room, dinner should be ready,' said Audrey. 'William should be here any moment. He must have been held up.'

At the mention of William's name, Daphne stiffened, but Audrey was determined to carry on as if this was a fairly normal event. Once everyone was seated in the best room, with the finest crockery and cutlery set out, she brought in a Woolton pie fresh from the range cooker. The Woolton pie was a vegetarian pie inspired by Lord Woolton, the Food Minister, created to provide a decent meal using home-grown ingredients. Audrey knew it didn't beat a Sunday roast, but the butcher had had very little in the shop when she called in – only brains and knuckle and kidneys – so she decided to try the vegetable pie instead.

'Can't imagine the toffs eating this in the Savoy, can you?' said Audrey, referring to the fact that the pie, packed with potatoes, swede, cauliflower, turnips, oats and cheese, was first created at the Savoy Hotel. 'Victor, can I tempt you to a slice?'

Sitting up in his chair so straight he might as well have had a rod up the back of his shirt, Victor nodded and granted Audrey a small, tight-lipped smile. For some reason, perhaps because she was so nervous, the whole occasion suddenly made her want to laugh out loud. What would Charlie think if he could see this, she wondered. Controlling herself, she cleared her throat and served everyone around the table: Elsie, Victor, Daphne, Lily and Mary.

'It's wonderful to have you here,' said Audrey, trying to break the silence as everyone tucked into the pie. 'It's a shame Charlie's not here to meet you, of course. What prompted you to visit, Mother?'

Daphne paused from eating and took a sip of water, before addressing Audrey, with eyes that darted about like the sand martins on the cliffs.

'Victor has been missing Lily somewhat,' she said slowly, as if carefully selecting her words before she spoke. 'And we witnessed some terrible goings-on in London through the Blitz. We lost some good friends and neighbours—'

'I'm sorry,' said Audrey. 'London has suffered so badly.'

Daphne smiled at her, before continuing, 'With the outlook so grave, the world over, we thought it best that we try to overcome our differences. Is that… did I hear…?'

There was the sound of a door slamming shut downstairs and a 'hello' from William, before footsteps and crutches could be heard on the stairs. Audrey leapt from her chair and opened the door, to where William was standing, leaning on his crutches.

'William,' she said, 'come in. Mother and Victor have arrived, so we made a start on lunch. You'll be wanting to say your "hello", I'm sure…'

Audrey's heart was in her mouth as she watched William's face. She could tell how difficult it was for him to hold himself together. The last time he and Daphne had been together, a row had broken out that had split the family in two – no wonder his hands were trembling so terribly. This was also the first time that Daphne had seen William's injuries. Audrey had written to her to tell her about him, but she hadn't responded. Now though, she couldn't hide her horror and pain. She stood from her chair and moved around the table to where he was standing. Timidly, she outstretched her arms and embraced him. William, unsure at first, suddenly relented and grasped hold of Daphne, desperately trying not to weep.

'Oh, how could they do this to you?' Daphne said, staring down at his foot and gently touching his face. 'How could I not have been there for you? Victor, this can't go on! William needed me and I wasn't here…'

Audrey was stunned by Daphne's reaction. Stunned and heartened. For the first time in a decade she was behaving how a mother should. Victor, taken aback, cleared his throat and also stood from his chair. He took William's hand in his and shook it. 'I think I owe you an apology,' he said. 'I'm hoping we can put all that business in the past behind us. There are much bigger fights going on these days, as you very well know.'

William nodded but didn't speak. The emotion in the room couldn't have been more heightened, and Audrey felt momentarily lost for words.

'Come and have some of this pie, William,' said Elsie. 'Daphne, Victor, William and I are soon to be married. I'm sure he'd love for you to be there.'

'Thank you, Elsie,' said Daphne, her cheeks going motley pink, as she returned to her plate of half-eaten food. 'And there's another reason we're here, isn't there, Victor?'

Victor sighed and nodded, his eyes shining. He looked at Lily, who was holding Joy.

'Lily,' he said, 'we'd like you to come home. I was wrong to treat you in the way I did. When I met Joy, it was like I was meeting you again, as a baby. I thought about your mother and how she would treat you. She would want you at home...'

Audrey couldn't eat any of her pie. Victor and Daphne's revelations felt nothing short of small miracles. It was so wonderful to see that it *was* possible for people to change.

'But Lily *is* at home,' piped up Mary. 'Joy and Lily's home is here, isn't it? Are they going away too, now?'

Audrey picked up Mary's hand and squeezed it. 'Of course this is Lily's home,' she said. 'But she has another one too.'

'Thank you both,' said Lily. 'I can't tell you how wonderful that is to hear, but being here, with Audrey, Mary and everyone, the bakery has become home. I've found a job helping refugees with their spoken English too. I'm making a life for myself, but I would love for Joy to be a part of your life. There's nothing I would like more.'

'Victor doesn't mean now,' said Daphne, imploringly. 'London is too dangerous for a baby, but after the war. We both wanted you to know you are welcome back whenever you need, or want to come home. Henry Bateman led us to believe that you are struggling down here, but I see you have been made very welcome.'

Audrey beamed, feeling, finally, that her mother acknowledged her way of life in Bournemouth to be as warm and comforting as the bread Barton's baked. 'Lily is my family,' she said. 'I would never turn her away, or indeed anyone in need.'

'You've a big heart,' said Daphne, shame passing over her features. 'You're just like your father. He would have been proud of you. Was always proud of you. I am… proud of you.'

Even though she was twenty-seven years old, with a marriage and a bakery to her name, and Mary to care for and a brother to help rehabilitate and customers to provide for, something in Audrey's heart rejoiced at her mother's words. She felt as if a piece of a jigsaw puzzle, which had been missing for years, had finally slotted into place.

When Victor and Daphne left late that afternoon, Audrey joined John and William in the bakery, where they were mixing up dough and lighting the ovens for the week ahead.

'What a day!' she said to the men. 'I never thought we'd see the day that they visited Bournemouth. Did you, William?'

William turned to face her and smiled, just like the way he used to smile when he was a young boy. If it wasn't for his scars and his injuries, it could have been ten years earlier.

'Folk are full of surprises, that's for sure,' said John, before dusting off the blade of his long-handed peel. 'I'll be buggered if I can work 'em out!'

Chapter Twenty-Two

'I've borrowed this from Mrs Cook,' Audrey said, self-consciously touching her saucer-style hat with a green ribbon bow on the front. 'She says she has no use for it now, but is it a bit grand for me?'

'Not at all,' said Lily, with a smile. 'It suits you. Will you hold Joy for a moment, please?'

They were standing outside St Katherine's Church, with William and Elsie, in the afternoon sunshine, waiting for Maggie to arrive. The wedding had been arranged in haste, slotting into the few days that George had left in Bournemouth before he was to be posted elsewhere.

Audrey had done her best with the cake, baking a fruit cake flavoured with orange, cinnamon and cloves. A dense cake, it was the best she could do with the ingredients available – and had used gravy browning to enhance the colour. The icing was a plaster of Paris mould and she had carefully attached the cake topper Maggie loved the most, the couple sitting on a crescent moon. With a gold ribbon wrapped around the bottom, it looked beautiful for a 'make-do' cake. Brides were definitely having to 'make do' during wartime on all fronts, but judging by the look of utter happiness on Maggie's face as she arrived at the church, she didn't care one jot.

'Doesn't she look a picture?' said Lily, joining a long line of admiring glances.

Dressed in a delphinium blue dress, with tucked bodice and a knife-pleated skirt, Maggie wore white shoes and long white fingerless gloves. Over her face she wore a short veil, through which her red lips and blue eyes dazzled. She carried a Victorian posy, arranged by Pat, of delicate spring pink and blue flowers, surrounded with frilly ivory broderie anglaise, and from which long strips of ribbon fluttered in the breeze.

'She really does,' said Audrey, feeling tears leap into her eyes. She blinked hard, focussing on her fingers, which were red and sore from working in the bakery. Moving her wedding ring around her finger, she was overwhelmed by a desperate need to see Charlie or even hear his voice. It was a horrible feeling, but sometimes she felt she couldn't remember what he sounded like, and though he had written a couple of times, he wasn't a natural letter writer. Today, despite being surrounded by people she loved and for such a happy occasion, she felt her heart might burst with longing for the one she truly loved.

'Looks like trouble is on the way,' whispered Lily into Audrey's ear, interrupting her mournful thoughts. 'Who on earth is *that*?'

Snapping out of her reverie, Audrey looked up and followed Lily's gaze to Maggie's grandmother, who was staggering towards the church. Maggie's sisters were trailing close behind, looked concerned and embarrassed, Isabel tugging at her grandmother's arm.

'Is that Maggie's grandmother?' said William. 'She's three sheets to the wind and heading inside!'

Audrey handed Joy back to Lily and marched over to Gwendolen. Swaying slightly in her shoes, the old woman focussed on Audrey and sneered.

'Here she is,' said Gwendolen, pointing her gnarly old finger at Audrey and twice jabbing her in the chest. 'Miss Goody Two Shoes coming to put me in my place! Well, I'll tell you something, you've no right. Maggie is my granddaughter and she's not getting married without my consent. I've not even met this George fella yet.'

'I'm so sorry, Mrs Barton,' said Isabel, blushing madly. 'Please excuse my grandmother, she's not herself. I tried to convince her not to come, but she wasn't having any of it.'

'Don't you worry, Isabel, just go inside and see Maggie,' said Audrey, grabbing hold of Gwendolen's arm and steering her around the corner to the other side of the church. The rest of the small congregation had gone inside.

Isabel, rooted to the spot with anxiety, followed Audrey with her eyes until Nancy pulled at her shoulder and instructed her to go inside. When Maggie's sisters were finally in the church, Audrey addressed Gwendolen.

'Gwendolen,' said Audrey, 'you're in no fit state to go inside. That home-distilled alcohol you're drinking, it's very strong and could be dangerous.'

'And what's that got to do with you?' she said, slurring and stumbling over onto the grass.

Audrey rubbed her forehead in dismay, then helped pick up the old lady. With one hand firmly holding her arm, she led her to a bench, where a seagull was perched. Audrey flapped her arm at the gull and it flew into the sky, cawing at the top of its lungs.

'Eh?' said Gwendolen, her eyes narrowed. 'What did you say?'

'Nothing,' said Audrey, with a sigh. 'Look, I'm sure you have your reasons for being so angry with the world, but this is Maggie's big day. If you go inside the church like this, she will be mortified. You can hardly stand up.'

'But I want to tell her what I think…' she cried. 'I've not even met this George, and in my experience these fellas are bad news!'

'Why don't you sober up a bit and come along to the food and drinks reception in the café afterwards?' Audrey said. 'I can walk you back to the bakery now where I work, if you like, and you can have a nap? I'll make you a brew and find you a slice of cake too. Come on, let Maggie enjoy her day. There's not much for young women to enjoy at the moment, is there?'

Grumbling, Gwendolen consented, and though Audrey was desperately disappointed to be missing the wedding ceremony, she walked the old lady back to the bakery. After settling her down in a comfortable armchair, with a cup of tea and a slice of gingerbread cake, Gwendolen softened considerably. Audrey realised the poor woman was vulnerable and probably needed a bit of looking after. She told her that she planned to return to the wedding, but that Uncle John was in the bakehouse, should she need any help. The next moment Gwendolen fell into a deep sleep – the cake plate sliding to the floor with a crash. Clearing up the shards of broken porcelain, then quietly closing the door on the snoring old lady, Audrey walked back to the church as quickly as she could.

On her way there, she thought of her own wedding day, when Daphne and Victor hadn't attended, much to her huge disappointment – yet now they wanted to make amends. In the same vein, there was hope for Gwendolen changing into a nicer woman, wasn't there?

By the time Audrey got back to the church and crept through the cool stone entrance into the congregation, the ceremony was over and Maggie and George were embracing and kissing.

Once everyone was back outside in the church grounds, Elsie caught up with Audrey.

'Where did you go?' Elsie said. 'Are you okay?'

'Yes,' said Audrey. 'Just making a thirsty person a cup of tea.'

Both women were watching Maggie, the picture of happiness, as she turned her back to the assembled gathering and prepared to throw her bouquet. Maggie's sisters were elbowing each other out of the way to find the best position for catching the posy, shrieking and laughing.

Audrey caught Isabel's eye and smiled, so glad and grateful for the joy of weddings when all the other news in the world was so depressing.

'Thank you,' mouthed Isabel.

'What do you mean, a thirsty person?' said Elsie, frowning. 'Gwendolen?'

'I'll explain another time,' said Audrey, her eyes following the posy, which was soaring through the blue sky, tumbling this way and that, and heading towards Elsie. 'Oh Elsie, look out! Catch it!'

Elsie raised her hands in the nick of time and caught the flowers, collapsing into shocked laughter. A small cheer and a smattering of applause went up from the crowd, and she looked bashful as William kissed her on the cheek.

'You two are next,' said Audrey, smiling.

The reception afterwards was in the community hall, decorated with bunting and where Audrey had set out the food on borrowed tablecloths and Maggie's sister, Isabel, had strung up a banner saying 'Congratulations' over the entrance. It reminded her of the wedding party she had arranged for Elsie and William's wedding the previous year that never happened, but she tried to push that thought aside.

George's parents had had to return to the city due to travel restrictions, and all of his brothers were overseas, but several of his peers were there, determined to enjoy the party.

'This war has made every party even more fun!' one pointed out.

Gwendolen, who had sobered up and was clearly feeling ashamed of herself, sat looking perplexed in the corner of the room. Earlier, she had approached Audrey and muttered her apologies, which Audrey quickly accepted. Like many of the older people, she wore too many layers and must have been boiling hot, but she refused to take off her coat. George, bless him, treated the old woman like a member of the royal family, collecting a plate of food for her, before sitting down next to her and engaging her in conversation.

'Whatever can he be talking to her about?' Maggie asked nervously, biting into a beetroot and horseradish savoury split. 'Goodness knows what she's saying about me. She's never had a nice word to say where I'm concerned...'

They both watched George and Gwendolen for a moment. It seemed George was doing all the talking while the old lady was shoving sandwiches in her mouth, ten to the dozen.

'She doesn't look like she's saying much at all,' said Audrey. 'It's not every man that would have the heart and patience to talk to a woman who has been so cruel to his beloved. You've got a good one there. And hopefully your grandmother will see the error of her ways. I think she's perhaps just lost her way a little.'

'She's an old bag,' said Maggie, her voice low. 'But I know she has her reasons. She lost my grandfather in the Great War. She never really moved on from that. Then when my parents died, she was left to look after us girls and couldn't take any more.'

'Poor old dear,' said Audrey, suddenly noticing that William was sitting on his own at a table, staring into a glass of beer. Though he seemed to be on the mend now that he'd patched things up with Elsie, there were still moments when she felt desperately worried about what was tormenting him. Occasionally he just seemed to disappear somewhere else in mind, if not in body. Here, where everyone seemed delighted to be able to enjoy a few hours of celebration, a welcome relief in wartime, toasting Maggie and George's happiness, his sombre mood made him stick out like a sore thumb.

'Why don't you go and ask your new husband to dance, Maggie? I suspect he'd like to be rescued from your grandmother!' Audrey said. 'I'm going to check on William, then I'd better get back to the bakery.'

*

As the gramophone record played out, a cheer rippled through the room, and people began to dance. From his seat at the table William glanced up to see Elsie talking animatedly to Lily, as they danced together. William was taken aback by Elsie's beauty. Her glossy black hair piled high on her head and dark eyes seemed so definite – if this were a painting hanging on a wall, she would leap off the canvas, having been painted in the boldest, brightest colours. He, on the other hand, felt as if he were a shadow in contrast. Watching her move with energy and grace, he suffered a tremor of doubt about whether he could be a good husband to her. Did he have what it takes? He hadn't told her what a coward he had been overseas – and if she knew, would she still love him?

Pull yourself together, he told himself, rolling his shoulders and sitting back in his chair. *You need to let this go.*

'William?' said Audrey, suddenly by his side at the table and taking a seat. 'Are you okay? It can't be much fun watching everyone dance. Where's Elsie? I should probably get back to the bakery if you're okay here?'

William smiled and cleared his throat, placing his hands flat down on the table, while he nodded towards Elsie in the throng. 'She was just dancing with Lily,' he said. 'Yes, I'm fine. I'm okay. I was thinking…'

'About…?' Audrey asked, looking at him questioningly, but William flapped his hand dismissively in the air.

'Nothing,' he said. 'It's nothing at all. Or should I say, all and nothing.'

Brother and sister sat for a moment together in silence, when Elsie rushed over, grinning broadly. She sat on William's knee and pulled off her shoes, wriggling her toes and pulling a relieved face.

William tried to iron out the frown he knew he was wearing, forcing himself to smile.

'These shoes are giving me blisters!' she said, holding up her heeled bow court shoes. Slinging an arm joyfully around William's neck, she kissed him on the cheek and he felt himself melt.

'I hope you're not having second thoughts,' she said to William, half smiling.

He put his arm around her waist and hugged her tight, squeezing his eyes closed for a moment, suppressing the emotion that was threatening to wash over him, catching the hand of a drowning man.

'Never,' he said into her ear, breathing in the lavender scent of her shampoo.

'I can feel another wedding cake waiting to be baked,' said Audrey, laughing and standing, then winding her way through the revellers to find little Mary and take her home.

Chapter Twenty-Three

It was late when Elsie cycled home from Maggie's wedding on her Raleigh, her head full of songs and dancing. Maggie had looked beautiful in her 'going away' outfit, accessorised with a silver fox fur, thoughtfully gifted by the groom, Elsie thought, as she opened the front door. George was such a handsome groom too, in his made-to-measure suit – single-breasted, of course, since double-breasted jackets and turn-ups on trousers had been prohibited by the Board of Trade.

'What a day!' she said to her mother, Violet, as she placed the posy of flowers she'd caught on the kitchen table, where Violet was sewing an elbow patch onto her overall. She sat down on a creaky chair, which rocked slightly on uneven legs, and sighed happily. In the background, the wireless droned on with the Home Service news reporting on the German invasion of the Soviet Union – but Elsie didn't want to listen. Instead, her mind was brimming with thoughts of her own wedding to William. They didn't want anything big, couldn't afford anything grand – they just wanted to be together and put the uncertainty of the last eighteen months behind them and face the future hand in hand.

'Maggie looked beautiful tonight,' she told Violet. 'It's made me so excited about my wedding. I can't wait to be married to William, Mother. Some certainty in these uncertain times would be good, wouldn't it?'

Violet glanced up at Elsie from her sewing with her big brown eyes – full of concern and love – before putting down the fabric and needle for a moment, and drinking the cool remains of her earlier cup of weak tea.

'Those poor people in Smolensk,' she said, not picking up Elsie's thread of conversation. 'Hitler will stop at anything. I sometimes wonder what his mother thinks of him. Apparently, she was an unmarried kitchen hand, would you believe?'

Elsie raised her eyebrows. She'd never really thought about Hitler as a person before, someone who had parents and maybe brothers and sisters. He was a crazy monster and a dark force who seemed to stop at nothing to get what he wanted. Murmuring her response, she stood and moved over to the wireless and switched it off, even though her mother objected with a tut.

'I need a break from the war,' she explained. 'Just for tonight. It's all I hear on the buses, it's all people want to talk about.'

Flickering her eyes around the small kitchen, Elsie's high spirits suddenly dipped. Though Violet did her best with Elsie's help to keep on top of things, the house needed attention. In her father, Alberto's, absence, Elsie made a mental list of all the jobs that needed doing: she needed to get pot-menders from the ironmongers to repair the hole in the kettle; all the chair seats needed re-webbing; the enamel milk jug needed fixing with sealing wax; the cupboard handles needed tightening up and even the rug on the floor needed patching up. On top of her job as one of Bournemouth's 'clippies', plus her fire-watching duties and helping take care of her sisters, there weren't enough hours in the day.

'I think I should wear the dress I was meant to wear last year, do you?' Elsie continued, returning to her seat, but her mother didn't respond. 'I've heard there's some parachute nylon available and girls are making their own dresses, but I will wear the one—'

'He must have been born under a blood moon,' Violet interrupted, before reciting a line from the Bible: '*Before them the earth shakes, the sky trembles, the sun and moon are darkened, and the stars no longer shine.*'

Elsie shook her head and rested her head in her hands for a moment, before pulling in her chair, closer to the table and putting her palms down flat. 'Mother,' she said. 'What's wrong? Don't you want me to marry William or something?'

Violet looked pained and picked up her sewing again, accidentally jabbing her finger with the needle. 'Ouch!' she cried, before sucking the dot of scarlet blood from her finger. 'It's not that I don't want you to marry him,' she continued, 'it's just he's messed you about something rotten. Last year he didn't come to his own wedding, this year he broke off your engagement and now it's on again. In my mind, love is straightforward, and he's made it more complicated than it should be. Can you be sure you can trust him? I do so wish your father was here.'

Elsie knew her mother was just wanting to protect her from further heartbreak, but she felt herself bristle. Was it that she was voicing concerns in the deepest, darkest depths of her own mind? No, she told herself firmly, that wasn't it at all. William had been through a difficult time – more difficult than she could possibly imagine – and he was doing his utmost, now, to find his equilibrium.

'Did I tell you that the clippies' uniform is changing?' said Elsie, deliberately ignoring Violet's question. 'Girls have been wearing whatever they want under the ticket punching machine, the cash bag and the cap, but that's going to change. The uniform is now going to include slacks.'

Her mother stared up at her, with a small, knowing smile on her face. 'Just you take care,' she said. 'That's all I'm saying. Take good care of your heart. You can be pig-headed at times, Elsie.'

'Slacks are much more convenient for running up and down the stairs,' said Elsie. 'More than eighty-five per cent of clippies voted for slacks over skirts.' She looked affectionately over the table at her mother, giggling into her hand.

'You…' said Violet, shaking her head and joining her daughter in laughter.

*

William returned to the bakery after the wedding reception to work in the bakehouse alongside John. Rhythmically preparing trays of tinned dough to prove, he felt his mind slip into the familiar black hole that was his all-too recent memories of the battle in France. It seemed whenever he let his mind run free, it returned to the same place, to the same suffering and bewilderment that nothing could have ever prepared him for.

'I love her, you know, John,' he said suddenly, not pausing from his work. 'I mean, I love Elsie.'

The bakehouse was warm from the heat of the raging ovens, dimly lit and hazy with flour. The bread peels, like boat oars, leaned up against the brick walls, and a broom for sweeping up the flour stood alongside. It was a hot night, anyway, and William worked in a vest, with a white apron over the top, while John wore a pristine long-sleeved shirt, apron and cap. Clipped to his apron were his spectacles, which he occasionally lifted to his eyes, to check the dough.

'I know that,' said John, who was now turning his attention to sweeping the flour from the floor with the broom. 'That's clear for anyone to see.'

Without facing John, William continued to work and talk – he had to tell someone what was burdening him. 'I think I need to tell her about what happened when I was away. What I did in France, it has changed me—' he started, but John slammed the broom down.

'I've told you about this, son,' he said, pulling at William's shoulder so he was forced to face him. 'You can keep going back, living in fear of what you've done, turning it over and over in your mind, or you can bury it. Lock it away and throw away the key. We all do bad things – we all have regrets – but we're 'uman. Let yourself off the hook, young man, let yourself off the hook! You're a good man with a good heart. You have a beautiful fiancée. Don't trouble her with what's behind you and what you cannot change. Get on with your life, William – it's no good fighting for freedom if you come back a prisoner.'

William nodded and, sighing deeply, he chewed on his bottom lip, throwing all his frustrated strength into his work, until his back ached and his right leg throbbed. He repeated John's words to himself: *It's no good fighting for freedom if you come back a prisoner.*

*

Audrey frowned as she stood outside the bakehouse door, a pile of freshly laundered and pressed dishcloths in her hand. It was very late now, and she was tired after the wedding knees-up, but she'd heard William and John's conversation and felt suddenly wide awake. What was William talking about? What terrible thing had he done in France – and what did it have to do with Elsie? Just when she thought things were coming together, was this a sign they were unravelling?

She sighed. She would have to talk to him about it, to get to the bottom of what was bothering him. Of course, it must have been the awful fighting he had seen and been involved in – nobody would be able to forget it and especially not someone like William. Oh gosh, Audrey could hardly stand to think of the violence! What was Charlie going through this very minute? The last letter she'd had from him said he was in Crete, where the newspapers had reported on 'unparalleled ferocity' and said that thousands of the British military had been captured. She shivered. It seemed so very far away, she thought, looking at the sepia photographs of Charlie's relatives who had started up Barton's bakery hanging on the wall.

Heading into the shop to check the blackout blinds, she felt her eyelids grow heavy. But before she could turn in, she must sit down at the kitchen table and write a list of the orders for the next day. Checking the door was safely locked, she stood still for a moment in the dark shop, silently telling Charlie that she was taking care of the bakery as best she could. Empty now, of course, the shop seemed to echo with the gossip from the customers, their faces as visible to Audrey now, in the darkness, as they were in the day.

Turning from the shop floor to climb the stairs to finish off the paperwork, she yawned when she entered the kitchen, thinking how, mercifully, it had been at least a week since the last air-raid siren and how, in Bournemouth at least, they had escaped bombing raids at night for some weeks, and—

Chapter Twenty-Four

There was no warning. No siren. No shout or rattle from the Air Raid Patrol warden. Nothing. The explosion, followed by the roar of aircraft overhead and heavy gunfire, seemingly came from nowhere, and lifted Audrey from her feet like a giant pair of invisible arms had picked her up and hurled her across the room, slamming her body into the kitchen dresser. Glass jars of marmalade, jam, pickles and bottled fruits fell from the shelves, smashing onto the floor tiles, as heat and bright light scorched her eyes, clouds of dust and smoke filling the air.

Audrey lay on the floor with her arms protectively over her head, stunned, blinking in the darkness, trying to make sense of what was happening all around her. Sounds of what could only be masonry, or the ceiling collapsing, stirred her into action, as she became aware of the taste of blood on her lips, then the sight of flames leaping up through holes in the floor like dancing devils into the kitchen. Reaching for a bucket of sand, she threw it onto the flames, to little effect, and staggered across the room to the stairwell.

Lily, home earlier from the party, emerged from the bedroom, clutching Joy, who was crying hysterically.

'Get outside!' commanded Audrey. 'Into the shelter!'

Her mind rushed through where everyone was. John and William were in the bakehouse and hopefully by now in the shelter, but Mary was upstairs in bed.

'Audrey!' called John from behind her at the bottom of the stairwell, a handkerchief over his mouth. He came up a few stairs and tried to grab her arm, but Audrey was heading up to Mary's room. 'The front of the building is on fire,' he said. 'We got hit. Go outside to safety, I'll go up for the girl.'

'No!' said Audrey, pulling away from his grasp. 'I have to get her. Put out the ovens – they'll make the fire worse! Get the AFS! Find the sandbags!'

Audrey felt her way through the weaving trails of thick black smoke that were rising up the stairs like snakes and burst into Mary's bedroom. It was pitch-black and impossible to see.

'Mary!' she cried. 'Get up! Quickly!'

Throwing open the blackout blind, so at least the moonlight would fill the room, she flew to Mary's bed, but Mary wasn't in it. Feeling under the bed with her hands, in case she was hiding, Audrey found she was there, curled up in the foetal position. Grasping hold of her little arm, she tried to pull her.

'Come out, Mary love!' she said. 'We have to get out now!'

But Mary did not move.

Her heart pounding, as screams of 'Audrey, come down now!' came from outside the building, she tried pulling Mary again, but to no avail. It was as if the girl was frozen solid, utterly paralysed with fear.

*

Moments earlier, on the other side of Bournemouth, Maggie and George were welcomed into their room in the Ocean View guesthouse by Fanny Chandler, the kindly proprietor, an elderly lady who had laid out a silver tray with a small decanter of port on the table by the window, with two small crystal-cut port glasses and a red rose in a vase.

'Oh, it's just lovely!' said Maggie, clasping her hands as her gaze ran over the room. The heavy curtains were pulled shut across a large window, and the floral carpet was thick underfoot. Near the fireplace were two inviting velvet-covered armchairs, and the bed – a double with a mahogany headboard – was freshly made up with starched white sheets, perfectly pressed. Above the fireplace hung an oval mirror and when Maggie caught her reflection she was taken aback. She'd never seen herself look so radiantly happy. Feeling like a movie star in her dark blue 'going away' outfit and silver fox fur given her by George, she suddenly felt she had no cares in the world. Finally, she was where she wanted to be, with a man she truly loved. Placing down her handbag, she moved over to the decanter and poured herself and George a nip of sherry, wanting to squeal with joy.

'Congratulations,' Fanny said. 'It's lovely to have something to celebrate. If Hitler had his way, we'd never celebrate again, would we? This war is hard on young people, I know that. You must enjoy every moment together as if it were your last, my dears. Tomorrow is not guaranteed.'

As she closed the door of the room behind her, informing them of the location of the air-raid shelter in the basement and wishing them both goodnight, George walked towards his new bride, his arms outstretched.

'Here we are, Mrs Meadows,' he said, beaming at her. 'Alone at last.'

Maggie put down her glass, smiled at George and took his hand, leading him over to the bed, where they sat down next to each other – and kissed. For all her flirtatious ways and movie-star looks, Maggie wasn't experienced with men and she blushed, amazed at how her body felt almost electrified by George's kisses. For a blissful few moments the pair were oblivious to everything else around them, until the awful wail of the air-raid siren shattered their intimacy.

'Oh, for heaven's sake!' said George, standing quickly and holding Maggie's hand, to lead her to safety. 'We'll have to carry on where we left off a bit later. Let's hope this is a false alarm and over quickly.'

Chapter Twenty-Five

Crawling under the narrow bed until her whole body was next to Mary's, panic coursed through Audrey's veins. Trying to steady her thoughts and control her fear, she wrapped herself around the little girl's trembling body and spoke to her as calmly and softly as she could.

'Mary?' she said, gently. 'We must get out from under the bed now. Do you know why?'

But Mary shook her head and kept her eyes firmly closed.

'Because we need to go and get your rabbit from his hutch in the yard,' she said. 'If you're feeling frightened, imagine how that bunny feels. Why don't you hold onto my hands, nice and tight, and I'll lead us downstairs and out the back door, where we can collect your rabbit and take him into the street to safety? You can cuddle him there and tell him that he's going to be all right. How does that sound?'

After a moment, Mary nodded and opened one eye, a huge tear dripping down her cheek. Audrey's heart broke for the girl, whose short life had been blighted by fear and trauma and tragedy.

'Hold onto my hand and don't let go,' said Audrey. 'I'm not going anywhere without you.'

Together they slid out from under the bed and the room was now thick with smoke. It was literally impossible to see or breathe, so holding her breath, Audrey felt her way through the darkness, all the while clutching on to Mary.

'I think your rabbit is going to need a fresh carrot after all this,' she said, desperately trying not to slip on the stairs.

Finally reaching the back door, she burst through it and into the yard, gulping in the fresh air. Rushing over to the rabbit cage, quick as a flash she unlocked the door and put the terrified creature into Mary's waiting arms, then steered her by the shoulders to the street, where the AFS had arrived and were pumping water onto the fire at the front of the building, while others were throwing buckets of water or sand onto the flames.

'Oh, gracious me!' said Audrey, hand over her mouth in shock, as she staggered towards John, William and Lily, who was holding Joy. They were all trying to offer soothing words of comfort, but each was stunned and horror-struck by what was happening. As they stood on the road, fire officers battled to get the blaze under control, looking on in desolate helplessness as more of the ceiling collapsed, sending wood and bricks and plaster crashing to a heap on the shop, and spilling out through the broken window, into the street.

'My bakery will be destroyed...' Audrey stuttered. She could barely form a sentence. 'I just can't believe it's happened...'

Sitting with Mary and the rabbit in her lap, on the pavement kerb, the group watched in stunned silence as the fire officers bravely battled to control the flames. Running her eyes over the damage, Audrey's heart broke as she looked at the smashed front windows, the blackened walls, the usually pristine black and white tiled floor covered in rubble...

'Mrs Barton?' asked a fire officer, with black soot on his face. 'Are you injured? This must be such a shock to you, my dear. I'm so sorry for you.'

Audrey shook her head, in a trance.

'How will I get tomorrow's bread delivery out?' she whispered. 'Was the bakehouse directly hit?'

'No,' he said. 'Just the front of the house. Luckily a fire-watcher spotted the fire and reported it, so we were quickly on the scene. May I suggest you get to the rest centre, where they'll treat you for shock and any minor injuries, and they'll make you comfortable for the night?'

'You may suggest that,' said Audrey, standing up and dusting off her apron, gripping Mary by the hand. 'But I'll do no such thing. I have to get the bread out.'

'But the building's not safe, Mrs Barton,' he said. 'You can't go back inside.'

'Watch me,' she said. 'Mary, I'll take you to stay with Pat, but then I must help John with the bread.'

'I'm here, love,' said John calmly, dabbing his forehead with his hanky. 'There'll be no bread tonight. I dampened down the ovens completely – I didn't want to make it worse if the fire took hold. The loaves will all be ruined. We're going to have to let folk down in the morning, but they'll understand, Audrey. I'll get word to Crowne's, to expect some more customers than usual, and I'll ask Albert to tell our delivery customers what's happened. The best thing you can do, my girl, is get washed up, sort out Mary's cuts and bruises and get some sleep.'

'But what would Charlie say?' asked Audrey, her eyes filling with tears. 'He's never not got the bread out on time for the customers. How will Mrs Cook, and Flo and Elizabeth and all my ladies manage? This will be the first time in years that the bakery has been closed.'

Audrey looked on helplessly at the half-destroyed bakery – their business literally up in flames. She felt all the fight drain out of her as she silently wept.

'Charlie and all your customers will thank their lucky stars you are alive,' John said, putting his arm over her shoulder. 'You'll come back from this, Audrey. Don't you worry, my girl. Let's get you to Pat's, she'll sort you out.'

*

Maggie, her spirits high, giggled as they headed towards the door of the bedroom as the air-raid siren wailed, noting the way her heels sank into the carpet, a touch of sherry and George's lingering kisses on her lips. They continued to kiss one another as they went out into the hallway, when an almighty thunderous clap hit their ears and a blinding flash of light ripped through the darkness.

'George!' Maggie cried, as she grabbed hold of his hand and the couple were thrown to the floor, like rag dolls, and plunged into absolute darkness. With their fingers entwined, they lay there for a moment, before George leapt into action, scooping Maggie up from the floor and carrying her in his arms down the stairs, through the hotel's front door and out into the street.

'Oh my goodness, George!' she coughed, blinking in shock as he set her down and the roof of the hotel half collapsed behind them.

They looked at one another in disbelief before being ushered into a nearby public shelter by an AFS warden, who explained that high-explosive bombs and incendiary bombs had been released across Bournemouth from a German plane, falling on both the hotel roof and the roof of the house next door.

'What a way to begin married life,' said Maggie, half-smiling, trying to lighten their shock as they huddled together in the dimly lit public shelter with dozens of local residents.

The couple held hands and gazed lovingly into each other's eyes, both of them remembering the landlady's words: 'You must enjoy every moment together as if it were your last, my dears. Tomorrow is not guaranteed.'

*

'I just heard about the bakery,' said Elsie, rushing into Pat's house, where Pat, Audrey, Lily and Joy, Mary and John were huddled at the kitchen table, Mary wrapped in a blanket. 'How could this happen? I'd wring Hitler's neck if I could get my hands on him! Apparently there was no warning. They just came out of the night, from nowhere. Someone said that they were dropping bombs they hadn't used, like litter, on the way back from another raid on a different part of the country. Are you injured? Is Mary okay?'

Audrey smiled a small grateful smile and shook her head. She felt totally and utterly disorientated. A few hours earlier, she had been celebrating Maggie's wedding and now this. She gently patted Mary's hair. The little girl was asleep against Audrey's chest, her forehead still smeared with dust. It was now 3 a.m. and though Mary and Joy slept, none of the adults thought they'd be able to get even a wink of sleep.

Pat's kitchen was warm and welcoming, a pot of tea was on the table and she'd put a few biscuits out on a plate – even the milk had been poured into a jug ('You'll never catch me putting a milk bottle on the table,' she'd said. 'Even in a crisis.') A little black vase decorated with a painting of a mallard duck was filled with lavender from the garden – and the scent was a welcome relief from the acrid stench that seemed to have permeated Audrey's clothes.

'It was a close thing,' said Audrey quietly. 'Mary froze, poor dear, but we got her out in the end.'

'No wonder she's so frightened,' said Pat, pouring everyone more tea. 'That poor child has lost everyone she loves. Thanks be to goodness she's got you, Audrey. You'd make a fine mother and Charlie a fine father, wherever in the world my beloved son might be right now. I'm looking forward to you two making me a grandmother.'

Audrey smiled gratefully at her mother-in-law, who rarely gave out compliments. She considered explaining that, after six years of trying unsuccessfully, she didn't think that she and Charlie would ever be able to have a child of their own – and that's why last year she'd offered to adopt Lily's baby girl Joy before Lily had decided she couldn't part with the child – but now wasn't the right time. She knew how much Pat wanted Charlie to have his own child.

'What on earth would Charlie say if he knew about this?' said Pat. 'His heart would break, wouldn't it? All those years of building up a business.'

The mention of Charlie brought tears to Audrey's eyes. She'd become so used to working in a partnership with him – they were like a well-oiled machine running the bakery – the idea of telling him that the business was collapsing without him filled her with dread. She was convinced he would feel that she hadn't looked after it properly.

'Charlie will understand,' said William. 'He will have seen whole cities being devastated by war – he'll know that in the face of a bomb, you have no chance.'

'I'll have to think about what I should do,' Audrey said. 'I need to get some sleep and think about how we can fix this as quickly as possible. I have cakes to make, orders to fulfil. The customers need their bread, what with the meat ration at almost nothing, and food becoming scarcer. You know, I had a letter from the Ministry of Food about the introduction of the National Loaf? In a few months' time all the bakers might be having to bake the National Loaf with wheatmeal flour, to ensure the health of the nation, and there'll be no choice about it. That's why I have to find a way through this.'

'I can't imagine not having my white tin,' said Pat despondently.

'That's the last of our worries just now,' said John, yawning loudly and causing Mary to stir in Audrey's lap.

'Get that little mite into bed,' said Pat. 'I'll find somewhere for you to sleep. You've all had an awful shock. Tomorrow we'll think about the bread.'

Chapter Twenty-Six

Unable to sleep, with adrenalin still coursing through her body, Audrey rose before sunrise, pushed her feet into her dust-covered shoes and crept out of Pat's house.

'Back later,' she told Mary, who stirred in her sleep. 'Go back to sleep.'

Before she left the house, she caught sight of her face in the mirror by the front door and gasped. Smudges of dust and soot covered her face, a gash on her forehead that Pat had cleaned up was sealed with dried blood and her eyes were pink from sleep deprivation. She hardly recognised herself, but she didn't have time to dwell on it – there were more important matters to attend to.

Walking swiftly back to the bakery in the cool morning, she stared in disbelief at the state of the shop and the first floor of the house. Fisherman's Road was quiet, as, after the disturbed night and various evacuations, the business owners were catching up on a few hours' sleep before the working day started. The AFS had cordoned off the bakery, but Audrey walked past it and stepped inside, her feet crunching on broken glass.

'Heavens above!' she said, as she stared up at the decimated shop. The front windows, bearing the word 'Bakery' in elegant gold lettering, were blown out, the door had been blown off and strips of wood from the doorway were hanging like stalactites from above. The first-floor window had smashed and a fraction of the roof collapsed. The ceiling of the shop had caved in, leaving the beams and the lath and plaster exposed, where the lime plaster had crumbled. The shop was covered in thick grey dust, the shelves fallen, the walls blackened, the clock and counter broken. Her chocolate-box bakery shop had been turned upside down and inside out, as if the devil himself had visited.

Audrey lifted her hand to the brass bell still in place and sounded it gently – she smiled sadly as it released its merry little jingle. Walking through the shop, slowly and carefully avoiding the debris underfoot, she moved into the cake room, which was, thankfully, relatively undamaged, though she dare not look in the stockroom at her labelled boxes and jars of precious ingredients.

With her heart pounding, she continued on through to the bakehouse.

'Thank heavens!' she whispered into the room, which was strangely cool after John had extinguished the bakery ovens. Quickly scanning the small outhouse for damage, it seemed the bakehouse and the ovens were unscathed. Audrey's tired mind whirred with questions. Even if the ovens were working, where would she make the cakes and sell the produce if the shop was out of action? It probably wasn't even safe to be in the building at all.

Deciding to go back outside, she felt something shatter underfoot and looking down on the floor to see what she'd stepped on, she cried out: 'Oh no! Oh, heavens above!'

Flashing her torch onto the floor, tears poured from her eyes as she realised she'd trodden on the framed photograph of Charlie's Uncle Eric and his wife Edith, who had started up the bakery with little money, but elbow grease, skill and passion, decades earlier. She dusted off the photo, which was now scratched and soiled, and stared down at Charlie's ancestors, blinking madly when she felt sure she'd seen Uncle Eric's eyes move.

I'm that tired, I'm starting to hallucinate now, she thought to herself, but it was as if she could feel Uncle Eric's presence in the room with her. Audrey shivered, cold with exhaustion and shock. *What nonsense*, she told herself.

'At least nobody was hurt,' she said out loud, carefully wrapping the photograph in a hessian sack to protect it. She would take it to the Photography Studio to see if there was anything that could be done to repair it. A shiver passed from head to toe, as she thought about what might have been: they could have all been killed.

'It could have been so much worse,' she muttered to the empty room, though to Audrey's exhausted and emotional brain, it felt as if someone was listening.

It was Maggie's sister, Nancy, that came to tell Audrey the news.

'Is anyone here?' Audrey heard Nancy's voice calling outside the bakery and, drying her eyes, she carefully negotiated her way out to greet her and warn her not to come inside as it was too dangerous.

The sun was just beginning to rise now, above the homes and businesses on Fisherman's Road, turning parts of the sky the colour of deep golden honey. Nancy, wearing just a short-sleeved dress and clearly shivering, looked pale as milk.

'What are you doing here so early?' said Audrey in surprise. 'Maggie's not here, love – she's enjoying her wedding night, I should hope. As you can see, we've had some trouble overnight.'

Audrey gestured to the bakery and watched Nancy's face crease with concern, though she hardly looked at the building at all. Wrapping her arms around her waist, Nancy blinked away tears.

'Maggie sent me,' she said. 'She wanted me to tell you that she wouldn't be coming in for a few days. She didn't know the bakery had been hit in the raid. Her hotel was hit and she spent the night in a shelter, but we've had some awful news.'

Nancy swallowed hard and Audrey tensed, sensing something dreadful.

'What, love?' said Audrey. 'What is it?'

'Isabel,' said Nancy. 'Our sister Isabel was killed last night. After the wedding I went to work my night shift, and Isabel was apparently trying to get our grandmother into the public shelter down the road from our house when the siren sounded, but she was hit by a motorcar. The driver panicked when the air-raid siren went off and was driving too fast in the blackout. Course he didn't even see Isabel until it was too late. Maggie's with our grandmother now.'

Nancy's face blurred in front of Audrey's eyes, as she tried to digest her words. Steadying herself on the gas street lamp that stood outside the bakery, she felt light-headed and nauseous.

'I don't believe it,' she said, barely able to speak. 'Isabel is dead?'

Nancy nodded her confirmation – and in her sister's face, Audrey saw the wretched truth: Isabel was gone. And what of poor Maggie? Only yesterday she was a happy bride, dancing into the evening with her great love, George. Today she was facing the loss of her sister, who she deeply loved. Audrey's heart broke into a million pieces and she felt she might collapse under the weight of the news. It was more than her heart and shoulders could bear.

'I have to go,' said Nancy. 'I have to get home. I borrowed my neighbour's bike. I can hardly ride—'

'Yes… go,' said Audrey, softly, taking Nancy's hand in hers and dropping it gently. 'I'm lost for words.'

Audrey stumbled and sat down on the edge of the kerb. Watching Nancy get on her bike – obviously a man's and much too big – and ride off down the road towards the munitions factory, her narrow body balancing precariously on the saddle, she felt paralysed in disbelief. If the siren hadn't sounded, the driver of the motorcar wouldn't have panicked and Isabel would be alive today.

'This heinous war!' Audrey said, picking up a shard of broken glass and hurling it across the pavement. 'This sickening, wretched, blasted war! I want nothing more to do with it! I wish it would stop! I *hate* it!'

Standing now and marching along Fisherman's Road, not knowing where she was going, but wanting to go somewhere, *anywhere*, Audrey walked until she reached the Overcliff. Here, she stared out at the ocean, her arms folded across her chest, the breeze blowing her hair across her face and her dress against her legs. Outrage and horror coursed through her as she longed to blame someone, to find the pilot who had dropped this bomb, to make him accountable for everything that happened as a result. Maggie's wedding night ruined, the death of her young and gentle sister. Who was he? she wondered. A young man, perhaps no more than twenty years of age, dropping bombs on people he knew nothing about, in the name of what? And, Audrey knew very well, the British army were doing the same overseas – bombing innocent people and devastating civilian areas in Cologne and Dusseldorf, dissolving people's hopes and dreams in a split second.

Feeling as though she would burst with anger and grief, Audrey swept her gaze over the coastline, which was pockmarked with hideous reminders of war: 250-foot high metal masts from the radar station, the pillboxes, dragon's teeth, trenches and weapons pits and reams of barbed-wire barriers. It was all so ugly and in conflict with the beautiful coastline. The early morning sun threw a long, golden spotlight over the quivering water. Another day was beginning. A day without Isabel in it.

'Mrs Barton?' said a voice from behind her, making Audrey jump. She swiped at the tears running down her cheeks and turned to face Arthur, the engineer working at the radar station, who had returned her wedding ring and stayed for dinner. Concern was etched on his face when he saw her expression. He rested his hand on her arm, in comfort, and put his head to one side. 'Please, can I help you, Mrs Barton?' he asked, in a voice so caring and gentle and in contrast to the fire and death and destruction, that Audrey was lost for words.

The fury rushed out of her and she felt suddenly empty and utterly alone. She longed for Charlie's strong arms to be around her, to bury her nose in his skin, to listen to his warm, serious voice reassure her. But Charlie was on the other side of the world. Was he even still alive? She stared down at her hands and couldn't hold it in any longer; she started to weep and when Arthur tentatively put his arms around her, she didn't move away but rested her face against his chest. He was as good as a stranger, but he was there.

'Let me buy you a hot cup of tea,' Arthur said when she managed to pull herself together. 'Seems to me like you need a bit of looking after.'

Holding the tea in her hands in the café, the steam drifting up towards the ceiling and clouding the window by her side, Audrey's nose and eyes were swollen and red from crying. She knew she must look a dreadful sight, but it didn't occur to her to care. Once she'd told Arthur the whole terrible story of the bakery fire and Isabel's untimely death on her sister's wedding day, and he'd sat quietly listening, shaking his head and occasionally murmuring his sympathies, she wondered if she'd said too much.

'I've taken up too much of your time and burdened you with my troubles,' she said, wiping her eyes with her handkerchief, which itself was dark grey from the fire. 'I'm ever so sorry, I don't know what came over me. I just felt like I couldn't take any more.'

Arthur was a good listener and seemed genuinely affected by what Audrey had told him, and she sensed he had something he wanted to share too. She waited quietly as he chewed his lips, looking as if he was contemplating whether to speak out or remain quiet.

'My wife was killed in the Blitz,' he said, eventually. 'She was a schoolteacher in east London, and she was killed when a bomb fell, along with dozens of the children in her care. Her body was found with her arms around three children, trying to protect them, I expect – she was like that.'

Audrey's hand flew to her mouth and she let out a gigantic, shuddery sigh. 'Goodness me!' she said. 'I'm so sorry. Here I am, pouring out my troubles when you have your own heartache. I don't know what I'd do if my Charlie was killed. How do you get through the days?'

Arthur folded and unfolded the napkin on the table, seemingly not knowing how to answer this question. His silence spoke a thousand words and when he looked up at her, he rolled his eyes at himself.

Audrey smiled at him and he returned the smile – something passed between them; an understanding, a mutual respect, a glimmer of another life, in another time.

'Thank you for the tea,' said Audrey, standing now, brushing down her dress and neatening her hair, which had escaped the pins. 'I must get going, there is so much to sort out.' She held out her hand to shake Arthur's. He took it and gave it a gentle, reassuring squeeze; tenderness and warmth travelling between them.

They walked out into the morning, where people were going about their business as usual – how quickly life carried on – and Audrey realised she had dropped her handkerchief as she was leaving.

Entering the café again, she called out to the owner. 'Sorry,' she said. 'I just dropped my hanky.'

The owner, a woman she didn't know, rushed out from behind the counter and spoke to her in low, urgent tones. 'You don't want to be seen with that fella,' she said, jerking her head towards Arthur, who was waiting outside.

'Why ever not?' Audrey asked, frowning.

'He's a member of the Peace Pledge Union, ain't he?' she said. 'One of them bleedin' conscientious objectors. He's been stationed here to do a non-combatant job, but he's a traitor, a spineless coward. And cowards have no place in this town.'

Chapter Twenty-Seven

Lily stared out of the library window at the huge weeping willow trees dipping into the River Stour. She'd hardly slept and couldn't concentrate. The eleven male refugees, or 'friendly aliens' as they were called, in the room looked at her expectantly, waiting for the conversation class to begin, but she felt lost for words. This was the first session of her new role – part-time work that would finally help her feel she was doing her 'bit' for the war effort – but the thought of the previous night's devastating raid and the knowledge that Audrey was suffering weighed heavily on her mind. She was desperate to be able to help her stepsister, but she didn't know where to start and these men, who had found themselves in Bournemouth, just as she had done, were becoming impatient.

'Good morning?' said a Czechoslovakian man, enquiringly.

'Yes?' Lily said, spinning on her heel, turning to face him, her mind whirring. There must be something she could do to make a difference to Audrey, but it would take days to clear up the mess in the bakery shop. The building would need 'first aid'; repairing, clearing up and repainting. Everything broken would have to be fixed – they would need a number of helpers to get the job done as quickly as possible. And then, like a flower blossoming, an idea formed in her head. She grinned at the men in front of her – all fit, healthy and willing to help. 'Today we're going to do something different,' she said. 'Wait here a moment, gentlemen, please.'

Met with confused expressions, Lily dashed out of the room and checked with the supervisor that her outlandish idea was permissible, as some of the men's movements were under controlled 'conditions'. Making sure Joy was happy in the crèche for a while longer, Lily returned to the classroom and told the group of men that she had a friend who needed some help, explaining that it would involve manual labour, and that she would pay each of them a few pennies if they would assist.

'Who's in?' she said. 'Please raise a hand if you are.'

Those men with poorer English didn't really understand what was going on, but as the other students translated, each man's hand rose tentatively into the air.

'Anything but classroom work!' Lily said, to a bemused response, but she was galvanised by their agreement and keen to get on with helping to restore the bakery to normality. It wasn't an entirely selfless act either – she knew she would become a hindrance if she had to stay at Pat's house. Joy still didn't sleep through and woke up several times a night, crying at the top of her lungs. The sooner the bakery was back up and running, the better, and who better to help than eleven fit young men?

Showing the men out of the classroom and leading them to the bakery, Lily felt something she hadn't felt in a long time: she felt useful.

When they reached the bakery, there were a couple of the neighbours, alongside William and John, leaning on the front brick wall, sawing wood to put boards up in place of the blown-out windows. Elsie was there too, dressed in dungarees, with her hair tied up and gloves on, but there was no sign of Audrey.

'What can we do to help?' Lily said, tapping William on the shoulder. 'There are twelve pairs of hands here. All willing and able in return for a bit of conversation.'

*

Audrey couldn't get the café owner's words out of her head. *Spineless. Coward. Traitor.* None of them seemed apt to describe Arthur, who had just listened, with the patience of a saint, to Audrey's tear-stained woes. What right did that woman have to condemn Arthur without knowing a thing about him? People were too quick to pass judgement, too quick to read the headline but not digest the whole story. Audrey sighed, berating herself for not giving the woman a piece of her mind.

Walking home towards Fisherman's Road in an exhausted and emotionally drained daze, she couldn't think clearly about Arthur right now. There were too many other things fighting for her attention. Just the thought of relaying the news about Isabel to Elsie and Lily, who had been so happy yesterday at the wedding, made her feel broken. Oh, there were no words to lighten the pain, to reduce the shock or lessen the suffering – this was the stark reality of wartime.

And then there was the bakery, she thought, approaching Fisherman's Road, dread growing in her heart. Turning into the street, she felt her legs turning liquid and specks and stars of light fill her vision. For a moment, she thought she might faint at the prospect of viewing the wreckage of her home and business in the harsh daylight, but biting her lip, she forced herself to continue.

'Oh, gracious me!' she said, sucking in her breath when she saw the group of people working on the bakery. Lifting her hands to her mouth, she stood stock-still on the street, a sudden gust of wind blowing her hair up wildly, watching in amazement as men she'd never even seen before were giving the building 'first aid'. There was a man up a ladder fixing boards onto windows, several clearing rubble, another clearing broken glass – and William, Elsie and Lily were getting stuck in too. The sight of all the people helping choked her and she bit down on her lip to suppress the tears.

Elsie was the first to see her. She waved, pulled off her work gloves and walked towards her up the street.

'We've just heard the news about Isabel. Poor Maggie, however must she feel?' she said, throwing her arms around Audrey. Lily ran over too and the three women hugged one another, weeping, before eventually drying their eyes, pulling away and walking towards the bakery with their arms linked in a daze. 'It's all too much to digest, I think we need time for the news to sink in. Lily brought her language class with her to help clean up. They've been so helpful.'

'Thank you,' said Audrey, standing outside the bakery, addressing the men. 'Thank you so much. Let me get you something, there must be something left.'

Feeling unsteady and drained after the emotional outpouring, she cautiously made her way through the bakery, opening the store cupboard door to find that most of the tins were unharmed. There was a box of biscuits she'd made for Maggie's wedding that hadn't turned out as well as she'd hoped, so she opened the lid and took them outside onto the street, offering them round to the workmen and women, who gratefully accepted.

'John's out back,' said William. 'He's getting the ovens going.'

'What? But the building's not safe yet,' said Audrey, going through the yard to the bakehouse and throwing open the door to find John had already lit the ovens and was hand-mixing the flour, yeast and water in the trough. He didn't look up from his work when she came in.

'I'm sorry, but I can't talk about that poor young girl just yet,' he said, his voice cracking. 'Instead I'm putting myself to work. I've thought it through and we can serve the loaves from the bakehouse hatch for a few days while the shop is getting repaired. That way people will still get their bread. They might have to do without the counter goods, but it won't be long until you're up and running again, Audrey.'

'But…' she said.

'But nothing,' said John, breaking out into a cough. 'Have you read the newspapers lately? There's a war on, you know. This is the way it's got to be, but we will not give up.'

After his speech, he coughed and coughed. Audrey patted him gently on the back.

'John,' she said quietly. 'You're ill. I can't let you work here with that cough.'

'I'd rather die on the job than die in that hospital bed,' he said. 'Let me be, Audrey Barton. Just let me be.'

Chapter Twenty-Eight

'I've made some soup,' said Audrey, placing a steaming pot of vegetable soup on Pat's kitchen table, where they would be staying until the bakery was deemed safe to return. 'I know nobody really feels like eating after today, but we have to keep our strength up.'

Isabel's funeral had been packed. The congregation, made up of young and old, flowed out of St Katherine's Church and onto the street, and even when the wretched air-raid siren had sounded its warning, nobody moved from their pews and the vicar continued the service with his head held high. Her death, on the night of Maggie's wedding, had stirred something in the whole community – a determination and need to pull together and be together. When the congregation's voices joined in the hymn 'All Things Bright and Beautiful', Audrey was so moved by the passion with which people sang, she felt as though the roof of the church might lift off at any moment. Seeing Maggie so unhappy, after previously being on such a high, broke her heart, but she'd resolved to stay strong in the face of adversity, to not allow sadness to defeat her.

Now, Audrey, Lily and Joy, Elsie and Mary, sat around Pat's kitchen table. William had gone on fire-watching duty and John was at the bakery, seeing to the ovens. Maggie had returned home with Nancy and Gwendolen, having to abandon her first few precious days of marriage.

'I don't know what will happen to Gwendolen now,' Audrey said, ladling the soup into bowls. 'I think she needs some kind of help, really.'

'Perhaps this will make her pull her socks up,' said Pat, sitting up straighter in her chair. 'The woman's got to take responsibility for herself and her family. She doesn't have a choice, does she? Just like the rest of us! It's black and white, Audrey, there's no "wondering" about it!'

Audrey sat down in her seat and thought for a moment, while Pat tutted irritably. She knew Pat thought her daughter-in-law was a soft touch, and she was going to let her comments pass, but the thought of Arthur popped into her head.

'People aren't black and white, though, are they?' she said. 'They're a bit of every colour in between, if you ask me. It's like that man, Arthur, that I met. You know, the one who brought my ring back? The woman in the café told me he's a conscientious objector…'

'He never is!' said Pat, putting her spoon down on the table. 'What good would a conscientious objector be if Hitler was marching down the high street and knocking on the door?'

'Maybe he's brave,' said Audrey. 'Maybe it's braver to stand up for what you believe in, than go with the crowd.'

'Fiddlesticks!' said Pat. 'I don't know how you can say that when your own husband is out there fighting somewhere, Mary's father was killed, and William has come back wounded. Elsie's father is in a prisoner-of-war camp. You can't stick up for a man who's basically a coward—'

Audrey knew she should button her lip and control her tongue, but she was sick of war and fighting and violence and bad news, and no matter what, she always found herself fighting the corner of the underdog.

'All I'm saying,' she said, as calmly as possible, 'is that people are not black and white, they're complicated. People's reasons for doing things are complicated, aren't they? Arthur is a very nice man and we have no right to call him a coward, just as people have no right to call Elsie's father a spy or Lily "shameless" for having a baby even though she's unwed. I've said it before but I'll keep on saying it till I'm blue in the face: if we showed more empathy and understanding and simple human kindness, we would all be much better off.'

'You're entitled to your opinion,' said Pat, her cheeks pink, 'but my son is out there putting his life on the line for people like Arthur and—'

At this Pat, uncharacteristically, burst into a smattering of tears. Audrey put her arms around her mother-in-law. 'I'm sorry,' she said. 'I shouldn't have spoken out like that.'

'Oh, don't take any notice of me,' said Pat, quickly recovering. 'Goodness me, I don't know what came over me.'

She fussed around with her handkerchief, while the others murmured words of comfort. Despite the soup being delicious, nobody could really eat anything at all.

'I think all our feelings are a bit raw,' said Lily, resting a hand on Audrey's arm. 'It's no wonder after today, is it?'

'I think maybe William and I should wait until next year to marry,' said Elsie. 'It seems insensitive.'

Audrey glanced at Elsie, who had suffered disappointment after disappointment, but who had worked her socks off to keep her family going and her relationship with William alive, despite his trauma. She had been so excited about marrying him and wasn't that what they all needed? A love story with a happy outcome? The whole community needed it, not just their family – especially now. Someone had to make something good happen.

'No,' said Audrey. 'We've all had a lot of knocks to deal with lately, and your wedding will be just what we need – something to look forward to and work together on. Elsie, you and William deserve a nice day to celebrate your being together. God knows, life is short! Let's make the most of the good times.'

Pat, clearly knocked for six by her own display of emotion, stood up from the table and went over to the dresser, where she fetched a bottle of sherry and the sherry glasses. She poured everyone a small glass and handed them round.

'Let's raise a toast to the good times,' she said. 'And to the memory of Isabel.'

'Isabel,' the women said in unison, lifting up their little glasses of sherry while sitting in the kitchen, with the light fading beyond the nets.

Audrey smiled at the assembled group, smoothing out the tablecloth with her palms, remembering Isabel's sweet smile on Maggie's wedding day, silently promising to carry a little of her essence in her heart, forever more.

With a deep sigh, Maggie sat on the edge of Isabel's narrow, creaky bed, still wearing the simple black dress and cloak that she'd worn to the funeral. In her fingers, she held a small lock of Isabel's soft hair that the undertaker had given her. George had promised he would get the lock of hair made into a brooch, a mourning brooch, so that she would always be able to treasure her sister's memory.

'Sweet George,' Maggie whispered, thinking of her new husband who had been such a gentleman these last few days, helping with the funeral arrangements and paperwork. Their wedding night had been so tragically interrupted and while Maggie had returned to the dank, tiny house with Nancy and Gwendolen, George was preparing to be posted overseas. The wedding now felt like a distant dream, her happiness utterly crushed by the loss of dearest Isabel. Her poor sister had never been fortunate and had absolutely hated her job at the laundry – and now she was dead before her life had even really started. Glancing around the bedroom and seeing ghostly images of Isabel everywhere, Maggie felt overcome with sadness. She would never see her again, never hear her laugh, never wash her one pair of blasted socks.

'Oh, gosh!' said Maggie, as tears spilled onto her cheeks. 'What will we do without Isabel?'

'I'll tell you what we'll do,' said Gwendolen, suddenly appearing at the bedroom door, with Nancy just behind her. Maggie jerked her head up and wiped her eyes, surprised by the steely expression on her grandmother's face. Isabel had been killed while helping to get a drunken Gwendolen to safety – and though she would never say as much, Maggie couldn't help but blame her grandmother in some way.

'I know you blame me and that's just the way it is,' said Gwendolen, taking the words right out of Maggie's thoughts. 'But blame won't get us anywhere. What we need to do, what *I* need to do, is look after you girls properly. We need to brush ourselves down and get on with our lives. Folk round 'ere 'ave all lost someone, thanks to this war. Isabel's death has been a wake-up call, I can tell you. I know I've been poisonous, but—'

Suddenly unsteady on her feet and with tears in her eyes, Gwendolen seemed to lose every ounce of her energy and Nancy held her by the arm to lead her to sit down on the bed. Gwendolen wiped her eyes and sat up straighter, admonishing herself, before addressing Maggie and Nancy again.

'I promise you I will change,' she insisted, her voice trembling with emotion. 'I've lost my 'usband, my daughter and son-in-law and now my granddaughter, and for so many years I've tried to blank out my sadness. It's 'bout time I stood up for what's left of m' family. I'm sorry, girls. I'm sorry, Nancy. I'm sorry, Maggie.'

Maggie and Nancy shared a wary glance at their grandmother's words, though both girls had tears on their cheeks. Maggie, who normally seethed with resentment whenever her grandmother spoke, saw Gwendolen through new eyes: she was a woman who couldn't withstand all the tragedy life had dealt her. Once she had been young, just like Maggie, with a new husband she loved and hopes for the future. Life had taken her on an unexpected journey that she hadn't been able to cope with.

'I want to make it up to you,' said Gwendolen quietly. 'For Isabel.'

With gnarled, liver-spotted hands that were criss-crossed with protruding blue veins, Gwendolen shakily reached out for Maggie and Nancy's hands. For a long moment neither sister moved, until Maggie took the lead and curled her own hand around her grandmother's. It was the first loving gesture they'd shared in years.

'For Isabel,' said Maggie, offering all she had: a small, sad smile.

Chapter Twenty-Nine

'This is a very peculiar arrangement,' said Flo, irritably, waiting for her bread. Weeks later, and the bakery shop was still being repaired – and the sound of sawing and hammering was a constant background noise – but Audrey had created a makeshift 'shop' from the hatch window on the side of the bakehouse building. The gate to the backyard was fixed open and the customers lined up, next to the cucumber plants, chickens and Anderson shelter, where leeks and lettuces sprouted from the roof, for their bread. Even rain didn't put off the customers. Since Lord Woolton had said on the wireless that housewives should keep one day's worth of bread in their house as a standby, the queue never seemed to go down.

'Won't be long before we're back to normal again,' said Audrey, optimistically. Her body ached all over from working all hours in the bakehouse and on the shop, but she understood Flo's frustration. Women had to spend hours waiting in shop queues, and the bakery shop had always been a place where the customers gossiped in relative comfort. 'Meanwhile, would you like to try the "National Loaf"?' she asked.

Audrey lifted the dense wheatmeal loaf up for Flo and the rest of the queue to see. The women tutted, turning their noses up at the grey-looking loaf that was gradually being introduced in bakeries across the country, and that Barton's was obliged to bake.

'It's grey!' called out one customer. 'And there's no crust on it at all.'

'Looks like you could knock someone out with it!' said Maggie, with a wink.

Audrey grinned at Maggie, who in spite of all she'd suffered – and with George now posted overseas – still managed to bring a smile to work. She was full of admiration for her.

'Not on your life, Audrey!' said Flo. 'Looks like Hitler's secret weapon to me! White tin and two rolls, please, and you'll never find me ordering anything else!'

'Didn't you say white bread is going to be banned?' said Elizabeth, who was standing behind Flo.

'There's been talk of it,' said Audrey, thinking of the letter she received from the Ministry of Food saying the matter was being discussed, since there was a shortage of white flour and wheatmeal was better for the nation's health. 'But no decision has been made. For the time being, we're baking as normal, but trying out this wheatmeal or "National Loaf" recipe too.'

'Can you imagine life without white bread?' said Flo, paying for her bread. 'It doesn't bear thinking about, does it? Give me some good news, Audrey, please! Have you heard from that husband of yours? My boys haven't written in weeks.'

Audrey stood with her hands on her hips, framed by the hatch. Thinking about Charlie, her heart sank. It had been weeks since she'd heard from him too and though she refused to believe the worst, doubts about his safety crept into her head. She opened her mouth to reply to Flo when a young woman, no more than twenty, carrying a baby, appeared in the yard, looking rather lost. Dressed in skirt and blouse, with her mid-brown hair pinned back from her face, she carried the baby in one arm – and with the other hand, she carried a suitcase. All the ladies in the queue stopped gossiping and peered at her.

'Can I help you?' Audrey said, inwardly rolling her eyes at the 'inquisitive' customers.

'I'm looking for a convalescent home around here,' the young woman said. 'We were sent here by the Invalid Children's Aid Association, but I seem to have lost the address – I had it written down. A man in the street said you might know where it was?'

Audrey nodded. She'd heard about the convalescent home in Southbourne where women brought their babies who had suffered in the Blitz in London and Bristol. The babies, aged between one and three, had been sent to Bournemouth with their mothers for some rest and recuperation.

'I can show her the way, Audrey,' said Flo.

Audrey came out from behind the hatch, with two hot rolls. 'What's your name?' she asked. 'I'm Audrey Barton. Pleased to meet you.'

'Christine Johnson,' said the young woman.

'Take these,' Audrey insisted, even though Christine protested. 'And if you don't know anyone around here, why don't you come back and visit us again? My stepsister Lily has a young child. You two might be good companions for one another.'

Christine smiled and, as she turned to leave, bumped into Pat, who was hurrying into the bakery yard, clearly bursting with news.

'Sorry, dear!' said Pat, rushing towards Audrey, a lock of grey hair escaped from her hat. 'Did you hear? About the pilot?'

'What pilot?' said Audrey, her mind fretting over the names of all the pilots she knew – the sons, brother and nephews of customers. Scanning the customers' faces, she felt sure they were all feeling the same nerves.

'A plane came down off Hengistbury Head during a training exercise last night,' she replied. 'The plane landed in the sea and was spotted by a soldier who was on the Head. He jumped into the sea and tried to get to the pilot, who was tangled up in the wreckage. Sadly, the pilot drowned, and when the soldier tried to swim back to the beach, the rip current was so strong and the water so rough and the weather so bad, that he got into terrible trouble. Another man, passing, got into the water and rescued him from drowning.'

'My goodness!' said Audrey, accompanied by expressions of intrigue from the other women in the queue.

'And guess who the man was, who jumped into the sea?' asked Pat, raising her eyebrows and looking pointedly at Audrey. 'Arthur, the man who found your wedding ring in his bread.'

Audrey felt a smile burst out onto her face. She lifted her hands to her cheeks, which had turned pink.

'Perhaps he's a braver man than I gave him credit for,' said Pat, sharing a smile with Audrey.

Chapter Thirty

'Beauty is duty, eh?' said Christine to Lily, as they stood next to one another in the gardens of the convalescent home in Southbourne, where Christine and her baby Aggie were staying, and dahlias and geraniums bordered a green lawn. Christine was referring to the government's instruction that girls and women should stay pretty in wartime to boost morale, but was jokingly applying the phrase to baby Aggie and Joy, who were sitting on a blanket, pretty as new roses.

'A beautiful face is a brave face,' said Lily in reply, and both girls laughed. They'd seen the posters and advertisements in magazines, aiming to encourage women to keep up their appearance, no matter what troubles they faced.

Audrey had told Lily about Christine and that she might need a friend, so she had visited the home, with Mary in tow and instantly liked her. They sat in the grounds of the grand white villa on Viewpoint Avenue now and played with the baby girls, who were picking up and dropping, or trying to chew two wooden cubes. Mary's face was smeared with blackberry juice stains, since she'd spent the afternoon collecting blackberries from the hedgerows. The Ministry of Food were offering threepence per pound of blackberries for preserving – and scouts and schoolchildren were making the most of the offer. Mary, it seemed, had probably eaten her fair share too!

'Talking of beauty, I think we better clean you up, Mary,' Lily said, wiping her hanky over Mary's face, rubbing at the stains. At that moment, an aeroplane roared over the roof, terribly low, and Aggie burst into tears.

'Oh, it's okay, baby girl,' said Christine, quickly picking up her daughter and holding her close to her chest, covering her ears with her hands and rocking her gently from side to side until she calmed down. 'It's part of the treatment programme,' she told Lily. 'The babies here are traumatised by the sound of aircraft, so we have to sit outside and expose them to the sound, but make them feel safe afterwards so slowly they don't see the aircraft as a threat.'

'Poor little thing,' said Lily, gently rubbing Aggie's back as she sobbed. 'Was it bad then, in Bristol?'

Christine nodded and seemed unable to speak. She swallowed and looked up at the clouds, as if to stem the tears.

'Five months of bombing,' she said. 'The houses in my street were decimated. Hundreds of people were killed. We knew we'd be a target as an industrial centre, but I never expected it to be like it was. And poor little Aggie was frightened to bits. Even in our cupboard under the stairs, she just couldn't stand the noise. Some of the babies here were stuck in rubble for twenty-four hours before being rescued. They're properly traumatised, poor lambs.'

Lily shook her head sympathetically and picked up Joy, kissing the top of her head. Her gaze dropped to Christine's hands, where she saw an engagement ring and a wedding ring. 'And where's Aggie's father?' she asked. 'Is he fighting?'

Christine's eyes filled with tears, which she wiped away quickly, before putting Aggie down on the grass again and busying herself with unbuttoning the tiny cardigan.

'He's a prisoner of war in Germany,' she said, without looking at Lily. 'He went missing in Crete but was reported as being in Germany. He was my best friend my whole life. We always said we'd get married when we turned eighteen, but then he was called up. We organised a wedding in forty-eight hours and managed to get married before he left. He was home on leave from military training for a week and that's when I got pregnant. He's never met Aggie and I've no idea when he'll come home again. People have been so kind, sending their sympathies and enquiring over my anxieties about him. How about you? What about Joy's dad? Is he fighting?'

Thinking of Henry, who hadn't been in touch since their awful meeting at the hotel, Lily found herself blushing and her pulse quickening, wondering how judgemental Christine would be. She never knew how to answer this question and though sometimes she was tempted to lie and pretend she did have a man overseas, she always told the truth and hoped that people would understand.

'He's a clot!' she said and Christine laughed. 'He's married to another woman. He wasn't at the time I knew him, but anyway, I think you can probably guess the rest. I was very foolish and made a mistake.'

Christine nodded. 'Did your parents support you?' she asked. 'I know lots of girls who have been in the same situation but their family wouldn't have anything to do with them.'

'My father didn't like the idea of me being unwed, so I came to stay with my stepsister, Audrey, the lady you met at the bakery,' explained Lily. 'She's been so kind to me and made me so welcome. My father has recently been to visit and I think he was bowled over by Joy. He wants us both to go and live with him when the war is over, but even though that's what I've always wanted, I've started to feel part of the community here and now I have a new job teaching English to refugees at the local college. I'm happy here.'

She fell silent, thinking that she loved her family at the bakery more than she could say and also enjoyed teaching her students – men from all over the world who found themselves in Bournemouth. Teaching them English made her feel as though she was doing something really useful.

'Christine!' said the matron of the centre, interrupting Lily's thoughts. 'Please come in now!'

Christine rolled her eyes discreetly at Lily. 'The other people here are lovely, but that one's an old cat,' she whispered, making Lily giggle.

'Why don't you come to the bakery for your tea?' Lily suggested. 'Audrey asked me to invite you.'

'I'd like that,' she said. 'Thank you.'

Chrisine cleared it with the matron and the young women left the home. As another plane roared overhead, prompting Aggie to burst into tears again, Christine comforted and kissed the child until she calmed down, and Lily was struck by the ability and power of women. Carrying their baby daughters in their arms towards the bakery, she realised what an important job she and Christine had to do – get on with life in spite of the war, while making sure they brought up their daughters to do exactly the same.

*

'Savoury onions,' said Audrey, placing a casserole dish on the kitchen table. 'Onions that I had to register for, stuffed with breadcrumbs, of which I have plenty, egg, a little bit of cheese and crushed sage from the garden. Help yourself to bread and cabbage and hopefully this will keep the wolf from the door. There's pudding, of course – flaked barley cake, Mary's favourite.'

Mary smiled at Audrey, from under her fringe, and tucked into a slice of bread spread thinly with margarine. The news of her father's death had devastated her, but shown plenty of love and patience: she seemed stronger. Now, one of her front teeth was wobbly and she was having to shove the bread into the side of her mouth and into her cheek to chew it properly, making Audrey chuckle.

'Mary, I think we should tie a piece of cotton to that tooth and tie the other end to the door handle, then slam it shut, don't you?' she said. 'It needs to come out!'

'But then I won't be able to eat the barley cake!' said Mary.

'You know what they say about pudding, don't you?' said Christine, putting her petite shoulders back as if ready to make a speech. 'Reflect, whenever you indulge, it is not beautiful to bulge. A large, untidy corporation is far from helpful to the Nation. It's from the Ministry of Food – I saw it in the paper.'

Everyone at the table – Lily, Elsie, Mary and Christine – laughed, and Audrey was heartened by the fact she was back in her own homely kitchen, putting a meal on her own, albeit fire-damaged, kitchen table. Finally, after help from the Assistance Board and with favours from friends and neighbours, they had been able to move back into the bakery, leaving a quietly relieved Pat to get on with her life. Now, with the shop about to open again, she felt as if she was getting back to 'normal' – as normal as life could be in wartime – and that she could finally concentrate on Elsie and William's wedding.

'We're preparing for a wedding, Christine,' said Audrey, serving up the onions. 'Elsie here is marrying my brother William. You're more than welcome to join us for the reception.'

'Thank you,' said Christine, grinning at Elsie, who yawned an enormous yawn.

'Excuse me!' Elsie said. 'I've been working long hours. I look and feel exhausted! My skin looks grey, doesn't it?'

Audrey laughed and shook her head: 'No, Elsie love,' she said. 'You look lovely.'

'You should use used tea leaves in muslin bags as a face mask,' said Christine. 'And if you've any lard, it works a marvel on the skin, instead of cold cream. And do you have any lipstick? If you melt the pieces you have and mix it with lard, you'll have a new blusher. Then you'll look and feel brighter.'

'Oh, you know all the tricks!' Audrey said. 'You'll be a useful girl to have around. How long are you staying in Bournemouth, Christine?'

'A month or two, I think,' she said. 'It depends on Aggie. I'm not sure what we'll go back to, but I do want to go back. Being here is lovely and thank you for the welcome, but Bristol is my home.

Makes me realise what all the little evacuee children must feel like. Homesick, I should think.'

Audrey checked Mary's reaction, but she was too busy eating, thank goodness. She was doing everything she could to protect Mary from upset at the moment – she just wanted her to feel at home at the bakery, not to be reminded of feeling homesick. But, of course she knew exactly what Christine meant. In the mass evacuation of children from the major cities, Bournemouth had received thousands of evacuees – from Southampton, Portsmouth and London – and while some, she knew, were content, others missed their parents immeasurably. Who the children were billeted with made a difference too: some local women loved their evacuee visitors like their own children, enthusiastically introducing them to life on the coast, while others treated the city children with disdain, complaining of fleas, foul mouths and bad manners. Audrey shuddered at the thought of any child being neglected, wishing she had a house big enough to take care of them all. It was a cruel irony, she thought, that she loved children so much, yet she wasn't able to have one of her own. Motherhood, it seemed, was out of reach.

'Audrey…?' Lily said, smiling and waving a hand in front of Audrey's face to attract her attention.

'Hmm?' said Audrey, blinking. 'Oh, I'm sorry, I was just thinking. What did you say?'

'I said I think someone's at the door,' Lily said. 'Shall I get it, or are you expecting someone?'

Audrey slid back her chair, suddenly flustered. 'No, no, I'll get it,' she insisted. 'You carry on with your dinner and make Christine feel at home. Find out all her beauty tricks!'

Quickly making her way to the door, Audrey took off her apron and tucked her hair behind her ears. Expecting a neighbour perhaps, she didn't let her mind go to the dark, dreadful place that feared the arrival of a telegram reporting on Charlie's whereabouts. The tension slipped out of her when she saw Arthur standing on the doorstep, holding a bunch of roses. His eyes were twinkling as he smiled at her and presented the flowers.

'I hope you are feeling better now, Mrs Barton,' he said. 'I wanted to wish you luck for the shop opening tomorrow. I've seen the repair work going on and I'm impressed by how quickly you're back up and running.'

'Thank you,' said Audrey, accepting the flowers with a smile. 'Will you come in for some pudding? We're about to have barley cake – there's plenty to go around. I've a new girl stopping in for dinner. She's from Bristol, I'm sure you'd like her.'

Arthur laughed and held up his hand in refusal, just as the memory of Pat's story popped into Audrey's mind. She touched his sleeve and left her hand there for a brief moment.

'Arthur,' she said, seriously, 'I should be giving *you* flowers, not the other way around. I heard about the incident off the Head and how brave you were. Lesser men would have turned away. Everyone is talking about you and they're so grateful – you're a hero.'

At this he burst out laughing and shook his head. 'One minute I'm a coward and the next, I'm a hero – I can't keep up,' he said.

Audrey felt her face redden. 'No, I didn't mean—' she started.

'It's all right,' he replied, kindly. 'I'm used to it, Mrs Barton – the gossip, the hard stares, the mistrust. I rescued that man because he was in trouble, not because I want to be considered a hero or to get people to like me.'

He gave a slight bow, and left, walking away down Fisherman's Road, leaving Audrey holding the bunch of flowers, with the uncomfortable feeling she'd been misunderstood. She longed to call him back and correct him, but wasn't sure what it was she wanted to say. Watching him disappear into the distance, she was struck by a thought: *I liked you anyway, Arthur, I liked you anyway.*

Chapter Thirty-One

The kettle steamed on the range, as Audrey made sure the kitchen was gleaming, before preparing a late-night hot drink for William and John. Her pocket watch told her it was 11.20 p.m., and time to put down the blackout blinds, as listed in the *Echo*, but to Audrey, it felt more like 2 a.m. Suppressing another yawn, she made two mugs of OXO and took them, on a small wooden tray, into the bakehouse for the men.

'They were saying earlier on the wireless that there were hundreds of bombers over Germany last night,' she said, setting down the tray in the warm, floury room and yawning once more. 'Berlin, Boulogne and Kiel felt the brunt of it. Doesn't bear thinking of, really, and it makes me worry for Charlie.'

'Get to bed, young lady,' said John sternly. 'If I know Charlie, he'll be all right. Shop's open again tomorrow and that's what you should be concentrating on, not what Bomber Command are up to.'

Audrey rubbed her eyes and shrugged, rather put out by John's dismissive comments, and said goodnight to the men. He was a kind, fair and hardworking man, was John, but he had absolutely no time for fretting.

Alone in her bedroom, she opened the envelope she kept under Charlie's pillow and, by candlelight, read the last letter he had sent her, weeks ago now. It was only a few lines long, but included a dried stem of a little blue flower he'd picked. Holding the delicate bloom in her fingertips, she tried to conjure up an image of him, smiling and laughing, in her mind. Whispering goodnight to him into the empty room, placing the envelope safely under her pillow, she blew out the candle and lay in the dark, blinking up at the ceiling, trying to quieten her thoughts.

Hearing the drone of distant aircraft, she suddenly felt incredibly alone. John might be able to see the German people as the enemy, but Audrey couldn't help but think of the ordinary people, just like her, trying to go about running their homes and businesses but whose lives were being turned upside down by the RAF. Women and children, in the wrong place, at the wrong time, would be yet more victims of this war. *There but for the grace of God go I.* On the other hand, she'd heard stories of the German army burning down villages in Crete, murdering old people and children in their beds and forcing others to dig their own graves before executing them.

Sighing in dismay, Audrey pulled the eiderdown over her head and curled up. She must make sure, she thought, as her head whirred, that in the shop at least, she brought a little joy into her customers' daily lives. Warm bread, cakes, bakes and a smile… that much she could do. There was so much wild fruit this year, particularly blackberries and crab apples, she thought, before falling into a deep sleep, that she should make fruit loaves and fruit buns. The scent of them baking would be enough to raise people's spirits…

Hours later, when John was working alone in the bakehouse, knocking back dough ready to be baked in the hot ovens, and the neighbourhood was silent apart from a fox skulking through the vegetable patches, Audrey's heavy sleep was disturbed by the warmth of a familiar body climbing into the bed beside her. In the thick of a dream, she sleepily opened her eyes to see Charlie's face, opposite her, in the dim light.

Suddenly wide awake and sitting bolt upright, her heart racing, she reached out her hands to cup his face, to make sure she wasn't imagining him. 'Charlie!' she said, incredulous. 'Charlie, is that really you?'

Heart pounding and body trembling, she wept with joy when Charlie gently embraced her, his body melting into hers. She held him tightly in her arms, resting her cheek against his. Blinking in the darkness, she felt relief and love wash over her.

'I've got three days' leave,' he said quietly. 'I didn't have a chance to write.'

They lay back down together in the darkness, unspeaking, but facing one another under the cover, just breathing in each other's scent and warmth, knees and toes touching. As time passed, they moved closer and explored one another's bodies, gently making love in the darkness, forgetting everything and everyone else and eventually falling asleep in each other's arms.

When Audrey woke with a start at dawn, looking across the bed to Charlie's side to find it empty, she wondered if she'd dreamt the whole thing but then she saw his kitbag on the floor beside the bed, draped over with his uniform. Straining to hear the sound of voices in the bakehouse, Audrey's heart leapt. It wasn't a dream – Charlie had come home.

Springing out of bed and skidding on the floorboards as she did, she dressed quickly and ran down the stairs to see him again with her own eyes. In the light of dawn and working the ovens, he looked exhausted and much thinner than he had when he'd left eight months before.

'Found this fella inspectin' my bread,' said John, with a laugh.

Audrey grinned and, hiding her shock at Charlie's undernourished appearance, she ran towards him, suddenly feeling foolish and shy, but he welcomed her with open arms. 'I've missed you, Charlie,' she said. 'We've all missed him, haven't we, John? So much has happened. To you too, no doubt.'

Charlie nodded. 'I wouldn't know where to begin,' he said, swinging round to shovel a tray of bread tins into the oven. 'I heard the sorry news about Maggie's sister, poor girl. And John tells me the bakery took a hit, but you've got the place up and running again. Must have been 'ard work. I've never felt so proud of you, Audrey, I 'ave to say.'

Audrey felt suddenly overcome with emotion. The months of missing Charlie and the strain of the bakery's repairs suddenly gripped her. Unable to speak for a moment, she gestured towards the bakery shop, and staggered into the corridor, where, leaning with her back against the wall, she gathered herself. She couldn't start crying on Charlie's shoulders. If those news reports on Crete were anything to go by, he would have witnessed horrors more terrible than she could possibly imagine. Only last night she was thinking that she had to work her hardest to lift people's spirits – and that would start with her own husband. Taking a deep breath, she opened the door to the store cupboard and checked various boxes until she found a string of bunting once used for a birthday celebration and took it out to the front of the shop, where she strung it over the window.

'Have we won the war or summat?' said Flo, arriving at the bakery for her bread.

Audrey smiled and shook her head. 'No,' she said. 'But the bakery shop's back open today and my Charlie's home on leave for three days. That's reason enough to get the bunting out in my book!'

She couldn't stop herself from beaming.

Flo pursed her lips and took a sharp intake of breath. 'There'll be those not so eager to celebrate your good fortune,' she said. 'Some husbands never come back, you know, Audrey.'

Pausing from hanging up the bunting, Audrey ignored Flo and privately rolled her eyes. 'Put a sock in it, why don't you?' she muttered. 'I'm celebrating and that's that!'

The day went quickly and cheerfully, with customers and neighbours keen to welcome Charlie home and shake his hand. Dressed to bake, wearing his long white apron and hat, a flour-covered Charlie quickly had his nose in the order and ledger book, the ingredients supply and paperwork from the Ministry of Food and the Bournemouth Food Office. He repaired a door handle that had broken, patched up a gap in the side of the Anderson shelter and strengthened the bunks, and had gone for a very quick ale at the Carpenter's Arms with John and William to congratulate William on his upcoming wedding. He squeezed a lot into a few hours and by the end of the day, he was quiet and tired, but didn't want to sit down and stop working.

When Audrey finally convinced him to sit down at the kitchen table, for a corned beef sandwich and a cup of tea, she couldn't decide whether or not to broach the military action he'd seen overseas. Knowing Charlie, he wouldn't want to talk about it, but she had to let him know she cared. Placing a hand over his and squeezing it gently, she just came out with it.

'Charlie,' she said, 'no words seem right. How's it been in the army? Are you… okay?'

Charlie rested his elbows on the table and his head in his hands as if it were too heavy to stay upright on its own. He smiled a small sad smile at his wife. Written across his face she saw a myriad of emotions: fear, anger, regret, bewilderment, resignation.

'I hope you will understand when I say I never want to talk about the war at home,' he said. 'I'm a man of few words, you know that better than anyone, but I don't have the words to explain or make sense of what I've experienced. The one thing I can say is that this is not just a war of brute force, but also psychological. I'm trying, with everything I have, not to let my mind be crushed. Am I making any sense, love?'

After a long pause, where Audrey floundered for an answer, she nodded. 'If that's how you want it to be,' she said, 'then I respect that. As long as you know that I'm willing and able to share your troubles, if you want me to.'

She stood up from the table and put their dirty plates in the sink, where the dishwater had grown cold and grey.

'I don't know what this country would do without women like you,' said Charlie. 'You're a good woman.'

She smiled at Charlie and, dunking her hands in the water, decided to broach the subject of Mary – and the possibility of adopting her.

'I'm in agreement, if it's possible,' said Charlie, once Audrey had explained the situation. 'Though I don't know what will happen to me in the future. The responsibility might well fall on your shoulders, love.'

Audrey frowned. She knew he was talking about his own life and the danger he was in, but she refused to think the worst could happen. After the war, she told herself, Charlie, Mary and herself could be a family.

'I still hope that one day we will have a child of our own,' said Charlie, reading her mind. 'It's a lot of work for you, Audrey, taking on a stranger's child. Mary's a sweet girl, but she's not our own flesh and blood… I have to be honest and admit that I dream of having a son to follow in my footsteps. A boy with baking in his blood.'

Rolling her eyes, affectionately, Audrey let Charlie dream about the son he'd always wanted, but deep down, she feared she would never fall pregnant and that adopting Mary was the closest they would ever get to being parents. Besides, she loved little Mary with all her heart. Charlie would come to accept that and love her just as much in time too.

*

Clutching the ankle of her precious but tatty porcelain and cloth doll in one hand, its hair skimming the floorboards as it hung upside down, Mary stood outside the kitchen door, hardly daring to breathe.

She'd heard every word Charlie had said with such clarity – it was as if he had been shouting through a megaphone. Involuntarily, as she stared at the closed dark brown door, Mary's teeth chattered, despite it being a warm night and being dressed in a warm nightgown. Thoughts of her dead brother, Edward, her mother and father besieged her. Was Audrey now going to desert her too? Charlie's words repeated in her mind: *It's a lot of work for you, Audrey, taking on a stranger's child. Mary's a sweet girl, but she's not our own flesh and blood… I dream of having a son to follow in my footsteps. A boy with baking in his blood.*

Moving her hand to the doorknob, the blood drained from her face as she felt warm liquid on her leg and noticed a small puddle on the floor, near her right foot. Blazing with embarrassment as she chastised herself for not realising she needed the privy, she quickly found some sheets of newspaper from the table in the corridor and mopped up the mess.

'Stupid Mary!' she hissed to herself, freezing when she heard noises in the kitchen.

'Mary?' she heard Audrey's voice from within the kitchen. 'Is that you out there?'

A big part of her wanted to burst into the kitchen and rush into Audrey's arms, which were always warm and welcoming and topped with her smiling face, but the other part of her knew she should make a plan. Charlie didn't want Mary. He wanted a son, born with baking in his blood – not one that had blown in from the slum district of London like a discarded paper bag.

Whispering her dead brother's name, Edward, Mary tried to conjure him up, right there and then in the corridor, and for a second, she thought she saw a ghostly movement in the shadows. Sometimes she felt she saw him, and those sightings always made her feel better. He would come with her, wherever she had to go next. He would help guide her when she had packed up her bag, collected her rabbit and stole away from the bakery. A tremor ran through her when the door opened and the light from the kitchen spilled into the corridor, illuminating Audrey.

'Mary, sweetheart, can't you sleep?' said Audrey, resting her hands on her shoulders.

The little girl gazed up at Audrey and shook her head, scrunching the damp newspaper up behind her. Audrey's eyes skittered from floor to newspaper, and Mary crossed her fingers in the hope that she hadn't noticed the accident.

'Never mind,' was all Audrey said, holding her hand and leading her up to bed, before tucking her in. 'Chin up,' she said, as always, and Mary lifted her chin. 'Chin down,' she said, neatly tucking the sheet under her chin.

I'll miss this, thought Mary, as her heart ached with thinking about what she would do next. She closed her eyes tightly, wondering if she could survive a whole night all by herself. Those babies in the convalescent home had managed it, she thought, so she could too.

Chapter Thirty-Two

'Where did the time go?' Audrey asked Charlie, as she packed up a parcel of provisions for him to take, as he prepared to return to active service. Two doorstep sandwiches, a gingerbread cake and two fruit buns would keep him going, she thought, handing him the parcel. Knitted socks from Pat were in there too, as well as a new shaving stick. If Audrey had been able, she would have put everything he loved in there: the gramophone, the view of Southbourne beach, his chair by the fire, where he rested briefly on a Sunday afternoon, the fat seagull he called Captain and threw scraps of bread to. Herself.

Charlie and Audrey were in the kitchen after the bakery closed, with the window open to a beautiful view of the Overcliff and the sea beyond. Steeped in golden sunlight, that scenery was the backdrop to life in the bakery and both of them loved it dearly. Since he'd been home on leave, Audrey had seen her husband staring out at the view and sensed he was internalising it, perhaps so that when he was in the battlefields, he could visit home in his mind.

'You blink and it's over,' she added, quietly batting away the tears threatening to fall, finding a teacup to take over to the sink and wash up.

Watching her husband polish his boots with a brush, the small tin of boot polish open and emanating a clean, crisp smell, Audrey's heart contracted. She longed for Charlie to reach over to her and put his arms around her, whisper comfort and reassurances in her ear, tell her when he would next be home, but she knew he wasn't able. He would never admit it, but this parting was impossibly painful for him too. She could read the fear on his face, see it in the slight tremble in his fingers as he cleaned his shoes. Knowing this truth about him, she resolved to stifle the anxiety and sense of foreboding that had been threatening to consume her the whole day. Flo's words rang out in her head: *Some husbands never come home.*

'I'm not convinced the Vienna rolls are perfect today,' Charlie said, finishing cleaning his boots but not meeting Audrey's eye.

'No?' said Audrey, too quickly. 'What do you think went wrong then?'

'I think we proved the dough for too long,' he said. 'They've not risen quite how they should – William needs to watch out for that. The boy needs to pay attention, he does seem distracted. Oh, I've got pins and needles in my leg!'

'Stamp it out, love,' she said, demonstrating with her right leg. 'Like this.'

Charlie watched her with a quizzical expression on his face. 'I know how to stamp, Audrey love,' he said, one side of his mouth twitching slightly as if he wanted to laugh. She stopped and blushed. 'Come here, you daft thing,' he said.

Audrey approached him with her arms outstretched and the two of them stood, leaning against one another, unspeaking, just being together for the last time in who knew how long.

'So, are you going to say a proper goodbye this time?' asked Audrey, still leaning against Charlie's chest, listening to the rhythmic thump of his heartbeat. 'I could get everyone up here and we could raise a toast to you, Charlie, for love and luck. It's a shame you won't be here for William and Elsie's wedding.'

He rested his hands on her shoulders and held her away so he could look her in the eye and shook his head. She shook her hair back over her shoulders.

'I can't say goodbye and I don't want to,' he said, kissing her gently on the lips. 'I'd rather just slip off, as if I was going out on deliveries, or up to see the miller, as if this was just an ordinary day.'

Choking on his words and letting his hands drop, he collected his bag, his food parcel and moved towards the kitchen door. Words of desperation bubbled up inside Audrey and, in her mind's eye, she imagined herself flinging her arms around Charlie and not letting him go. Instead, she took deep breaths and ordered herself to be still.

'Keep an eye on the bread, love,' he said, winking at her. 'The inside should be springy to touch, the crust, golden brown. Just as it should be.'

'I'll keep an eye on the bread,' she said, smiling, forbidding the tears from falling.

Listening to him walk down the stairs and go out onto the street, she moved quickly to the window, where she watched him stride down the street, kitbag over his shoulder. Longing for him to turn around one last time, before he went out of view, tears sprang from her eyes when, at the corner of the road, he did so. She smiled and raised her hand in reply, before letting it fall as she watched him disappear from sight.

Some husbands never come back.

Turning away from the window, Audrey nervously twiddled her wedding ring up and down her finger. Glancing around the kitchen, she decided she should give the floor a thoroughly good clean, but just as quickly as the idea came, it evaporated. Standing on a chair and looking at the plates and pots on the top of the dresser, she decided to dust them all, but after lifting one plate, her motivation slipped. She sighed and, climbing down from the chair, picked up the shoe polish tin, breathing in the astringent scent, allowing herself a quick cry, before wiping her eyes with a handkerchief.

'Pull yourself together, Audrey,' she muttered, thinking of all the other women, just like her, whose husbands, sons and brothers were away on the front line. Finding courage in the thought of their courage, she made a mental list of what needed to be done. Mary would be home from school soon – expecting dinner – and hadn't she promised the girl she'd show her the cake toppers that she might use on Elsie and William's celebration cake?

Checking her pocket watch, she frowned: Mary should have been back by now, even if she had been blackberry picking in the hedgerows again. Popping her head out the open window, she glanced out into the yard to check if she was petting her rabbit, but the yard was empty. In the distance, she could see William helping John spread the coal ash on the neighbourhood gardens that had been turned over to vegetable growing, but there was no sign of Mary with them either.

'That is strange,' said Audrey to herself as she left the kitchen, checked Mary's empty bedroom and concentrated on trying to work out where the little girl might be, a tangle of worries tying her stomach in knots. Had she been so involved with Charlie leaving she'd forgotten where Mary was?

Searching the Anderson air-raid shelter, followed by the bakehouse, the storeroom and the flour loft, Audrey lifted her skirt a little and navigated her way across the vegetable patch to where William and John were working. Both men stood up to greet her, William wiping his brow with the side of his hand.

'Charlie gone, 'as 'e?' said John, leaning on his spade.

'Yes, he's gone,' said Audrey, trying not to show her emotion. 'He wanted to go quietly – you know how he is. John, William, have you seen Mary? I can't find her anywhere. She should have been back home by now for her tea.'

The two men shook their heads and, spotting Lily pushing Joy in her pram coming into the yard, Audrey ran over to her, asking if she'd seen Mary. Lily hadn't seen her either, and with her heart now pounding in panic, Audrey rubbed her forehead.

'Have you tried the hedgerows near the river?' said Lily. 'I've seen her with some children sometimes picking blackberries there – there's such a glut this year. Shall we go and look? We'll come with you.'

Audrey, Lily and Joy went quickly to the banks of the River Stour, where an overgrown path led from the bridge at Christchurch to Hengistbury Head. The light fading a little as storm clouds gathered on the horizon, they headed towards the blackberry bushes, where some children could be seen picking.

'Mary!' called Audrey as they walked, her panic rising, and then turning to Lily, 'You know she can't swim. I told her I'd teach her to swim in the river, since the sea was out of bounds, but I've been that busy, I've not got around to it.'

Audrey suddenly felt crushed by self-doubt. Maybe she wasn't looking after Mary as well as she should be. Maybe she wasn't good enough to adopt the child after all! Being entrusted with the welfare of an evacuee was a big responsibility, and some local women she knew had failed miserably at the task, doing nothing but complain. One local woman had even been fined five pounds for pretending to have an evacuee and obtaining, under false pretences with intent to defraud the evacuee authorities, ten pairs of curtains, a bedstead, two overlays, a bolster and other bits and pieces! Perhaps Audrey was just as bad.

'This is all my fault,' she said, biting her bottom lip. 'What with the repairs on the bakery and Charlie coming home for a few days, I've been ignoring Mary, haven't I? Just when she's needed me most.'

She felt her throat thicken and she gulped, hating the thought that she might have neglected Mary.

'Don't blame yourself,' said Lily. 'Maybe she's just stayed out too long with the other children. Let's look down here.'

'Mary!' they called together, walking along the riverbank but finding nothing and nobody, before Lily had another idea.

'What about the Overcliff?' she said. 'Maybe she's gone down to the beach – she likes it down there. She might just be looking for lizards.'

'Yes,' said Audrey, frowning, then forcing herself to smile. 'Perhaps she's there looking for lizards and it'll be nothing more complicated than that.'

Chapter Thirty-Three

The light was fading by the time Audrey and Lily arrived at the beach, the orange sun hanging low in the sky and partially concealed by clouds. Though the flat and silver sea looked calm, she knew there were dangerous currents beneath the surface that could drag a person under and carry them off, miles down the coast. With no sign of Mary on the beach or on the promenade, Audrey shivered with fear. What if she'd entered the water and gone in too deep?

'I just can't think what's happened to her,' she said to Lily, chewing the inside of her cheek, deep frown lines across her forehead. 'She knows not to go in the water, but what if she did? Or what if she walked a different way home from school and got lost, or is laying injured somewhere? She'll be hungry and thirsty by now and I bet she doesn't have anything warm with her. What if the air-raid siren goes off? She'll be petrified, poor lamb. Oh, Lily, I don't know what to do! If only Charlie were here.'

Since Charlie had gone off to fight, Audrey had discovered that she could manage very well on her own, but now, with Mary vanished and after having had him home for a few days, she wished more than ever that her husband was here. While fear and anxiety was muddling her thoughts, his sensible, logical approach was just what she needed. For a moment, she felt she might collapse onto the sand in tears, but she took a deep breath and pulled herself together: Mary couldn't have gone too far. Lily put her arm around Audrey's shoulders and hugged her.

'Don't worry, I'm sure she'll be fine,' she said. 'Perhaps she's back at the bakery now. Should we go back, in case she is? She might be wondering where we are and waiting for her dinner!'

'You go,' said Audrey. 'And if she's there come and find me. I'll walk a bit further, just in case she's here somewhere. I need to find her before it gets any darker. We know only too well how dangerous blackout can be – and she's not wearing anything white.'

Audrey watched Lily walk up the zig-zag path, back towards the bakery, hoping she was right, and that Mary would be at home, but something told her that she wasn't. Briskly walking further, towards Hengistbury Head, she passed the ugly sea defences and rolls of barbed wire, her fear increasing with every step. 'Mary!' she called out as she walked, 'Mary!', but her calls were only met with the screech of a lone seagull, swooping overhead.

Returning home with sore feet and aching legs, Audrey found Lily, John and William sitting at the kitchen table. They all looked at her with expectant, anxious faces, clearly hoping to see Mary. Audrey shook her head and walked over to the window, staring out.

'She wasn't anywhere,' said Audrey. 'What shall we do? Should I go to the police station and speak to an officer?'

John poured Audrey a cup of weak tea and patted the chair next to him. 'Come and sit here, love, and have a cup of tea and a slice of bread and jam,' he said.

'Oh no, I couldn't eat,' said Audrey.

'Do as I say, young lady,' said John. 'You wait here and gather your strength, while I go out looking for her. William will take care of the ovens until I'm back. I'll ask Old Reg to telephone the police station.'

Audrey slowly sat down and John rested his hands on her shoulders, giving them a gentle squeeze.

'She'll be back,' he said gently. 'She wouldn't be without you, now, Audrey. You're a mother to her, make no mistake.'

Audrey patted John's hand in thanks, and gulped back the tears that were threatening to fall. John's words were true – she had become a mother to Mary and she loved the little girl with her whole heart. She realised it now with crystal clarity – she didn't need to have a baby of her own, she had Mary.

'I just love that little girl so much,' she said falteringly. 'As if she was my own.'

When the others had left, Audrey stayed in the kitchen, pacing the floorboards and straining to think where Mary might be, stopping dead every time there was a noise. By the middle of the night, her eyes were almost closing and, resting her head on her arms at the kitchen table for a moment, she briefly fell to sleep. Waking with a start minutes later, the silence in the bakery filled her with empty dread and she cried, longing for Mary to be found, or to come home.

'Oh, I can't sit here any longer!' she said to the empty kitchen. Grabbing her torch, she told William, who was in the bakehouse, that she was going out to search again near the river, where the boats were.

'But—' he started, a panicked expression on his face.

'I'll not be told otherwise,' she said, marching off before he could say anything else.

Walking towards the river, where the weeping willows rustled in the breeze, Audrey's heart jumped in her chest when she saw a flash of torchlight in the near distance. Running towards it, she stopped dead when she realised it was the man from the Home Guard, on night patrol, who had found Joy in her pram on the beach months before.

'Where are you going?' he said. 'You shouldn't be out. You're not wearing white and you don't even have your gas mask with you! Don't I recognise you?'

'I'm looking for my little girl, Mary,' said Audrey, stuttering. 'She didn't come home after school.'

'Now I know who you are!' he said. 'You're from the bakery, with that other young lady who left her baby on the beach! You're not very good with losing your littl'uns! You should take more care, madam!'

'Oh, do be quiet, old man!' Audrey snapped. 'I love my family more than I can possibly say and I'd do anything for them. Now let me past, so I can check the quay. It's the one place I haven't checked.'

'I better come with you,' he said.

Audrey shrugged, wishing he would just go away, as he huffed and puffed beside her, trying to keep up with her pace.

When they'd walked further along the river, much further than she'd walked with Lily, Audrey shone her torch over a group of three rowing boats bobbing on the water, moored near to the riverbank. One was covered in tarpaulin, which she felt sure moved.

'Shh,' she said, stopping and pointing at the boat. 'I'm sure it moved.'

Audrey strained to focus on the ancient-looking rowing boat, not knowing what to expect. What if it was the enemy? Heart in mouth, she called out Mary's name in a quivering voice. Moments later, Mary's little head poked out from under the tarpaulin and, when Audrey shone the torch directly into her face, she froze like a rabbit in headlights. A wave of relief and anger washed over Audrey as she marched closer to the rowing boat. Thoughts and images of what might have happened took her breath away. The girl could have drowned, or drifted away and out to sea, all alone in the darkness.

'Mary!' she said. 'Come out of there at once!'

'No, I shan't!' shouted Mary, grabbing one of the oars and trying to push the boat away from the edge. Audrey was taken aback. It was probably the first time the child had defied her – she was normally such an obedient and sweet little thing.

The old man, from the Home Guard, muttered under his breath and waded into the water. He pulled Mary from the boat and carried her, kicking and screaming, onto the riverbank.

'Now look here, young lady, just you stop kicking…' he started, setting her down, but she pushed him so hard, he stumbled backwards.

'Mary!' said Audrey. 'Stop it at once.'

'I'm not coming home!' Mary shouted. 'I'm never coming back!'

She started to run away from Audrey, through the bulrushes, but Audrey was quick to react and soon caught her up, grabbing the little girl's arm.

'Let go of me!' Mary screamed, but Audrey didn't let go. Instead, she clung to Mary for dear life, wrapping her arms around her frame and pulling her close to her.

'Calm down, Mary,' soothed Audrey. 'Calm down and tell me what you're doing here. Were you running away? Has something upset you?'

She had a sudden flashback to the evening she'd found Mary outside the kitchen. Had she overheard Charlie talking about her?

Mary, who had stopped struggling, started to cry and enormous fat tears rolled down her cheeks.

'Tell me what the reason is,' said Audrey. 'You can say whatever you like, it won't matter because I'll still love you.'

With her lips wobbling, Mary spoke: 'I heard Charlie say I was hard work and that he wanted a son of his own to follow in his footsteps and be a baker,' she said. 'I know you don't really want me either – you're just being nice. Nobody wants me. That's why everyone I love has disappeared.'

Audrey's heart broke into a million pieces. *Poor child*, she thought, *she doesn't believe that I love her*. Taking a deep breath, she wanted to say something that would leave her in no doubt she was loved.

'In my mind, you are my daughter,' said Audrey. 'I'm not leaving you and you're not leaving me, we're in this together. To tell you the truth, Mary dear, I can't have babies, and so Charlie's dream of a son is just a dream. I would have set him straight, but he's got to go off to fight in the horrible war, and I didn't want to crush his dreams. Sometimes dreams help keep us going, don't they? Now, why don't you come home? Your rabbit will be wondering where you've got to.'

After mulling over Audrey's words, Mary seemed visibly relieved. The old man from the Home Guard lifted his hand in dismissal and stormed off, leaving Audrey and Mary together. The sky was beginning to lighten and birds were beginning to sing – Audrey's thoughts flew to the bakery.

'It's almost morning,' she said. 'We need to get back, my love.'

'What about the bread?' Mary asked, as if reading her mind. 'Have I ruined the bread order? We need to get back to the ovens so you can put the rock cakes in.'

'You see,' said Audrey, folding her arms across her chest and grinning, 'you're going to make a fantastic little baker one day. There's no doubt about that. Later on I'll write and tell Charlie as much.'

And Audrey stayed true to her word. Yawning with exhaustion after a sleepless night, later that day she sat down at the kitchen table and wrote the longest letter she'd written to Charlie since he'd left. She told him that Mary was one of the family now and that she would never let her go. The bakery family, though unusual in shape and size, was what he should keep in mind when he was in battle. That she loved him and missed him more than there were words to describe. That he could rest assured that the Barton's bread was light and porous as ever, the crust golden and crisp. Just as it should be.

Chapter Thirty-Four

'Hold still,' said Violet to Elsie, as she fastened up her borrowed wedding dress. 'It looks like you've lost a few pounds since last year – this is loose on you. Perhaps I should take it in a bit? You want to show off your lovely figure on your wedding day, be the belle of the ball.'

Standing barefoot on a chair in her mother's living room, in front of a roaring fire, Elsie flicked her black curls out of the way, and twisted round to see how much spare fabric Violet had pinched in her fingertips. It wasn't enough to make a visible difference. After wearing her 'clippies' uniform all day, every day, consisting of slacks and jacket, this dress was feminine enough.

Her little sister June peered up from behind a book she was reading, a leaf from a beech tree that she used as a bookmark falling out and fluttering to the rug, where she sat cross-legged, humming, 'Here Comes the Bride'.

'No, Mother, it'll be fine,' said Elsie irritably. 'It's only a small do, nobody will notice. Be quiet, June!'

June stopped humming and put her nose back in her book.

'And what will you wear for warmth?' Violet said. 'It's autumn now, you'll be shivering if you go without a jacket or coat. I have that fur stole you could borrow, or perhaps you could wear a cloak until you get in the church? And what about your hair? Will Maggie be doing it—'

'Stop fussing!' interrupted Elsie. 'I'll wear my overcoat and I'll put my hair up myself. I have a little bit of lipstick left and some powder. I don't want a lot of fuss, Mother, you know that.'

She climbed down off the chair and sat on a chair near the fire, tucking her feet under her bottom, and stared into the embers. Without saying anything, Violet took off her spectacles and came to sit next to Elsie, resting her hand on her daughter's arm.

'What is it, love?' she said. 'There's something on your mind, I know it. Is it that your father is away? I know, I miss him terribly and I can't wait for the day he's returned home. Or is it something else, probably just nerves?'

Elsie stared at the engagement ring on her finger for a long moment, before lifting her head and meeting her mother's concerned gaze. Her creamy complexion and rosy cheeks shone in the firelight, and she radiated a natural beauty few girls had.

'How can I be sure he loves me?' she asked quietly. 'He was so distant when he first came home. Even though he says he wants nothing more than to marry me, how can I be sure? There's something he's hiding from me, I'm sure of it.'

She thought of the times she'd popped into the bakery and, despite him now working hard in the bakehouse with John, and being more affectionate towards her, William sometimes drifted off into his own troubled world.

Violet sat back in her chair, stretching out her legs in front of her and linking her fingers across her stomach. 'Do you love him?' she asked, to which Elsie nodded, in an 'of course I do' sort of way. Violet smiled. 'Marriage isn't just about loving each other. It's about understanding, not always easy with menfolk, but he's clearly been suffering,' she said. 'And as someone clever once said: "What do we live for, if it is not to make life less difficult for each other?"'

Elsie leaned into her mother's shoulder and digested her wise words, staring into the fire, watching the flames leap and dance in the grate, her anxiety and nerves dissipating and a feeling of certainty growing in her heart.

*

'I don't know who it was,' said Audrey, setting out the ingredients on the kitchen table, 'it could have been my granny, or it could have been Mrs Simpson for all I know, but someone once said that if a bride ate wedding cake made by a baker with love in his heart, she'd have a long and happy marriage. And if the baker had an empty, cold heart when he mixed the cake ingredients, her marriage would be miserable as sin. I wonder if it made a difference how much she ate?'

Mary, whose hair hung past her shoulders, laughed, while Lily, who was giving Joy the juice squeezed from raw blackcurrants, twisted in her chair to fix Audrey with a quizzical stare.

'Whatever's up with you?' asked Lily, affectionately. 'You've lost leave of your senses!'

'Wha-at?' asked Audrey, laughing. 'I heard that when I was a girl, and that's the truth of it. Oh, ouch, I have such a headache this evening! Must be a storm brewing.'

'There you go again with your old wives' tales,' said Lily, good-humouredly.

'In my view there's none that speak more sense than old wives,' Audrey grinned and rubbed her temples with her fingertips, waiting for her throbbing head to ease.

She scanned the array of tins and packets of ingredients on the table through narrowed eyes. The wedding was just days away and the customers had talked of little else all day, wanting to wish William and Elsie well, or dropping off small wedding gifts – some of them made from bits and bobs in the home. Mrs Cook had made Elsie a tea cosy out of offcuts of wool, and Mr Newton, the ARP warden, had fashioned a bracelet out of an old silver teaspoon. 'She can use it to stir her tea while she's wearin' it!' he had quipped when he handed it to a bemused Audrey.

Audrey's gift would be the food: a spread of cold finger food and, of course, the wedding cake, though, with ingredients now even more scarce and rationing worse than ever, just baking a tasty fruit cake was quite a challenge.

'Raisins, loganberries, cherries, sultanas and dates,' she said, tipping the remainder of her dried fruit stocks into a bowl. 'That's just about every bit of dried fruit I have left until the next consignment arrives. Mary, could you do the honours with the honey?'

Mary picked up a pot of honey and poured spoons of that into the mixture too, for sweetness, before Audrey handed her grated carrots to add for moisture and gravy browning for colour.

'Gracious me,' she said, winking at Mary and thinking of the rich and indulgent, intricately iced celebration cakes she'd made before the war. 'This wedding cake is going to be unique, I have to admit. Let's hope it tastes good!'

'It will,' said Lily, picking up Joy, who was starting to grizzle. 'I better get this one upstairs to bed, before she brings the house down.'

But Lily's dejected expression didn't go unnoticed and Audrey gently patted her back to make her feel better. She knew that Joy's crying wore her down, but it wouldn't last forever. Nothing lasted forever.

'Don't worry,' said Audrey, 'she'll grow through it. At least we know she has a good, healthy pair of lungs on her. Why don't you go up to bed too, Mary?'

Audrey gave Mary a hug and kissed her cheek, conscious that the little girl still needed plenty of reassurance that she was truly loved. When the girls left, William came in and helped himself to a glass of water. While Audrey was finishing off the cake, he sat down on a wooden chair near the fire, his leg outstretched. With his gaze firmly fixed on the flames, he looked deep in thought.

'Are you well, William?' Audrey asked, a memory of the conversation she'd overhead, where he had told John he had done some terrible things while away, popping into her head. Was he thinking about that now?

'There's been more talk of an invasion this autumn,' he said, leaning forward to stoke the fire. 'Churchill has met with Roosevelt, of course, so the Americans are getting involved, but still they warn of invasion. I try to stay positive, but sometimes the news gets the better of me.'

Audrey put the cakes in the range, murmuring her agreement and watching him put down the fire poker out of the corner of her eye. From the expression on his face, she knew he wasn't in the kitchen to talk about military operations, but of course she would humour him until he was ready to share what was really on his mind. She sat down on a chair next to him, waiting for him to continue.

Pulling his mouth harp from his pocket, William lifted it to his lips and started to play, but then, after playing a few dud notes, quickly stopped and stuffed it in his pocket with a deep sigh. Audrey opened her mouth to talk to him, but he spoke before she could.

'I need to tell you something,' he said, lowering his voice. Audrey nodded once and remained silent, her heartbeat quickening, waiting for him to continue. 'When I was in France, I made a decision I live to regret.'

She nodded again, biting down on her lip. Still looking straight ahead into the fire, he carried on with his story.

'I came face-to-face with a German soldier and I should have shot him instantly,' he said. 'That's what we're trained to do. I had the opportunity to shoot him, but I looked into his eyes and I saw a man just like me, no older than me, probably with a fiancée, like my Elsie, at home. I didn't shoot him, Sis. I couldn't bring myself to do it, I was too cowardly.'

He pressed his eyelids with his thumb and forefinger and sighed a ragged, exhausted sigh, as if the load he was carrying was crushing him with its weight. Though Audrey wanted to get up off the chair and fling her arms around her brother to console him, she sensed there was more to come. What he needed most, she knew, was to get the problem off his chest and for her to listen, but she couldn't stand for him to be thinking of himself as a coward.

'That makes you human,' she said carefully. 'It doesn't make you a coward.'

'No, you don't understand,' he interrupted, shaking his head. 'That soldier, the man I didn't kill, the man whose life I saved, ran away from me, before turning around and shooting and killing my friend, David. I watched David die in agony and he died because of me. I was helpless and hopeless. I tried to stem his bleeding as he lay there, but nothing I could do helped. I put the thrupenny coin in his palm, the one you gave me for luck – how futile!'

Audrey's heart shattered as William broke down in furious tears and sobbed into his hands. With tears flowing from her own eyes, she couldn't sit still for a moment longer. Standing close to him, wanting to shoulder the burden he carried, she rested her hand on his back and searched for words of comfort.

'William, you poor soul, I understand that you feel absolutely wretched about this,' she said, blinking away her tears, 'but these are exceptionally hard times. Your decision was made out of compassion, not cowardice. You weren't to know what that soldier was going to do. How could you? You are not to blame.'

Shaking his head, William closed his eyes and set his jaw, refusing to forgive himself.

'David is dead because of me,' he said. 'And his fiancée is left without her true love. I'm marrying Elsie and she knows nothing of this, of my failure to be the man I should have been. You said it yourself "act like a man". I've hardly acted like a man, have I?'

Watching her beautiful brother, once so full of music and laughter and life, in such anguish and turmoil was physically painful for Audrey. She wiped away her tears and stood straighter.

'You are a man with great integrity,' she said firmly. 'What you went through over there, I can't hope to imagine. Watching your fellow men die in agony in front of you, being so severely injured, and having your foot amputated, your face horrifically burned, it's—' She floundered, searching for the words to try and describe what William had been through. 'It's been a nightmare, and I'm desperately sorry for David, but his death was not your fault. You have to realise that.'

'I failed him,' said William, a tear dropping silently onto his lap. 'There's no doubt about that, and I think Elsie should know who she's marrying.'

Audrey took William's hands in hers. 'Elsie loves you, no matter what,' she said. 'While you were away, I got to know Elsie like a sister. If you tell her about this, it won't make a difference to her. And William, it's not her forgiveness you need, but your own.'

Chapter Thirty-Five

Perched on the edge of the wooden pew, Audrey held her breath as the priest addressed the congregation: 'If any person present knows a reason why these persons may not lawfully marry, you must declare it now.'

Warm October sunshine shone through the saints and patrons encapsulated in the decorative stained-glass windows, casting rainbows onto the bride and groom, who stood side by side at the front of the church in silence. William shifted position on his crutches slightly, a child wriggled and a guest coughed, before the priest continued the ceremony.

Twisting to smile briefly at Mary and Lily, who were sitting next to her on the pew, Audrey breathed out in relief, trying to calm her nerves. She wasn't sure what she'd expected to happen, but after everything Elsie and William had been through, she was determined that nothing would spoil their wedding day. After William's confession the other night, she hadn't stopped worrying about him, but she hoped he'd had a change of heart and decided to look forwards, not back. She knew he still hadn't told Elsie the full story about what had happened in France, but Audrey knew she would understand if he did. There had been other hiccups too: the photographer they had booked had cancelled because of ill health, and Victor and Daphne's plans to attend had been thwarted because of problems with the railway.

'William's hand is shaking!' whispered Lily, as the couple put rings on each other's fingers.

Audrey gave a little nod of her head, registering his nervous state, but strongly felt that when the wedding was over, he would feel a whole lot better. Her mind went to the food she had prepared, waiting in the back room of the café on Fisherman's Road. Despite rationing, she and Violet had whipped up a celebration spread and the cake, under the plaster of Paris mould, would hopefully be a delicious treat for the guests. William had selected the music and Lily and Violet had decorated the tables with jam jars filled with sea pinks and foliage picked from the clifftop. They'd all agreed that they wouldn't listen to the wireless news that day and would try to put the war out of their minds. Everyone needed a little gaiety and with any luck, the reception would provide that.

'…I now pronounce you husband and wife,' said the priest and the small congregation let out a cheer, as Elsie and William kissed. Audrey felt overwhelmed with emotion for William, who looked happier than she had seen him for a long time.

She glanced over at Violet, who wiped her eyes with a hanky, and the two women shared a knowing smile. With Elsie's father locked in a prisoner-of-war camp – and Charlie away overseas, they had much in common, but today at least, they had something to be happy about.

Later that evening, after the cake had been cut and Violet had made a teary speech about wishing the war would end so families could get on with their lives, Audrey distributed small pieces of cake to the guests, who closed their eyes in pleasure when they had a bite.

'Is it true what they say?' asked Elsie's sister, June. 'If the baker baked the cake with love in his or her heart, the bride and groom's marriage will be strong?'

'I like to think so,' smiled Audrey, patting June's head. 'Let's hope so. Though I know Lily here doesn't agree!'

Lily, whose copper hair was resting on her shoulders, hoisted Joy onto her hip and took a sip of sherry from her glass. 'I've decided I'm not the marrying kind,' she said. 'I don't want to be anyone's wife, really. Things are changing for women, aren't they? Since so many men have gone to war, women are filling their shoes, taking their jobs and proving not all women want to be at home and raise a family.'

Audrey smiled at Lily. She was a feisty young lady and was managing marvellously with her new part-time job. She wasn't surprised by her attitude to marriage – especially after her experience with Henry – but she didn't want her to close her heart to the possibility of love.

'You never know what the future will bring,' said Audrey. 'Keep an open mind and an open heart, that's what I say.'

After standing talking to family and guests, Audrey took a moment to sit down. When the air-raid siren sounded, there was a brief panic, but most people stayed where they were, as they had started to do, defying Hitler's army to ruin the day. However, the siren wasn't a false alarm. Over the centre of Bournemouth, a German bomber dropped two parachute mines on the Pier Approach and every window of the Russell-Cotes Art Gallery and Museum was shattered, but the wedding party continued as if nothing had happened – the gathered family and friends determined to see out Elsie and William's big day, no matter what.

By 11 p.m., with Mary yawning and Audrey realising she should get her home to bed, Audrey felt a strange dizziness hit her. She popped outside to get some fresh air.

'I think I've had too much sherry,' she told Lily, who came outside with her.

'You're ever so pale,' said Lily. 'You're not coming down with something, are you?'

Audrey frowned and considered her symptoms: dizziness, queasiness and food tasting a bit funny. Was she coming down with something? A thought flashed into her head: Or was she…?

Instinctively, her hand fell to her stomach, where she gently prodded the flesh through her dress. She remembered the night that Charlie had come home, the tender hours they had enjoyed together. Under the moonlit sky, a startling realisation occurred to her.

'That's not possible though,' she said quietly, not thinking about the fact that Lily was still there.

'Anything's possible, Audrey!' said Lily flippantly, before shivering and returning inside, leaving Audrey alone in the road, a surge of excitement coursing through her.

When the very last of the wedding confetti had blown away in the breeze, and Elsie and William's wedding day was but a precious memory, Audrey waited in the doctor's appointment room, nervously pushing her wedding ring up and down her finger. After that night at the reception, when she realised that she'd missed her monthlies and was feeling quite queasy, she'd waited for more weeks to pass until she was sure she had fallen. Seeing the doctor was just a formality, but he was still the only other person in the world who knew.

'Congratulations, Mrs Barton,' Doctor Bradwell said, after his observations were complete. 'I know you've been trying for a long time for a baby, and this is splendid news. I expect you'll want to inform Charlie at once? As an expectant mother you'll be entitled to the green ration book and extra oranges and bananas when available, eggs, milk and vitamin supplements. You'll have to work out what to do about the running of the bakery, of course. You won't be wanting to work for too long.'

'I'll work until the day I go into labour,' she said, in a stunned voice. 'The bakery needs me.'

The doctor looked at her with a kindly expression and sat back in his chair. 'You can't be all things to all people,' he said. But Audrey, vehemently shaking her head, didn't agree.

'I think in wartime that is exactly what women are having to be, Doctor,' she said, before standing, shaking his hand in thanks, and pulling on her gloves, ready to leave. 'One and a half million women are facing conscription and direction now, and most I know are desperate to help put an end to this heinous war.'

Doctor Bradwell stood up from his chair and laughed gently. 'Perhaps you are right,' he said. 'Perhaps women should be running the country!'

Audrey wasn't sure how to take this comment because there were still men in the town who were not able to accept and appreciate all that women were now doing since the men had gone to fight. Slightly aggrieved, she stood taller and straighter and lifted her chin. Thinking of the Land Girls and the WRNS and the WAAF and the girls in the munitions factories building Spitfires, and the grandmas knitting for the Forces and the mothers digging for victory, and the nurses tending the wounded soldiers and the housewives creating family meals from rations and caring for evacuees, she smiled.

'We pretty much are,' she said, as she left the surgery, and stepped onto Belle Vue Road, feeling a mixture of excitement, disbelief and trepidation. Her suspicions now confirmed, Audrey held her secret in her heart like a precious jewel. After years of longing for a child of their own, she had now fallen, but it was a bittersweet joy. Charlie was away and though she had written to him several times since he'd returned to active service, she hadn't had a letter back from him.

Whispering words of love to Charlie, wherever he was that morning and whatever he was facing, she longed to tell him this news. Imagining the surprised smile breaking out on his face when he read her letter, she found herself suddenly bursting out with laughter as she walked home. Covering her mouth with her hand, she told herself she must remain calm and sensible. She would write to Charlie and only after she began to show would she tell people their news. Mary first, because she didn't want the little girl to feel as if she didn't matter. It was all going to be hard work, organising the running of the bakery and her responsibilities with a newborn, but she would manage it – somehow. That's what women did, after all.

'Mrs Barton?' said a woman's voice from behind her when she turned into Fisherman's Road. Audrey turned and blinked in the afternoon sunlight, recognising the woman as Margaret Peak, the billeting officer. 'Do you have a moment, please?'

'Yes,' said Audrey, suddenly frowning, worrying about Mary. 'Of course. There's not a problem with Mary, is there?'

Margaret shook her head and smiled. 'I've spoken to Mary's aunt and she's more than happy for you to keep Mary here with you,' she said. 'There's paperwork to fill out to make it formal, but I thought I'd bring you the news in person. A letter will follow.'

Audrey's heart exploded with joy. Enthusiastically shaking Margaret's hand, she beamed in thanks and hugged the billeting officer's stiff frame, before laughing and bidding her farewell. When Mary had arrived at the bakery last year, neither of them had known what the future held, but now, thankfully, Audrey could offer the little girl stability and love. The bakery family was growing.

Overwhelmed with all the news, Audrey rushed past Old Reg, who was wiping down the grocery window, and into the bakery, not saying 'hello' to anyone. She flew upstairs into the kitchen, where she pushed shut the door and pulled out her writing paper. Sitting at the kitchen table, she started a letter to her dearest Charlie, a tear of joy blurring the ink on the paper.

Darling Charlie, I hope above all that this letter finds you safe and unharmed. I have some news to brighten your day, a nugget of gold to carry in your heart during the bleak days I know you are enduring. In these dark times we find ourselves living in, there are still moments of light and hope and joy. Oh Charlie, I have some wonderful news... you're going to be a father.

Resting the pen on the table, listening to the sounds of the busy bakery shop beneath, she folded the paper and held it lightly to her lips, staring out of the window at the sun setting over the sea, leaving the most glorious red and purple sky in its wake.

A Letter from Amy

Dear Reader,

I want to say a huge thank you for choosing to read *Wartime Brides and Wedding Cakes*. If you did enjoy it, and want to keep up-to-date with all my latest releases, just sign up at the following link. Your email address will never be shared and you can unsubscribe at any time.

www.bookouture.com/amy-miller

I've so enjoyed writing this book and during my research and reading, continue to be amazed and inspired by how women coped in wartime. Often dealing with dreadful heartache, worrying about their sweethearts and family members in active service, as well as the everyday realities of working in industries previously dominated by men, and putting a meal on the table during rationing, it's clear that women pulled together to give one another emotional and practical support. This is particularly evident in accounts I have read about weddings in wartime. Quickly organised, sometimes in just a matter of days, communities worked together to ensure the wedding celebrations were as joyful as possible, against the dark backdrop of war. Sharing wedding dresses, donating food – even contributing wedding cake ingredients at a time when iced cakes were banned from sale by Food Minister Lord Woolton – women did all they could to help give the bride and groom a day to remember, sometimes with the groom returning to active service the day after, or, in one case I read about, the bride having to go on Fire Watch duty on her wedding night. I'm moved and inspired by people's remarkable resilience.

I have tried to base events around those that happened in Bournemouth and the wider world during 1941, the second year of war, but there are some fictional events, such as the bombing of the bakery. Though the location of the bakery exists in reality, near the cliff in a beautiful part of Bournemouth near where I live, I have changed street names.

I hope you loved *Wartime Brides and Wedding Cakes* and if you did, I would be very grateful if you could write a review. I'd love to hear what you think, and it makes such a difference, helping new readers to discover one of my books for the first time.

I love hearing from my readers – you can get in touch on my Facebook page, through Twitter, Goodreads or my website.

Thanks,
Amy Miller

Acknowledgements

Building on research I did for *Heartaches and Christmas Cakes*, I am once again very grateful to have read *Bournemouth and the Second World War*, 1939–1945, by M.A Edgington, a brilliantly researched and detailed documentation of exactly what happened in Bournemouth during the war years. Also helpful was the information in the Heritage section of Bournemouth Library, where I enjoyed many hours studying the archived *Bournemouth Echo* from 1941, using the microfilm reader. In terms of the baking content, I am grateful for the conversations I had with John Swift, of Swifts Bakery, and team members at Leakers Bakery, Cowdry's Bakery, Burbidge's Bakery, as well as various relatives of wartime bakers, including Anita and Betty. I am also indebted to the residents of the Bournemouth's War Memorial Homes, who gave their time to share memories.

Other books I must mention are the brilliant book *Wartime Britain 1939–1945* by Juliet Gardiner; *Cardboard Wedding Cakes*, Chris Neale; *The 1940s Look*, Mike Brown; *We'll Eat Again*, Marguerite Patten OBE; *Baker's Tale*, Jane Evans; *Bread: A Slice of History*, Marchant, Reuben & Alcock; *The Wartime House*, Mike Brown and Carol Harris; *Eating For Victory*, Jill Norman; *Make Do and Mend*, Jill Norman; *Wartime Women*, Dorothy Sheridan; *The View From The Corner Shop*, Kathleen Hey; *Our Daily Bread – A History of Barron's Bakery*, Roz Crowley; *Spuds, Spam and Eating for Victory*, Katherine Knight; *Reader's Digest: The People's War*, Felicity Goodall; *Save Bread*, Susannah Walker; *A Woman in Wartime London*, Edited by Patricia and Robert Malcolmson; and *The Ministry of Food*, Jane Fearnley-Whittingstall.

Finally, I found looking at photographs from the era was really helpful, including those on the Imperial War Museum's website and many others, as well as wartime poster-advertising campaigns. I'm indebted to the incredible personal stories told on the BBC People's War website, an invaluable archive of Second World War memories, written by the public and gathered by the BBC.

I hope I have remembered everything and everyone. Heartfelt thanks to them all for making it possible for me to write this book.

Lightning Source UK Ltd.
Milton Keynes UK
UKHW02f0303230218
318346UK00006B/426/P

9 781786 813244